Burden of Shame

Burden of Shame

By

Veronica Perry

Published in 2004 by Stamford House Publishing

© Copyright 2005
Veronica Perry

The right of Veronica Perry to be identified as the author of this work has been asserted by her in accordance with the Copyright, Designs and Patents Act 1988.

All Rights Reserved
No reproduction, copy or transmission of this publication may be made without written permission. No paragraph of this publication may be reproduced, copied or transmitted save with the written permission or in accordance with the provisions of the Copyright Act 1956 (as amended). Any person who does any unauthorised act in relation to this publication may be liable to criminal prosecution and civil claims for damage.

A CIP catalogue record for this title is available from the British Library

ISBN 1-904985-10-6

Stamford House Publishing

1st Floor, 13 The Metro Centre, Woodston,
Peterborough PE2 7UH

DEDICATION

My thanks to my Great Nephew, Richard Wilson for his unwavering support and enthusiasm

'BURDEN OF SHAME'

CHAPTER ONE

The Guildhall clock struck four. A thin plaintive voice of protest all but lost in the screech of the wind swirling through the tormented trees, taunting the rain that waited poised in the lowering sky.

From the shelter of the War Memorial I stared out across the deserted park.

Four o'clock!

God, I was tired! Wearily I leaned against the wall, closing my eyes - cursing the searing torment of my throbbing head. Longing to sleep, yet reluctant to leave the domed shrine and the ghosts to whose memory it had been raised. Ghosts whose names were written in neat golden letters on the pale stone walls. Row upon row of them, dulled now with the passing of the years. The men who fought and died for freedom in what they called 'The War to end all Wars'!

Poor valiant fools! How posterity had mocked them! They died that their heirs might inherit the earth, little knowing that two decades later, the heritage of their sons would be the grave!

Some weeks ago workmen were busy here, removing part of the walls on either side of the arched entrance, to insert two panels recording the names of the fifty-two men of Sandworth who fell in the Second World War.

I read about it in the local 'Echo' when the unveiling ceremony was carried out in the presence of George Sweeney, the town's mayor and because of Arthur, promised myself I would come here at the first opportunity.

Outside, the wind paused for breath and with a roar of triumph, the rain came. Relentlessly, in straight, drenching abandon. Beating upon the slender half-grown daffodils and the purple hyacinths peeping from the dark earthy borders flanking the wide stretch of fresh green grass.

I lit a cigarette, flipping the empty carton into a wire basket. Swallowed the smoke greedily, pressing my head back against the cold wall. Savouring the soothing coolness.

Above the beating of the rain, the whispering silence of the place was strangely comforting. Opening my eyes I looked from the dull gold of the old heroes to the bright newness of their sons, and felt a sudden tightness in my throat.

I glanced away, upwards at the glass dome where the rain left a blurred visiting card between me and the grey brooding sky, and as my eyes rested on the words carved round the stone base of the cupola, I smiled bitterly.

'*Dulce est decorum est pro patria mori*'.

A damned and bloody lie! A worn out legend told by plausible hypocrites to camouflage the murder of youth! There was too much canting! What was glorious about death when the blood of youth coursed through the veins!

But no bitterness. Not today. There was no time. This day was different from all the others I'd spent in this sheltered shrine. A day when I envied the dead their right to everlasting glory.

To a point, I was one with them.

I fought as they did, though maybe my reasons weren't the same. Men go to War for a variety of reasons. I went to forget, and found only more to remember.

A game leg and half a hand testify to that experience. Little enough back in Civvy Street where the bitter disillusionment of returning youth condemned the whole ghastly travesty of a civilization seeking to secure peace by unleashing death and destruction, and a holocaust of horror upon the world.

Stiffly and painfully I eased myself from the wall. It wasn't my problem. Not any more.

Today my life had gone full circle. Now I had no choice...

Gripping my walking stick, I took a step forward and stopped, my attention focussed again on that single name - the last on the tablet to the left of the entrance.

'**Leading Signalman Arthur Ryan**'.

Arthur! Just at that moment I felt him very close. Close like we used to be, before he learned to despise me.

Oh it is warm, the allegiance of the dead!

Outside, the menacing growl of thunder split the heavens, and the rain fell with renewed violence. I shuddered, and buttoning my raincoat stood undecided, while the past and the future merged into a kaleidoscopic pattern of my own inevitable destiny.

What lay ahead was my rightful heritage. I'd no quarrel with that. Since I'd ignored the lesson, I must take the consequences. Full circle... Retribution.

Sometimes it's hard to reconcile Christianity with the Law and the stern and terrible threats which make up a large part of the Bible.

My father was hanged for the murder of my mother. The Law demanded a life for a life. The inexorable Law! A law unto itself! The god heads of civilization must be appeased, and to hell with Saint George and the dragon!

Yes, they hanged my father for the murder of my mother, and damned him to an unmarked grave. Yet he was a good man, while she, well she was like Rose, a lying, foul-mouthed, soul-destroying bitch! Like Rose...

My father and mother! John St John Stevens and Cara Tesseli. They met in Florence where he had a temporary job teaching the piano in an Academy of Music. Details of her family were obscure. Apparently her father had deserted them, leaving her mother to bring up six children. This she managed as a seamstress, apparently working many hours for very little reward. Dressed dolls in national costume for Cara and her two sisters to sell to the many tourists who thronged the city.

I'm not sure how they met, but I know my father became besotted with the girl more than twenty years his junior. They were married on her eighteenth birthday, and four months later, I was born. I'm sure she never loved him. That the marriage offered her a means of escape from the frugal life she led - and she was pregnant. I've never dared to question whether or not John St John Steven was my father. He was a fine figure of a man. Educated, and undoubtedly a good catch for a young woman with nothing but her beauty to commend her.

This I do know, Cara never forgave me for being born. All through the years of my growing up, we carried on a sort of love hate relationship, and in those years I marked the gradual change in her. She coarsened. In appearance and behaviour. Men ogled her and she flaunted herself. Brazenly encouraging. Taking delight in seeing my father squirm. Seeing his manhood disintegrate as more and more, he sought solace in the bottle.

I suppose I grew to hate her because I loved my father, and I knew she had other men. He would hear nothing against her. She was young, he said. There was no real harm in her. I could have told him different. Told him how she embarrassed my friends so that eventually they stopped coming to the house. And worse. Told him how she teased my lips with the tip of her tongue when she insisted in kissing me goodnight. How as she pressed herself against me, I pulled away from her, flushed and ashamed, and sought the sanctuary of my room. Guiltily aware of the hardening in my loins. She had a superb figure, and her skin was soft and smooth as she wrapped her arms around me. Mockingly aware of my body's response. But I was her son for God's sake! And she shamed me. Made a fool of me. How could I tell my father those things? She could twist him round her little finger, and with what lying accusations would she have tried to destroy me?

I felt myself tremble as the past engulfed me. I remembered another day when the firm green shoots of tulips thrust their way through the yielding earth, firm and certain in the hour of rebirth. A day similar to this. A day, seven years ago, when leaving the council office where I was employed as a clerk in the rating department, I found my father waiting for me on the rain-swept forecourt.

How clearly I remember him at this moment! John St John Stevens. A tall, broad-shouldered man wearing his shabby suit with quiet dignity. An imposing figure always, but on that day, the day that ended so many things, one look at him told me that something was wrong - terribly wrong. His expression was strained. The blue eyes clouded, the jaw set firm.

"Dad," I said surprised. "What brings you here?"

"Thought I might catch you," he mumbled, not meeting my eyes. His speech sounded slurred. It was obvious he had been drinking. "Must talk," he said, catching me by the arm. "Let's go into the park."

A stab of fear ran through me.

It seemed the wrong time to tell him I was on my lunch break and Franklyn wanted me back on time. Un-protesting, I allowed him to propel me across the square into the park. The wind had risen, driving the rain before it as it tore through the trees with a kind of baffled fury. In silence, he led me to the shelter of the War Memorial and sat down.

"All right, Dad, what's all the mystery?" I asked, striving to keep my voice steady.

For a while he didn't speak. Just sat, head in hands, staring at the floor.

"It's not easy," he said at last, "and there's not much time."

"Don't worry about me," I told him. "Just give it to me straight."

"You know what's been going on."

"You mean Mum?" I said hesitantly, and my voice sounded a long way off. "I might have known. What's she been up to this time?"

He shook his head. Struggled for words but no sound came. I sat beside him.

"You should never have taken her back," I said, my mouth inexplicably dry, "Can't you get rid of her. Divorce or something?"

He gave a deep sigh.

"I'll never get rid of her now, son," he answered wearily. "A man like me needs a woman around. I took her back because I loved her, and I was thinking of you."

"That's more than she ever does," I told him bitterly. "If she's cleared off again, I'm glad. We'll be okay. It's been rotten these last few months. It didn't matter so much about her, but now it's you, and you know drink's not the answer. Things get around in this damned place!"

I saw him flinch.

"I know," he said. "You can't stop tongues wagging. I know what people think of me! I'm a failure. I should have realised it years ago, but a little talent, like a little learning, is a dangerous and damnable thing. Music should have been my hobby, nothing more. Instead, I let it obsess me heart and soul. I've gone on dreaming of success and all that goes with it, and all the time, I should have known the dream was too big for my fingers to cope with. All my life, music's been inside of me, but somehow it never reached my fingers." He looked up searchingly, and as I struggled to find words to answer him, he went on. "It's the same with you, son. I've taught you all I know but it's not enough. It's all somewhere inside you, but when your fingers touch the keyboard, it's just notes they play."

"D'you think I don't know that!" I told him with a show of bitterness, "I've known for a long time. It's not the end of the world, Dad. I play to amuse myself, that's all."

"Good boy," he said quietly. "No. You won't make a fool of yourself like I have. I know that. You'll never know the destructive force of frustration. Anyway, you can always teach. There's a lot of satisfaction in that."

"Hell, Dad!" I exclaimed. "What's brought all this on? This isn't the time or place to remind me of my short-comings as a pianist. It's never meant anything more than a hobby. I've got a good job and it's pretty safe. Old Faulkner told me this morning he's recommending me for a rise after Easter, and with a bit of luck, at the end of the year I'll be taking over Packham's job. He's going to Kenya."

It seemed as though he hadn't heard me. He stared across the park to where the Municipal Buildings stretched stark and white against the leaden background of the sky.

"There'll be changes," he muttered after a while. "A lot of things can happen before the end of the year."

"War, you mean? All right, so there'll be War. I'll have nothing to worry about then will I? I'll probably be called up, and if I'm not, there'll be plenty of jobs to..."

"Things may not work out that way for you," he interrupted me. "I'm trying to tell you why, and I want you to understand. You know I could never make enough money for your mother - not even in the beginning - and she couldn't do without it. I'm as much to blame as she for what's happened. Make no mistake about that. I've no excuse. I turned a blind eye to what was going on. I neglected her. Not wilfully you understand, but I believed music was my destiny and I came to begrudge any moment away from it. I put it before everything. That's why I lost my job at Gibson's. I was never there when they wanted me. Used to slip away to the church to snatch an hour's practise on the organ - or to the Club - or any place where there was an instrument I could play on.

"After Gibson's, no one gave me another chance. I was a 'crank' - a 'dreamer'. Commerce had no place for me. Not that I cared. Now I had all the time in the world to do what I wanted. To play! Your mother started to go out more often. God knows where she went. I never asked her - never questioned where her money came from. The music grew like a canker inside me. I spent hour after hour at the piano seldom knowing whether she was in or out of the house. I evaded the truth by ignoring it until, as I became more and more dependent on her for the necessities of life, I came to despise myself.

"We had quarrels. Noisy, sordid quarrels. You heard them. Realised that your father was living on the immoral earnings of the slut your mother had become."

He was looking at me now, his eyes boring into mine, and I fidgeted uneasily, sick with embarrassment.

"Why now, Dad?" I asked him. "You're not telling me anything new. I've heard it all before."

Suddenly, I felt a peculiar detachment. A remoteness from him that was frighteningly alien to our relationship. It was true. He hadn't told me anything I didn't already know, but despite my words to him, I felt instinctively, it all had to be said. That what had happened in our home that morning, would alter the course of both our lives. That things could never be the same again because of it.

I'd heard their ugly quarrels all right! I was only ten when I first became aware of their violence. Then, cowering at the top of the stairs, I'd heard my mother's slurred, drunken voice, hurling taunts and obscenities at my father. And between each wild tirade of hers, I'd hear his quiet intercession.

My father seldom raised his voice, but the expression changed.

Sometimes he'd be pleading, sometimes contemptuous, and sometimes there'd be so much suppressed loathing in his voice that a great shiver would pass through me.

Through the years of my adolescence, I came to believe that what he endured, he endured for my sake. So much did I feel my mother's growing resentment of me. Perhaps she always hated me. Even now, my earliest recollections bring to mind nothing but the feelings of hurt and bewilderment with which I retired after each effort to find in her the understanding and affection I believed it right to expect.

It was my father whose patience, counsel and complete unselfishness, formed the structure of my childhood contentment, and above all else, through all the years in that seething cauldron of domestic strife, there was our mutual love for the piano. It had absorbed me in my early teens. Strengthening the bond between me and my father. Something of which my mother had no part. I remember how the knowledge used to satisfy me - but then I knew nothing of my father's suffering.

Then, just before my seventeenth birthday, she went! Suddenly, without warning, and for the first time I learned just what she meant to him.

He was like a man dazed. A stranger, withdrawing into himself so utterly, that it seemed he had forgotten my existence.

That was when the drinking started in earnest, and I heard the dreadful sound of his sobbing. I felt so damned helpless. I'd recently started my first regular job as a junior clerk in the office of the Borough Engineer, and when I got home from work, I'd find him locked in the sitting room night after night, thumping out chord upon chord of savage longing. It was then, as the hours dragged by and discord after discord crashed through the quivering piano, I knew the masochistic ferocity with which he tried to expurgate the misery in his soul.

Lying baffled and helpless in my bedroom, when at last the noise stopped, I'd hear his restless pacing through the house, and sometimes, the sound of the front door closing. That used to scare me! I'd get out of bed and go to the window, pulling back the faded blue curtains to peer out into the dark. And there I'd see him! Standing by the post box at the corner of the street. Almost motionless he'd stand. An hour. Perhaps two. Waiting for her to come, and then, when the waiting got too much for him, he'd walk from one end of the road to the other. Backwards and forwards between the rows of gaunt grey houses.

And then, just as suddenly as she'd left us, my mother returned.

She was there one evening when I got home. Painted like a street walker, with her thick black hair bunched up on top with a lot of curls, and dressed in some dark red thing pulled tight to show her shape.

I remember the revulsion I felt when I looked at her. Cheap and brazen and oozing sex, but in my father's eyes was the look of a man restored to life, and because of that, I tried to be glad she was there.

For a few weeks it seemed things would be different. My father was almost gay, though he still drank more than was good for him. They even went out together sometimes, and when I spent an evening with him at the piano, she'd curl up on the shabby old couch reading, or sewing some brightly coloured material into a seductive frippery for herself.

Then it started again! The interminable nagging! The petty quarrels, growing in bitterness until, less than six months after her return, things between them were worse than they had ever been.

The picture of the past faded suddenly as my father's voice cut across my reflections.

"Things haven't been easy for you, Mark. I know you've only stayed at home because of me. I'm grateful. Things are bound to be pretty rough for you for a while. People can be damnably cruel. You'll have to take it on the chin my boy. It'll turn out all right in the end."

I spread my arms. Keep calm, I told myself.

"You're talking in riddles, Dad," I said, "Give it to me straight. What's happened? Look! I promised I wouldn't be late back from lunch. I ought to be going."

I wanted to leave him. To run somewhere and hide. To sort out this nightmare that had imposed itself upon reality. And yet, I found myself powerless to move. I just sat staring at him. Waiting. Expectant. It was like listening to a charade where the actor went on too long and I already knew the answer. Knowing there was much to remain unsaid.

"You're not yet twenty, Mark. Just starting out in life. You've got yourself engaged." he said earnestly. "Things may change. Don't..."

"Nothing's going to change between Susan and me," I interrupted him. "The sooner we're married the better. We're planning on this summer. I'll be glad to get fixed up in a place of my own. It'll be somewhere for you to come when things get bad at home."

"That's how it ought to have been," he said with a sigh. "A couple of grandchildren on my knee."

I knew panic! His choice of tense had frightened me.

"Dad..." I commenced hoarsely.

But suddenly he was on his feet.

"You'd better be getting back now," he said resolutely. "And I must do what I have to."

We walked from the park as we had entered it - in silence. Vague, uneasy notions crowded my mind. The whole time we had spent together seemed to have passed in an aura of unreality, and what should have been said, remained unspoken. I knew it, just as surely as I knew my life in that drab, unhappy home, was at an end.

We reached the steps leading to my office.

"Well, this is it, Mark," he told me, curiously calm. "Here's where we say goodbye. You're a good lad. You'll understand. Be brave and... forgive me."

His voice faltered, I thought I saw the glint of tears in his eyes, and as I struggled for words, I felt the firm grip of his hand, a brief embrace, and then he was gone, striding away, head in the wind.

He walked, I thought, faster than usual, and with an unmistakable air of finality.

He didn't turn round.

My head felt curiously numb. It was as though I strove to stop my brain thinking because I dare not face the certain knowledge of what was about to happen. Forgive him, he'd said! Remorse. Guilt. The prospect that he had gone out of my life forever... Surely if there was a God?

I don't remember going back to the office. Sitting at my desk. Waiting. For what? I dared not think. And then, at three o'clock that afternoon, it could no longer be evaded. I was summoned to the office of the departmental chief where a plain clothes man was waiting.

From him I learned that my mother was dead - strangled - and my father, having confessed to the proper authorities, was being held in custody...

CHAPTER TWO

It was the Ryans who made bearable the first few weeks following the tragedy.

Since my father had surrendered himself to the Law, a strange calmness had taken possession of me, and after a little while I braced myself to return to the place where the thing had happened.

Turning the corner into Lawson Street, I saw, about fifty yards away, a uniformed constable standing outside the house, and all around, little whispering groups of people.

I hesitated, walked on a few steps, and suddenly I was the cynosure of all eyes and a great hush descended over the street. Were these my neighbours I wondered? Those same people I had lived amongst, and talked with, and joked with all my life? These faces, agape with mawkish curiosity? Strangers. I was no longer one of them. An outlaw. An object to be stared at. Gaped at and whispered about as though I was some creature from another world.

And suddenly I knew I couldn't go home. Not yet. I wasn't ready to face the haunted emptiness of the place. Standing there, undecided, I began to shiver uncontrollably. How could I turn and retrace my steps before that gathered wolf pack? It was then, Arthur Ryan put his hand on my shoulder.

"I've been looking for you, Mark," he said quietly. "Mum's expecting you."

I looked at him dumbly, my eyes filled with humble gratitude. Relieved. Choked with emotion.

I felt his grip slide down to my elbow and tighten as he propelled me across the street and turned into a doorway almost opposite the one that had been my home.

"Nosey lot of bastards," he muttered. "Ghouls, the lot of them!"

In the neat little back room, his mother waited. Without speaking, she gathered me in her arms and hugged me to her.

"Come and sit down," she said, when at last she released me. "No need to talk until you feel like it, but try and eat something. You'll feel better for it."

I mumbled my thanks and sat down. Surprisingly, I felt hungry. The smell of freshly baked bread hung about the room, homely and appetising.

I made a good meal despite the pretence of small talk which quickly fell away to silence.

And then,

"Have you seen your Dad?" Mrs Ryan asked quietly.

"Not yet," I told her. "I could have done, but he refused to see me."

I felt my mouth quiver. God! That had hurt like hell! I looked across the table and burst out passionately,

"Whatever he did, she asked for it! Everyone knows what she was!"

"We're not judging your Dad, Mark," Mrs Ryan assured me gently. "But we mustn't judge her either. We can't help her now, and there's little enough we can do for him yet, but if there's anything we can do for you..."

"You'll stay here with us, Mark," Arthur put in.

"Yes. You must think of this as your home," his mother told me. "You won't want to be over there, brooding by yourself."

"They'll hang him," I muttered through tight lips.

"You mustn't talk like that," Mrs Ryan chided me. "It's not right. We don't know what happened yet. You won't help him by thinking that way. It's like putting yourself against him from the beginning."

I stared at her incredulously.

"Against him?" I whispered hoarsely. "Oh, my God!"

I giggled. A high pitched, hysterical sound, and then it seemed a dark curtain came down over my mind. As though at a distance I heard someone laughing, not realising it was the sound of my own voice.

When the mist cleared, my head was resting on my arms on the table. My shoulders shook and my cheeks were wet.

"That's right. Let it come out, Mark," Mrs Ryan soothed me. "You've had a terrible shock. Don't try and bottle up what you feel."

With an abrupt movement, I pushed back my chair and stood

up.

"D'you mind if I have a wash?" I asked shortly. "I've got to see Susan."

"Of course," she answered. "And you'll come back here afterwards?"

I hesitated, then, "I'm very grateful to you, Mrs Ryan," I told her, "but I expect I'll be staying at Susan's place."

I saw her glance at Arthur.

"Well," she said dubiously. "I suppose you know best, but you're welcome to stay here. I've made up another bed in Arthur's room."

I murmured my thanks and went up to the bathroom. Oddly enough, their painstaking kindliness irritated me. Arthur was a good mate. We got on well together. Played snooker at the club where we shared a few drinks and chatted up the girls.

He was six years older than I. A quiet, unassuming serious sort of fellow. Keen on spouting politics if anyone would listen. He had a good job at the Walford Printing Works, and although he kept his widowed mother, he was never short of a pound or two. He'd lost his father somewhere on the Somme.

During the early days of our friendship, Arthur had been a frequent visitor to my home. Frequent until he'd stopped coming altogether. Hedging each invitation with uneasy embarrassment. Whenever I think of it, I see the laughing, vivacious face of my mother, and anger makes my blood run hot.

Bitch! Slut! She couldn't even leave my friend alone! Yes, Arthur and me! Friends who went everywhere together until I met Susan. After that, there never seemed to be time to go to the club, or anywhere else, with Arthur.

On the night of the day my mother was murdered, Lawson Street was almost deserted when I left the Ryans. In the gathering gloom, the police constable was still there, and a little further on, two women talked together. That was all, yet as I walked, it seemed that many eyes followed me. Furtive shapes in gardens - the movement of a curtain in a lighted window. I hurried on, the gathering gloom giving me anonymity.

It was raining again when I reached Susan's house, and as I

swung open the front gate, a sudden surge of misgiving swept through me. One thing I knew... the Garlands must certainly have heard the news! Bad news travels fast, and Harry Garland's butcher's shop was a notorious gossip centre. How would they receive me?

Susan's father had never liked me, and she herself was not averse to reminding me of the better offers she'd rejected in my favour.

Still, she had chosen me, and we loved each other.

Fortified, but with diffidence, I pressed the doorbell and after a little while Mrs Garland opened the door.

"We thought you'd come here," she greeted me tight lipped as she peered anxiously up and down the street. "You'd better come in."

Hostility amplified her harsh voice. I followed her into the kitchen where Harry Garland was having his supper. A big, red-faced man, he sat in his shirt sleeves, braces hanging down his back as he ate quickly and noisily, pushing the food into his wide fleshy mouth with an almost continuous movement, to reveal a profusion of gold filled teeth.

He cleaned his plate, mopping up the gravy with a piece of dry bread, and eyed me belligerently.

"You're not welcome here," he said aggressively.

I swallowed hard, struggling to keep calm.

"I never have been," I reminded him. "I came to see Susan." I watched anger emphasise the coarse ugliness of his face.

"You cheeky young bugger!" he ground out furiously, getting to his feet. "I'll soon..."

"Now, Harry," his wife hastily cut him short. "You know what we agreed. No use losing your temper. No need for that language either. Just say what you..."

"Shut up!" he snarled, standing aggressively in front of me. "We don't want you here, Stevens! Is that clear enough for you?" He thrust his bullet neck towards me.

"Crystal!" I said quietly. "But I came here to see Susan!"

"My girl's not going to get mixed up in any dirty scandal!" he shouted. "She doesn't want to see you, and if you try to get in touch with her, you'll get the end of my belt! You're bad stock! God knows I warned her!"

"Stop it, Harry!" his wife put in nervously. "There's no need for that. It's not Mark's fault."

"Thank you for nothing," I said tensely. "Okay. I know where I stand with you, Mr Garland. Now I want to see Susan. I've got a right to hear what she has to say."

"Not any more you haven't," Garland answered, and for the first time, he took his eyes off me and looked at the mantlepiece.

There, next to the tall brass candlestick, I saw Susan's ring. The sapphire winked wickedly from between the two diamonds, and something inside me turned cold. I remembered the pride with which I'd taken Susan to select the symbol of our engagement, and the sacrifices that had been necessary to make the expensive purchase possible.

"I see," I heard myself say. "At least she should have had the guts to tell me herself."

"After what your Dad's done!" Garland stormed. "I've seen something like this coming for a long time. I tried to warn Susan. Something bad was bound to happen. Both of them, your Mum and your Dad were heading for trouble. Oh yes, I could tell you."

"And you'd enjoy it wouldn't you!" I cut him short. "I know you've never liked me, but what's happened today doesn't make me a criminal, and you've no right to treat me like one. I hoped for Susan's support. She's supposed to love me - remember?"

"She got jolted out of that this afternoon," he said harshly. "She doesn't want to see you. Now or at any other time. It's over. Finished. And she didn't need me to persuade her either. Now get out of here."

"You must see our point of view," Mrs Garland put in. "Susan's a sensitive girl. She's deeply shocked. After the news got out, the shop was simply swarming with people. Just came to stare at her they did. She had a terrible time. We had to close up at four o'clock, she was in such a state."

I took in a deep breath.

"What about my state!" I shouted. "What a bloody fool I've been! In spite of what's happened, I've deluded myself with the thought that you and Susan would stand by me. I should have known better. There's more feeling in that fly-blown pig's head in your shop window! I'm well rid of the lot of you!"

And as Garland choked for words, I snatched up the ring, dropped it on the floor, and ground it savagely under my heel - then I went out into the rain.

Back at the Ryan's place, Arthur admitted me, seeing in my face all there was to know. He didn't speak. There was nothing to say. He watched me slump into a chair, then turned away and busied himself at the sideboard.

The first tot of whisky warmed me through, and each time he refilled my glass the hurt inside me lessened until I felt nothing at all...

The weeks before they hanged my father passed like a nightmare in which I hung suspended between the horror of what had happened, and the fear of what must follow. From the first, I felt he would not escape the full penalty of the Law. He didn't want to. Mildmay, his Counsel, had no chance, and I was sorry for him.

It might have been better if my father had had his way and pleaded 'guilty', and saved the farce of a trial. In all but the final act of extinction, life had already left him. There was an air of patient resignation about him. He seemed content.

When I went with Mildmay to visit him, I think we both knew his case was hopeless. Although for my sake, he agreed to plead 'Not Guilty', he would make no effort to defend himself, refusing to discuss any aspect of the tragedy which might have saved him from the gallows.

A few weeks later, in a crowded court room, I sat helpless, listening to the prosecuting counsel destroy him. Writhing as he painted an eloquent picture of an attractive, vivacious woman, twenty years her husband's junior, neglected through his obsession with music and his addiction to drink, with the inevitable result that she sought other company.

The smooth relentless voice went on to tell how the husband's jealousy, awaking like a demonic avenger had extracted the last, terrible payment from the unfortunate woman.

A cold, hawk-like man, Sir Sefton Larrimer, the prosecuting counsel. A tall, lean man, savouring the succulent certainty of success. Damning the calm, dignified figure in the dock.

The defendant, he said, was a waster who lived on his wife, well aware of the source of her income. A paranoid, existing on dreams of grandeur and success. A maudlin sentimentalist who, besotted with drink, would change from a cringing moral coward, into a veritable avenging colossus, and in a drunken fury became a fiend - a murderer!

Had he not brought witnesses to prove that on the morning of the crime, the accused had spent an hour and a half in the 'Rose and Crown', brooding and ill-tempered, as he consumed quantities of neat spirit?

And so it went on with the sure touch of a master's oratory. Stark, basic truths cunningly distorted, brutally misrepresented. A monstrous caricature that ruthlessly tore a good man's life away.

My own evidence fell strangely flat. I wanted passionately to help my father, but the stream of questions, continuous and dunning, caught me up in a maelstrom of confusion that damned him as surely as if I had set out to see him hanged. God knows I didn't... Even my thoughts were incoherent.

Oh, it was all there! The piano, the drink, his acceptance of her money and how she came by it. These things were irrefutable.

As I left the witness box, bewildered and frustrated, I glanced despairingly at the figure in the dock, and met his gentle smile.

I heard the final stages of the proceedings as though from a long way off, and suddenly, it was over. The mechanism of the Law, whilst admitting there may have been some provocation, could find in that no justification for murder.

The ominous black cloth on the Judge's head - the awful words that damned my father to an unmarked grave - my last glimpse of him, tall and unruffled as he bowed with quiet dignity to the judge - these are impressions that will never leave me.

As the court began to clear, a merciless hammer pounded in my brain. The sea of faces all around me, merged into a great gray shadow, and for a little while, as Arthur led me out into the street, a numbness of thought exorcised the dreadful significance of the verdict.

My father lodged no appeal, and as Mildmay wrestled for his life, it was as though the ponderous gait of the law frankly bored him. He had done what he had to do. For him, it ended there.

The day after they took him to the condemned cell, my boss sent for me. I'd been expecting it, and if it wouldn't have looked like running away, I'd have given up my job days ago. My workmates were treating me like a pariah. Isolating me. Condemning me, just like my neighbours. Whispering. Furtively watching me with cold hostility.

My misery became pent-up anger, and my wretchedness a smouldering hatred, and yet I felt something of pity for the bald, bespectacled little man who floundered uncertainly as he tried to find a kindly way of telling me my employment there was at an end.

It wasn't his fault. I knew he was only obeying orders. Dwarfed by the big oak desk, red-faced with embarrassment, he handed me my cards.

"I'm sorry, Stevens," he mumbled. "Really sorry. I don't know what to say to you..."

"Try calling a spade a spade," I answered bitterly. "There's no room for the son of a murderer here! You do a bit of preaching, don't you, Merrick? I've heard you and your bloody psalm-singers doing the heavy soul-saving act! A bloody fine lot of Christians there are in this stinking place! Think about me when you're spouting your piece next Sunday morning! It's not enough that I've lost my parents, my home and the girl I expected to marry, in one go, I've got to lose my friends and my job too! And why? I've done nothing!" My voice was rising hysterically. I stumbled over the words and a voice as though far away, was repeating nothing! Nothing! I struggled to control myself. Shouted at him,

"D'you hear, you old humbug! If that's your bloody Christianity, I want no part of it!" I broke off panting.

Merrick's face paled.

"It isn't Christ's fault that people behave as they do," he answered quietly. "Believe me, my boy, His suffering is beyond all earthly understanding because of the sins and sorrows of the world. I'm sorry for you, Stevens, believe me. Just now you seem to have lost everything. Try and keep faith. Christ will not forsake you. There are many things we don't understand, but believe me, they are all for a purpose. If you'd like to call and see me at my home I'll try and help you over this very difficult time. The teachings..."

"Thank you for nothing," I cut him off harshly. "Teachings won't bring back the things I've lost."

I left him then. Went out into the biting wind. Stood for a moment on the spot where I'd said goodbye to my father on that fateful morning. Staring across the park, it seemed strange that nothing there had altered, and I thought what an insignificant thing was one man's life against a background of things that last forever.

On my way back to the Ryans, I saw Susan. A tantalising wisp of a hat covering her tawny curls, the wind sporting with her short skirt, caressing her long slender legs. A chance to talk to her. She couldn't pass me by without a word. I hurried towards her. Scarcely half a dozen yards separated us when she caught sight of me, and the sudden look of fear on her face, made me wince.

For an instant, we stood staring at each other. I smiled reassuring. Called her name, and saw the fear replaced by a brief, wavering uncertainty, and then, as I took an eager step towards her, her carmined lips curled in arrogant disdain, and head in air, she hurried past me.

It was as though she'd struck me. Incredulity, fury and hurt battled inside me, and I wished savagely that I'd taken her, on the common, the last time we went out together. It would have been easy, I knew that. Maybe she'd have been glad enough to marry me then, but I hadn't touched her because I'd wanted our marriage to start right - even though she'd nearly driven me mad, and I hadn't slept at night through wanting her.

I ached for her then as she walked away. Loving her even as I cursed her, then I went on into the town where I'd promised to meet Arthur at the Flax Club. And later that evening, when he left me to go on night shift at the printing works, I tagged on to Cockle Ann, because I felt lonely and bitter, and Ann was the only one in the crowded bar, who treated me as she'd always done.

She was kind to me, Ann was. We sat and drank together, and each empty glass paid a dividend of forgetfulness. Forgetfulness of everything save Ann and her husky voice, her kindness, and the strong heady smell of her lusty flesh, and that night, I didn't go back to the Ryan's.

The day they hanged my father, I woke up early. In his bed on the opposite side of the room, Arthur slept soundly. Quietly, I got up and went to the window. Across the street, in the misty morning light, was the ghost of what had been my home. Empty now. Everything had gone under the hammer to pay for the defence. Everything save the piano.

I couldn't have let it go. It was all that was left of my father. A link between the two of us. A link to transcend the shadowy unknown to which he had been condemned. It stood now, in the corner of the Ryan's sitting room.

That morning, the last for my father, I wondered whether I would ever be able to raise that rosewood lid again. Dimly, across the street, I saw the newly erected board advertising the house **'To Let'**. Wondered who would live there. Many would apply. That much was certain. All eager to take over our legacy of notoriety. Ghouls, all of them. How they would magnify each lurid detail of my parents tragedy. How little would they think about mine!

I sighed and looked at my watch. Half an hour to go. Thirty minutes of life, and then... I closed my eyes. Thirty minutes, and then a broken puppet at the end of a rope would be all that was left of John St John Stevens. Gone! Silenced! Finished! Snuffed out like a candle flame!

I shuddered, feeling a searing pain between the shoulders. Flinched. Already I could see that awful swaying figure. Would death come at once I wondered? A single jolt and a broken neck, or would there be slow strangulation to squeeze his life away?

'*To be hanged by the neck until you are dead...*'

The awful significance of the words refuted an instantaneous death. '**UNTIL YOU ARE DEAD**'. I remembered a handbook on hanging I'd read. How it had been known for a man's head to be jerked from his body! I stifled a groan, and wondered how Merrick would justify the right of the State to torture and kill, and condemn a soul to damnation, and a body to unconsecrated ground.

I thought of my mother, who slowly and thoroughly had destroyed a good man. Betraying, belittling, giving nothing and taking all. Would she, by this one act of his, wear a martyr's crown. For an instant, a picture of her crowded my mind. Spreadeagled in the hall where my father had left her!

Oh God! It couldn't be true! Only it was! Cold, hard, ironic fact! The pain was stabbing at me again. Piercing my breath. Sweat was running down my face but I was shivering. Violently - uncontrollably!

Eight o'clock!

The bedroom door opened and Mrs Ryan came in carrying a tray.

"I've brought you a cup of tea, Mark," she said quietly, "with a spot of whisky to steady your nerves."

I muttered my thanks, trying to avoid her pale, pitying eyes. Took a step towards her, and a sudden searing pain across my chest, brought me to a startled standstill. I coughed, and white hot needles made me cry out.

I saw the look of alarm on Mrs Ryan's face. Saw Arthur, suddenly wide awake, push back his bed clothes and spring out of bed. Then came a confusion of sound - an impression of unbearable agony tearing at my body - a blurring of vision, and a sudden rush of darkness as my senses left me.

The weeks that followed, filled as they were with indescribable pain as Mrs Ryan and doctors wrested for my life, undoubtedly saved my sanity. A safety valve whilst the first tormented ravings of my tortured mind burnt themselves out in the dark oblivion of my delirium.

And when at length strength began to return, I tried not to think of my father. But he was always there, loitering in the crowded corners of my mind. Not as I remembered him, but twisted and broken as the Law had sent him to make his peace with his Maker.

Conversely, when I thought of my mother, it was always in the full, flaunting vigour of her life! It was hard to believe her dead, though I'd seen her once at the mortuary, when the grim farce of identification had to be played out. A distorted, broken figure stretched on a slab with an expression of stupid surprise on her dead face.

As the weeks went by, and under Mrs Ryan's care I regained my health and the ability to think rationally, I began to seriously consider my future. Mrs Ryan was a widow and although Arthur's wage provided a reasonable standard of living, I knew that providing for an extra mouth - a passenger - was not easy. I had to find a job. Any job. But where?

I scanned the newspapers, but there was nothing suitable locally. I was too well known in Sandworth... And then, Providence took a hand. An aunt of Mrs Ryan's died, and left her a thatched cottage and enough money to maintain it, in Ringwood, a thriving village in the next county.

It was a Godsend both to the Ryans and to me, for Mrs Ryan insisted that was now to be my home. I was one of the family! We moved to Lilac Cottage in the early summer of 1939. Mrs Ryan was ecstatic. It really was an idyllic place, its white stone walls a background for multi-coloured creepers, its garden ablaze with summer blooms. And so much space! Fields! Fresh air! Such a contrast after the grey huddled terraces of Lawson Street.

Arthur had bought himself a motor bike to make the daily journey to and from Sandworth, a distance of some twenty miles.

Now, I had to look for a job in earnest, but the newspapers were absorbed with the menacing threat of War, for the Nazi jackboot was crashing and crunching its way through Central Europe where, since the annexation of Czechoslovakia in the Spring of 1939, the German Fuhrer had strutted like a peacock, proclaiming to the world that he had brought a great peace to the countries he had 'liberated'.

Now he was at it again. The same old cant about having 'no more territorial claims', the stock phrase with which he had prefaced every major act of aggression.

This time, his sights were set on Poland, and Chamberlain had made a last minute flight to Munich in an attempt to avert the threat of War.

Not that I'd ever been one to interest myself in politics. Until my own life lay in ruins, Hitler's war had seemed a long way off.

Now, suddenly things had changed. The little Austrian housepainter's word could not be trusted. The newspapers were full of it. Gas masks had been distributed in London. There was talk of evacuating children from the Capital. Conscription! Suddenly I began to see a solution to my own problem.

In war, I told myself, a man could lose his identity. Bury his past. I thought about it a lot. I was thinking about it when Arthur came home one evening.

"Hello, Stevo," he greeted me. "How is it today?"

"I'm almost as good as new," I told him with a grin. "If you want a reference as a wet nurse, just say the word!"

"This place is just the ticket, isn't it?" he said, stretching himself out in an armchair.

"Couldn't be better," I assured him. "You've just got to look at your Mum's face! She's as happy as a sandboy." I picked up a newspaper. "Think there's going to be a war?" I asked him.

"Any moment, Stevo. Any moment now."

"Old Hitler's a bit of a boy," I commented. "But he wouldn't be daft enough to try anything on with us."

"He's dangerous," he returned thoughtfully. "Power drunk! So far he's taken everything in his stride. No one's been able to stop him."

"We haven't tried," I reminded him. "The Czechs had a damned fine army. Beats me why we didn't go in there and give them a hand."

"We weren't ready," he replied. "Even now we're not ready. We don't want war. We're only just recovering from the last. Mind you, Hitler's not predictable. Now that Germany's expanded to the east, maybe he'll go for Russia."

"I believe, they'll soon be at each other's throat. Stalin's more than a match for Hitler. Their Agreement is nothing more than a marriage of convenience. A stalling for time."

"What about Poland?"

"There's the danger." He sighed heavily. "If Hitler goes in there, so will we. We have to, ready or not, or Jerry will be in London before we know it. And it's my bet he'll move soon. Chamberlain's wasting his time. Hitler's promises won't mean a thing."

"The papers are on about conscription," I reminded him.

"I know," he answered. "Makes me sad. The bloody politicians make wars by manoeuvring us into a corner with their confounded word juggling. Then they have the damned cheek to believe we have to be forced to fight to defend the rights and privileges threatened by their own humbuggery."

He spoke with genuine anger, believing what he said, and feeling a soul-deep resentment towards those who would deny free men the right to exercise that freedom - to fight for it - and the things men hold dear, without the compellant of the law.

His eyes were suddenly bright with an expression I'd seen there many times before. He was going to talk - and I was going to listen. Perhaps I'd never listened to him before. My life had been too full of personal things. The misfortunes of the Fuhrer's victims, a long, long way from my own private world. I read the papers, finding in their contradictory leaders, a firm excuse for believing none of their pessimistic perorations. With Arthur it was different. Politics were his hobby. He was so earnest about them, and came in for a lot of good-natured ribbing from me and the rest of the lads at the club.

"Chamberlain might swing things," I muttered with no conviction.

"Rubbish!" he retorted. "The whole hocus-pocus of politics is a farce. We're forced like puppets into a scrap with other puppets. We've no personal quarrel with them. They're as bewildered and misled as we are, yet we destroy each other! At first we fight with a fine sense of righteousness, then the battle lust gets us. We're fighting for our lives, and all that matters is that we come out on top.

"We don't even notice the crack of the whip from the war lords who willingly sacrifice a generation of youth so long as vested interests are preserved with a well timed 'Halt'! And when it's all over, what then? For those of us who come through, the real struggle begins. The struggle for existence, for a place in the peace we're supposed to have won. For we will win the battle, make no mistake about that. And we'll find aliens in our jobs and in our beds, we'll put up with shortages and privations, while we put our former enemies on their feet.

"It happened after the last war. Ten years after her supposed defeat, Germany had recovered her trade, and re-established herself commercially, so that she was as strong as the countries who had beaten her. Inflation had wiped out her debts. She borrowed from other countries, made civic improvements of every kind, and within fifteen years of the end of the war, conditions inside Germany were as good as any, and better than most other countries. All paid for by foreign money, while her own was being absorbed in the production of armaments.

"Today, make no mistake about it, she is the mightiest country in Europe, and her territory greater than ever in her history. The Hun enjoys war, and whatever the result, experience has shown him he'll probably gain a damned sight more than he'll lose."

He broke off and stared at the floor. A frown creased his high forehead.

"I'll buy you that soapbox yet!" I laughed. "You'd be a riot in Hyde Park - or cause one! What's the use of getting all steamed up about things? What good does it do?"

"No use being an ostrich, Stevo," he answered quietly.

"Okay," I agreed. "So why believe in the invincibility of the British Empire? Face it! The German war machine if properly handled, is capable of conquering the world. So what? All great Empires fall in the end. Maybe it's our turn."

He shook his head.

"So far, Hitler's taken everything before him by force of arms," he answered slowly. "But man to man the Germans are no match for us. A war of diplomacy is beyond the conception of Hitlerism - the Führer's not a clever enough strategist to defeat us."

I stifled a yawn. Vaguely wondered why he had chosen this moment to indulge his favourite subject so deeply. Did he mean to channel my thoughts away from my own troubles? I tried to concentrate on his words.

Maginot and Siegfried vaguely suggested to me a parallel of the invincible force and the immovable object. The advance of Hitler's armies, the annexation of Austria and Czechoslovakia, these things were part of the unfortunate progression of might in a world where the weakest went to the wall.

Those things had been no concern of mine. Their significance confined to the newsprint that comprised my daily newspapers. Words - providing a topic for general discussion for those who were interested - and that hadn't included me!

The victims of the spreading tentacles of the Fuhrer's avarice were a long way off. The breath of their tragedy had never really reached me. My life had been too full. My father - Music - My eagerly awaited marriage - The security of a congenial job. These things had made up my design for living. Selfish perhaps. Narrow. Unquestionably trivial in the scheme of things. Perhaps that was why I had lost them!

I looked at Arthur's flushed face. His head was cocked expectantly, waiting for me to comment.

I grinned at him.

"You believe all that, don't you?" I said lightly. "You talk about it as though you *know*. It never interests me. I mean, there's no sense in getting all steamed up about something you can't alter, is there? Only brings on ulcers! Leave it to the politicians to work out. That's what they're paid for, isn't it?"

"It's not as easy as that, Stevo," he told me earnestly. "Every now and again, international politicians brew a strong emetic called War. They ladle it out with a few well-worn platitudes about overcrowding, and the balance of power. However we kick, we've got to swallow the dose - all of us. Believe me, it's in the pot now, and in a little while we'll all be up to our necks in the bloodiest war in history."

"Maybe that's what we need in this country," I muttered with a shrug. "Something to remind us we're all on the same side. Something to line us up together."

"You can say that again," he agreed. "It takes a war to get us all pulling in the same direction. Queer how we can always muster two things in the face of national disaster - an indivisible unity and an unshakeable faith. Men sink their private griefs and differences when their rights and liberties are at stake. Develop a new set of values. I always think the first great irony of war is the waste of fellowship which sustains it, and the premature death of that same unity once the issue of the battle has been decided."

"I won't quarrel with that," I said thoughtfully. "Maybe Hitler's done me a good turn. Provided me with an answer to my problem. I need a job. Well, what about one of the Services. Where better to bury the past. A new life. New interests. Comradeship."

As I looked at him, I realised suddenly, the reason for his oratory. This was what he had been leading up to, and at last the words had come from me. Maybe he was disappointed because they had been prompted by selfishness rather than the spirit of patriotism and the desire to join modern crusaders in their battle against the forces of evil seeking to destroy the world.

He sighed.

"It's a great idea, Stevo," he said at last. "Escapism! Well, I suppose personal reasons don't matter. The issue at stake is too vital. I've got to tell you - I decided today. I'm volunteering for the Royal Navy. How about it?"

I smiled suddenly. Already I felt better. He had decided for me. I reached out and gripped his hand

"You wasted an awful lot of wind getting to the point," I told him. "Okay. It's a bet!"

CHAPTER THREE

On Wednesday, 6th September 1939, three days after Chamberlain's precise voice broke the uneasy silence of a sunny Sunday morning with its solemn declaration of war, I kept my word to Arthur, and enlisted.

Six weeks later, the preliminaries completed, I exchanged the unhappy notoriety of my civilian status, to become a New Entry in the Royal Navy. Reporting to Portsmouth Naval Barracks I found myself one of a 'class' of thirty like-minded men between the ages of eighteen and late twenties who, for one reason or another, had renounced civilian life to serve King and Country

We were a motley crowd. The long, the short and the tall from all walks of life. Covertly sizing each other up as we were kitted out with uniform and hammock before being taken on the rounds by a leather-faced Leading Seaman who had been detailed to show us the ropes, and how to sling a hammock. My life in the Navy had begun!

To most people in England the Prime Minister's announcement came almost as a relief. After months of tension and uncertainty, we knew where we stood. Together, and with war only a few days old, it showed! People were beginning to look at each other with new faces - with warmth and friendliness.

Already, there had been casualties amongst ships caught between ports by lone U-boats, and on land, Jerry was knocking hell out of Poland, yet to me, on that grey October morning when I reported for duty, the idea of war was still unreal.

I was a stranger in a new world. A world of uniforms and regulations, where a man didn't need to think for himself - only to obey, and go on obeying until obedience became an instinct, and behaviour motivated by nothing more than a rigid formula of text-book discipline that made up the pattern of each day.

By the end of 1939, the Allies had lost more than a hundred ships to the U-boats. The battleship Royal Oak had been torpedoed and sunk at Scapa Flow. The aircraft carrier Courageous had been lost, there were many more, and although their names meant little to me their loss was etched in the grim expressions of the regular sailors with whom I was surrounded, and I learned that the German pocket battleships outgunned our heaviest cruisers, and were faster than most.

During those first weeks at Portsmouth, I was glad of the last minute emergency that stopped Arthur joining up with me. His boss had been rushed to hospital with a suspected duodenal ulcer, and Arthur had agreed to stay on at the printing works and manage things until other arrangements could be made.

My feelings were not disloyal to Arthur. It was just that I needed desperately to leave the past behind - and he was part of it. Later, when I'd had a chance to re-adjust myself I knew I'd feel different.

My days were full, obliterating all else but the endless panoply of drills and instructions, carried out by a succession of weather-beaten, poker-faced fanatics bent on making sailors of the motley assortment of raw material the National Emergency had channelled into the Senior Service.

A world full of uniforms and ranks. Of regulations and traditions dedicated with pride and humility to that exciting mistress, the Sea. The invincible Sea, and the ships and men to whom her ever-changing moods were a perpetual challenge, loving it, fearing it, hating it, yet unable to give it up, for the sea was in their eyes and in their blood, an integral part of them. It was tiring. All absorbing, and I drenched myself in it. Relieved for a while of the nightmare that had brought me there.

In the first few weeks, the thirty of us drifted into little groups, forming new friendships - new mates. I had been drawn to Lofty Yates from the beginning. Maybe because I'd watched him sitting at the piano in the mess, knocking out a one-fingered jingle. Obviously killing time. Magnetically drawn towards the instrument, I'd approached slowly. Stopped a couple of feet away.

The man on the stool appeared to be tall with broad shoulders and strong hands. A frown of concentration creased his rugged forehead as he stared at the keyboard. I decided he was older than I. Perhaps by three or four years.

I stood there watching him for a few moments, and at last, with a triumphant crash, he managed to synchronise the lower octave with the enormous forefinger of his left hand. Then he got up and looked at me. Fixing me with the darkest pair of brown eyes I had ever seen.

"Lofty Yates," he said without preamble, proffering his hand.

I introduced myself.

"You play this box of tricks?" he asked, nodding towards the piano.

"After a fashion," I told him.

"That makes us mates!" he laughed.

And so it was. Mates. Before long, Mike O'Leary, attached himself to us. Mike had been brought up with racehorses but grew too big for the saddle, and following the steps of his maternal grandfather, had turned his thoughts to the sea. An irrepressible character with an insatiable appetite for beer and a good fight to which his crooked nose and cauliflower ear bore testimony. And there was Mike's shadow, 'Beady' Doyle, a pale faced, aggressive individual who'd spent two years in Borstal for 'breaking and entering' - and bragged about it - his bulbous faintly bloodshot eyes, glaring and hostile.

Mike himself seemed content to have his morose companion around, and in time, Lofty and I came to accept him as one of our 'gang'. What he really thought of us, we never knew, but his devotion to O'Leary was proved the night he died.

But that was later. Much, much later when the bloody holocaust of the blitz was at its height.

The four of us spent much of our off-duty time together and in their company I could relax. Free my thoughts.

I remember the first night Lofty and I went out on the town together.

"What about a run ashore, Stevo," he suggested. "Pompey's famous for its night life!"

"Suits me," I agreed. "What about that place Mike was on about? On the Clarence Pier."

"Okay. Let's try it. Six o'clock boat then, eh?"

In Naval parlance, the barracks became a 'stone-wall frigate', and leaving them, was 'going ashore', and right from the beginning, we used the same routine phrases as sailors going ashore by ships' tender.

At six o'clock that evening, Lofty fell in beside me at the main gate where, handing in our station cards, we passed the inspection of the Officer of the Day, and went out into the Edinburgh Road.

It was a night of stars with a clear moon, throwing the blacked-out buildings into eerie silhouette as we made our way along Queen Street.

Drab looking shops alternated with numerous public houses, and from dark alleyways, loitering men and women emerged - shadowy, indistinct shapes with one clear purpose.

Voices called to us. Seductive. Harsh. Inviting and vituperative, as we brushed aside clutching hands and continued down the street to the 'Hard' - the area by the main dockyard gates that derives its name from the time when there were no jetties.

In those days, ships were taken into port on the tide and careened, or tilted, on the mud, to be left high and dry. The uppermost side of the boat would be cleaned before the incoming tide tilted the vessel the other way, exposing the underside for cleaning.

Alongside the South Railway jetty, the 'Queen Elizabeth' was moored.

"What price we get sent to her, eh Stevo?" Lofty exclaimed. "She's some ship!"

I knew nothing of ships, but even to me, she was beautiful. One of the great Dreadnoughts, she stood, a grey ghost. Powerful - proud - a veteran of the First World War when she had come to grips with the Turks and the Germans, and now, with her simplified superstructure and modern armaments, a formidable fighting machine, ready to do battle again.

"She's okay," I said quietly, as we turned back along the Hard. "Something like that would suit me fine."

"I know what you mean," he answered. "Something solid between you and the briny! Queer, me being in navy blue. I never was one for the sea. Always swore I'd go out with my feet on the ground. Now look at me!"

"Won't make any difference where you are when your time comes," I told him soberly.

"Guess not, Stevo. It's all marked out for us."

"D'you believe in God?" I asked abruptly, as we came to Sally Port where Nelson embarked for the Battle of Trafalgar.

"I've nothing against God," he returned, "but the canting baskets preaching Hell Fire and Damnation from the safety of the pulpit..."

He left the sentence in mid-air and spat viciously.

"I used to go to church 'til my old lady died," he went on harshly. "That finished me, I can tell you. We had her cremated. That's what she wanted. Christ! The bloody commercialization of it! D'you think that preaching humbug felt anything? Not on your Nellie! D'you think the identity of the corpse mattered a twopenny damn? Like Hell! Might as well have labelled it 'Burning up No 4'! Number Four in a nice orderly row of half-hourly cremations! For a couple of quid, the parson reeled off Burial Service Number so and so. Quick and unemotional as a bleeding parrot!

"There was me sobbing like a kid, and the perisher had the nerve to ask me if I was a relative, and tried to flog me a space in the Book of Remembrance - all the time edging me out of the place with a stupid smile on his clock - and spouting something about having to keep going. Might as well have said 'Next please!' Blimey, Stevo! I tell you there's more feeling in a railway timetable! That finished it for me, I can tell you."

"There are good and bad parsons, same as in any other profession," I said rationally. "Not that I'm sold on all the pomp and ceremony of the church. Far too many people pay lip service to Christianity by nothing more than a weekly couple of hymns and a few bob in the collecting box."

"You can say that again," he agreed. "I'll tell you what though. That padre in the mess last night seemed a good bloke."

"That's what I mean. About good and bad," I told him. "I felt good just talking to him. He was one of us. Flesh and blood. Not remote or someone apart from the human race - steeped in 'holier than thou' platitudes like..."

"Here," Lofty interrupted me, as the sound of dance music and voices cut stridently across the night air. "This is the place Mike was on about. Come on boy! Relax! Let's see if we can find a bit of spare to liven us up a bit!"

"If it's birds you're after," I warned him as we made our way into the hall. "I'm on a diet!"

"Depends what turns up to wet your appetite!" he grinned.

Inside, a motley crowd of servicemen and civilians milled round the floor to an off-key rendering of 'In the Mood'. Drink seemed to be flowing freely, the din was terrific, and the atmosphere thick with smoke and heaven knew what else!

We pushed our way to the bar and stood there taking in the surroundings and drinking beer. It was warm and oppressive, and after we'd downed two pints apiece, I began to sweat.

A plump bare-armed tart insinuated herself between Lofty and me, and stood staring up at him.

"How about a dance, Jack?" she invited.

Over the top of her straw coloured hair, Lofty winked at me, then grabbing her arm, swung her on to the floor. As her arms encircled his neck, I saw great patches of sweat discolouring the scarlet of her tight dress, and wrinkled my nose distastefully.

I downed another pint, and as there was no sign of Lofty, impulsively selected a partner from a group of giggling girls watching me with open invitation from the other end of the bar, and joined the dancers on the floor. The evening wore on. Sweating - drinking - dancing - necking - I began to feel pleasantly drowsy.

I tightened an arm round my partner and felt her immediate response.

"Coming home with me?" she murmured. "I've got a nice little place."

I nuzzled her neck, feeling hot, excited. Drew her close to me, feeling her soft eager body pressed against mine.

"Okay, Jack," she whispered. "I'll give you a good time."

My hands slid down her thighs. With a thrill of excitement I realised there was nothing beneath the flimsy black dress she wore. She began to steer me back towards the bar.

"How about a little bottle to take home then - eh dear?" she wheedled.

I stumbled against the counter, still holding her. My eyes were smarting - my throat dry. Hot with wanting her. Eager to go with her.

As I groped in my pocket, Lofty was suddenly beside me. An arm flung across my shoulder.

"Time we were on our way, Stevo," he said quietly.

"He's coming with me," my partner protested harshly. "You go and fix yourself up."

"Then it must be for love, darling," he told her cheerfully. "It's another six days to pay-day. We're skint!"

She pulled herself clear of me. Eyes narrowed to an anger obvious even to my fuddled mind. I grinned at her, reaching out an unsteady arm to draw her to me again.

"Bloody nerve!" she shrilled, backing away.

"Never mind. You go home and keep it warm," Lofty ribbed her. "We'll be back on Friday. Okay, Stevo?"

"Okay," I muttered thickly. "Christ! It's hot in here. Let's get some air."

We elbowed our way to the door to find a group of men pushing and shoving as two sailors struggled to get into the hall.

I heard Lofty's low whistle.

"It's Mike and Beady!" he cried. "Looks as though Mike's had a skinful. Let's break it up before he really gets his rag out. You get Beady, I'll grab Mike!"

We charged together. The nearest muscleman turned and saw us coming, and misinterpreting our purpose, swung a vicious right at Lofty.

That really started it! The next instant we were all at it hammer and tongs! Mike let out a whoop of welcome.

"Turn it in, Mike," I yelled at him, lashing out wildly. Felt the impact of teeth on my clenched fist. Winced as someone's knee caught me in the groin. Doubled up, momentarily winded, while all around me the melee of flailing arms continued.

Came a sudden crash - the sound of breaking glass - a confusion of voices, shrill and angry.

"Get him, Dave! Let him have it, Bill! Put that perishin' light out!"

And then, above all else, a sudden warning shout,

"Look out! Patrol!"

An instant of electrified silence, then I found myself hauled to my feet, and the next instant I was running beside Lofty. Haring back to the barracks. We stopped a few yards from the main gate.

"What happened to the others?" I panted.

"Reckon they bought it," Lofty said, looking back along the street. "Mike's a bloody fool! A gutful of beer and he'd fight his own grandmother!"

We hung around for a while, but there was no sign of Mike or Beady, so we picked up our station cards and turned in.

It was late afternoon the following day before we saw Mike again. One of his eyes was completely closed and his mouth distorted.

"Didn't I tell you it was a darlin' of a place?" he demanded blithely as we commiserated with him. "Sure it's the Mother of God's own gift to a fighting man like meself!"

"What good did it do you?" I asked. "Three days leave stopped, and no pay."

"Why, that's nothin' at all," he grinned. "Just long enough you might say, to recharge me batteries!"

"What about Beady?" Lofty wanted to know. "I heard he was in sick bay."

"And so he is," Mike confirmed. "He's having a couple of broken teeth drawn. It's nothing at all."

Oh I was glad of the three of them - Lofty, Mike and Beady!

The rest of my messmates would have been friendly enough I suppose, but I didn't give them a chance. There would have been too many questions. Questions that led back - and back - when I only wanted to go forward.

Like the night when someone asked.

"Where you from then, Stevens?"

"Dorset," I answered shortly.

"Not Sandworth by chance?"

The question came from Pete Williams, and I froze.

I nodded, my throat suddenly dry.

"I've got a sister lives there," Williams went on conversationally. "She married a chap called Rutland. He's a reporter on the Sandworth Herald. They're coming up for a drink sometime. Maybe you know them?"

I shook my head, not trusting myself to speak. A reporter... from Sandworth.

The ghouls were out again. Closing my mouth - setting a barrier between me and the others. In the midst of their lighthearted chatter, I remained silent. Suspicious of every question. Churlish! Unresponsive, until they came to exclude me altogether, tolerating my company only because of Lofty and Mike.

From the beginning I think Lofty sensed my loneliness. Knowing that when a crowd of us went into town, saturating ourselves in a pay packet's worth of beer, though it dulled the ache inside me, I stood on the edge of things, and the painted little whores, scarcely in their teens, who hawked their wares in every bar, filled me with anger, and a wild sense of frustration.

More than once I left the others and turned back alone to the barracks, and always, before I'd gone fifty yards up the road, Lofty was there, falling into step beside me, quiet and unquestioning. There was a lot of Arthur Ryan about him, and in those first weeks at Portsmouth, although we talked a lot together, it was soothingly impersonal.

I had been lucky enough to get Christmas leave and it was good to see the Ryans again. It was only the second time I had been back to Lilac Cottage since joining up. I thought Mrs Ryan looked frail, but she was cheerful enough and greeted me with warmth and affection. Certainly she was more like a mother to me than my own had been and I came to love her. She wrote me regular, cheerful letters filled with amusing anecdotes of village life in the black-out, and despite rationing, often sent me a parcel of cakes and chocolate although I told her I didn't really need them.

Arthur was waiting impatiently for the time when he would be released from his job in order to join the Navy, but I knew his mother was dreading the day.

At the beginning of January, having completed our preliminary training, Lofty and I started our gunnery course at Whale Island.

The world's most famous gunnery school. Mike and Beady had opted for HMS Vernon, the centre for underwater missiles.

At Whale Island we learned, and we learned fast. The routine, exhausting and rigid, relentlessly moulding us into machines. Like robots we responded to orders, subjugating the impulse to rebel - to argue - to question. At first we did it because it was easier, until at last it became a matter of pride.

And then, in the middle of February, I met Cora.

A couple of weeks before, Lofty had returned from an evening at the Gladstone Hall to announce that he had met a 'couple of smashers!'

"You'd have gone a bundle, Stevo," he said enthusiastically. "Real class."

"Sorry I missed out," I told him.

"They're in the band," he explained. "One of them's the pianist. Just up your street. Her name's Cora. She teaches at a kindergarden during the day. The other one, Kate, plays the fiddle. She's a hairdresser and boy, could I go for her! I've promised to take you along as soon as we can make it together."

"Fine," I agreed. "I'll look forward to it."

The days were grey and the war news did nothing to dispel the gloom. The U-boats were taking a heavy toll of our ships and the only brightness we could look forward to was in the nightly broadcasts of Lord Haw Haw from Hamburg, a British rogue spy who, in an attempt to sap the morale of the British public, only succeeded in making himself an object of ridicule.

One day I received a letter from Arthur telling me that Susan had announced her engagement to a Royal Marine stationed at Poole. Depression gripped me. I was back in Lawson Street and the life torn away from me. I lay in my hammock, brooding and bad-tempered, remembering Susan, and after a little while Lofty appeared.

"What's on then, Stevo?" he demanded in surprise. "Come on! Have you forgotten we're going ashore?"

"Count me out," I answered shortly. "I'm not feeling very sociable."

He glanced at the letter in my hand.

"Bad news?" he asked quietly.

"Does it matter?" I returned churlishly. "Look - just leave me alone will you."

For a moment he stood there looking at me, his lean, melancholy face twisted and questioning.

"You're a queer cuss," he said at length, "but you're all right."

"Thanks," I muttered dryly.

He hesitated.

"Come on," he coaxed. "Force yourself. You need a change. We both do."

"Oh turn it up will you," I protested. "I've told you. I don't feel like going ashore. What's wrong with that?"

He shrugged and turned away. Put one foot on the ladder then looked back at me.

"It won't work," he said deliberately. "I reckon you're burning bridges like me. You never came into this caper because you wanted to. Escapism - that's what it was. Only you can't run away from your thoughts. You've got to learn to live with them."

I sat up.

"Why the bloody sermon?" I demanded bitterly. "I don't know what the hell you're on about, but pack it up will you! I'm here, that's good enough. I don't need a post mortem about it! If I don't want to go ashore, it's none of your business..."

"Like I said, Stevo," he interrupted me. "I like you, but you don't make it easy. Some of the others don't go for you at all. You're a fool. You're trying to stand on the edge and it won't work! Your only hope of forgetting is to plunge right in at the deep end and..."

"Damn you!" I burst in furiously. "How the hell d'you know about me..."

A little smile creased the corners of his thin mouth.

"I've seen my own feelings reflected too often in your face," he said quietly. "I know the symptoms. Believe me, Stevo, to escape, you've got to hide, and that means getting right into whatever camouflage you've picked for yourself. No use brooding on the border. You sort of lose confidence. Don't inspire it either, and if there's one thing you won't be able to stand, it's being alone. See what I mean?"

I opened my mouth to answer, but stopped, uncertain what to say, then embarrassed, I hauled myself out of the hammock and stood looking at him.

"Message taken and understood," I told him ruefully. "All right, Lofty. Let's go ashore, shall we?"

"Sure," he grinned. "We're going to a party."

"Whose?" I asked.

"Kate's," he explained. "It's her birthday."

"Kate?" I muttered - and then I remembered. "You mean the girl at the Gladstone?"

"Right!" he agreed eagerly. "That's where we're picking them up."

"Them?" I repeated.

"You remember me telling you about Cora," he reminded me impatiently.

"So you did," I agreed. "Didn't know you had this all sewn up though."

We went ashore in silence. A fine rain was falling and it was getting colder.

"What about a pint at the Fisherman's?" I suggested.

He hesitated. The first time I'd known him jib at the prospect of a drink.

"Okay," he said quietly. "If that's what you want."

The bar was crowded. Lofty downed his beer and stood looking anxiously from me to the clock.

Watching him I began to catch something of the excitement he was feeling. A blind date - a date of Lofty's conniving.

What sort of a bird was she, this Cora? So far, Lofty hadn't struck me as much of a one for the opposite sex - not to go soft on them.

"Women," he'd say. "Women mean trouble, Stevo! A bad one brings out the worst in a man and destroys his faith in the whole sex, and a good one makes him so conscious of his own shortcomings, that he loses his nerve. Gets caught up in inhibitions and restrictions. Gets soft! Leave 'em alone, Stevo! They're bad medicine!"

His words had pushed me back to Susan and my mother. The one who had destroyed my father, the other, a snivelling, shrinking coward who'd gibed at sharing the ricocheting shadows of my notoriety.

The bloody Marine was welcome to her, I thought savagely.

My thoughts went haywire. Cora - Cara - she was there again. Laughing. Mocking. Triumphant. I closed my eyes tightly, trying to squeeze out that hated image. What was done was done. Surely time to let go! Opening my eyes I saw Lofty gazing at me intently, but he didn't say anything as we left the pub and crossed the street to the Gladstone Hall.

"What's she like, this Kate? Good or bad?" I asked lightly.

"Neither," he answered seriously. "Honest, and that's how I like 'em!"

We pushed our way inside. A great scraping sound met us. The thin strains of music. The chatter of voices. And couples dancing cheek to cheek sang to each other, and laughed and whispered.

Above the heads of the dancers, thin vaporish spirals of tobacco smoke writhed and twisted towards the arched wooden ceiling, coiling round the garlanded beams and the scintillating light fitments.

Mostly, there were sailors in the hall, but a few khaki uniforms showed amongst them, and here and there the odd pair of flannels and sports coat.

The din was harsh and ear-splitting, and it was quite some time before I could make out the tune to which the dancers swayed, and cavorted, and clung to each other. At my side, Lofty glanced at the wall clock.

"It's nearly interval time," he muttered, taking off his cap. "Let's get over to the band."

I followed him as he pushed his way down the hall to the platform.

The violinist was tall and thin with a mop of elaborately curled dark hair. As Lofty caught her eye, she gave him a wide, welcoming smile, and as her friendly eyes rested on me, held up one of her thumbs in an eloquent gesture of appraisal.

And then I saw Cora!

Afterward, I told myself it was the way she caressed the keys of the piano that caught at my throat. In her eyes was the look I'd seen in my father's when he played.

She was blonde, and nature had fashioned her that way. Her hair was smooth and shining, done in page-boy style, framing the calm oval of her face.

Cora was no classical beauty. Taken feature by feature, her nose was a trifle too long, her mouth too wide, and yet, my first sight of her, sitting there absorbed in the music, was the very quintessence of serenity and loveliness.

She wore a short white dress cut low at the throat and moulded gently to her firm young breasts. A single spray of scarlet roses at her shoulder. Her legs and arms were bare and golden and strong, and sitting there, she seemed to me like some virile Nordic goddess.

I remained staring at her, not realising that the music had stopped, and then getting up from the piano, she stepped down off the platform, and I heard the violinist say,

"How d'you do it, Cora? You've mesmerised him!"

Embarrassed, I murmured conventional greetings as Lofty introduced us.

I felt Cora's hand in mine, and a tremor of excitement surged through me - electrifying. I thought she withdrew her hand a shade too quickly, heard her sharp little intake of breath.

Her voice was quiet, so that the first words of our meeting were lost in the noise of the crowd surging across the floor to the refreshment tables. I scarcely noticed that Lofty and the dark girl had left us.

"So you're Cora," I heard myself say. "I didn't think you'd be like this!"

Her eyes, blue and smiling, looked into mine.

"Blind dates are always a risk," she answered gravely. "I promise not to bite!"

I looked at her seriously.

"You're all right Cora..." I muttered awkwardly and broke off abruptly, lost for words.

"Snap!" she laughed. "Well, that's a good start isn't it!"

Stupidly, I wanted to say a hundred impossible things to her. The words tumbled over each other in my brain as though, quite suddenly, I was alive again, and the numbness that hung like a pall over the memory of things past, lifted a while showing, not the past from which I had fled cringing, but the future, shadowy, but unmistakable.

Then Lofty was back to thrust a plate of sandwiches under my nose.

"All right, Stevo?" he enquired anxiously.

"Hundred per cent," I told him. "When does this show end."

"Nine-thirty for us," he answered with a wink. "I told you. It's Kate's birthday. She's got a couple of reliefs lined up to take over. Any time now, and they'll show up. Then we can go."

"They'll come," Kate put in confidently, sucking lemonade through a straw as I congratulated her on her birthday. "Got something stronger than this at home. Hey, Cora! What's wrong with you? You're very quiet."

Cora smiled.

"I'm fine," she said simply. "I'm happy, that's all."

"When I'm happy I make a lot of noise," Kate told her. "Let myself go. Ah - here's Andy and Sophie now."

An ascetic looking young man and a fluffy redhead made their leisurely way towards us.

"You boys wait outside," Kate said, smiling up at Lofty. "We'll be about five minutes."

"Okay," he said. "Come on, Stevo. Let's get cracking.".

Outside the rising wind was cold and sleet was falling.

"We're going to catch a packet if we're not careful," Lofty grumbled. "Perishin' cold! Don't want to hang around too long in this. How d'you like Cora then?"

"She's all right," I told him simply.

"On occasions," he said, almost to himself. "You've got to admit, I have flashes of almost brilliant inspiration. I knew she was for you, Stevo, the instant I clapped eyes on her."

I glanced across the street. A single placard on a news vendor's pitch announced briefly,

'CONNOR REPRIEVED'

"He's not going to swing after all," Lofty commented. "Join the elite at Broadmoor most likely. These trials confound me. All this bloody fanny about blackouts and loss of memory! Take this Connor! He criminally assaulted a school kid and she died, but he doesn't remember doing it, so the hangman is going to be ten quid worse off and Connor, with one eye tightly closed, and an inward raspberry at good old British justice, goes off to Broadmoor! Another poor devil, goaded to the end of his endurance by a bitch of a wife, gets the flamin' rope..."

Lofty's voice went on, low and vibrant with contemptuous anger, but his words were lost to me.

I felt the moisture gather on my forehead, and something inside me trembled. Beside me my father swung, broken and twisted on the rope, and involuntarily I recoiled. Anguish gripped me. The haunting horror of my parents' end, released now by Lofty's words, threatened for one fearful moment to overwhelm me.

Tears welled in my eyes. My throat tightened. I wanted to run - away from Lofty - to be alone in the darkness. Alone with my misery.

Subconsciously I must have started to walk away from him, because suddenly, I heard his voice behind me,

"Stevo! What's up?"

Hearing his purposeful stride, I stopped. Dabbed at my smarting eyes and folded my arms to rub my shoulders.

"It's damned cold," I muttered. I pushed a cigarette into my mouth, and as Lofty cupped a lighted match in his hands, I saw his anxious face. His eyes, kind and concerned, but questioning. For a moment, it was as though we took stock of each other, and then, as I turned away from him, we heard the girls and Kate and Cora came running to join us.

Simultaneously, the real rain came, bitterly cold and drenching.

"Quick, we'll have to run for it," Kate cried, tying a scarf over her head and grasping Lofty's arm. "Come on, sailor. Let's go!"

Cora was wearing a raincoat, the collar standing high. In the gloom, her face was featureless. Silently I reached out towards her, tucking her hand in the crook of my arm and taking my time about it. Savouring her nearness.

For an instant, shadowed silhouettes in the blacked out street, we stood facing one another, then we turned and ran after the others.

CHAPTER FOUR

I needed Cora, just as once I wanted Susan. It took just two weeks to find that out. Two weeks of holding back, unrelaxed, strained and churlish as I tried to stop her getting under my skin. I wasn't ready yet, I told myself. No emotional upsets. A bit of fun maybe. A laugh, but nothing deep. Nothing lasting.

Only I knew from the beginning, this was different. I thought about her all the time, wanting to be with her. Bursting with a thousand things to say to her, yet when we met, mute and brooding, shackled to a past that crucified the future.

I'd never known anyone like her. Her sweetness, and the calm serenity all about her. When I thought of her something caught at my throat as though the thought was a holy one. Perhaps it was.

Like me, Cora was an orphan. Her mother had died the previous summer, her father when she was only an infant. Once or twice I was able to meet her from the nursery school where I'd find her surrounded by youngsters and parents, flushed and happy, adoring and adored by all the kids.

Holding hands, we'd walk back to her flat together. Sit in the firelight.

This was my private heaven. The shining cascade of her loosened hair. Her quiet smile. The trembling of her soft lips when I kissed her. These were the visions that filled my days, and I wanted her, not just to be her lover, but in all the ways there were. To share my life with her.

To have and to hold... And then the dream broke.

Shattered to bits before the devils that hovered in the dark recesses of my mind.

My constant companions! Could I ask Cora to share them with me? Could I dare? Risk the horror in her eyes? Feel her recoil from me?

"What's up, Stevo?" Lofty asked one evening when, prey to my own dark thoughts, I sat with him in moody silence in the mess.

"Nothing," I muttered. "Browned off that's all. Feel like a walk. Coming?"

Silently, he followed me ashore, falling into step beside me as we turned towards the town.

"Want to get it off your chest?" he demanded suddenly. "It's eating you up."

"If it worries you, I can walk by myself," I muttered churlishly.

"Don't talk like a fool!" he answered. "It's Cora, isn't it?" and as I made no answer, he went on. "Gone on her, eh?"

"She's a nice girl," I told him carefully.

"Sort of girl a man could marry," he said, quietly insistent.

"Oh, for Christ's sake, Lofty! Give it a rest will you!" I shouted.

He stopped suddenly. A moment of incredible silence, then reaching out a long arm, he gripped me purposefully by the shoulder and swung me round to face him.

"Stevo," he demanded, his voice curiously stilted. "You're not married?"

His anger was a white hot thing between us.

"No," I said shortly. "I'm not married. Now let up, will you."

For a moment we stood there, measuring each other in the darkness - then slowly, he released me.

"Okay, Stevo," he said quietly. "If you say so. I'll get back to the ship."

He turned and strode away from me. Long striding. His tall frame straight. Head high, and as I watched him go, I remembered the other figure I had loved, striding away from me - from life.

Impulsively, I made a movement after him. Stopped, then went on aimlessly, undecided where to go. What to do.

Cora was in Bournemouth spending a couple of weeks with an aunt who was all set to go to the States for the duration of the war. An old lady who was trying her damnedest to persuade her niece to go with her. The thought frightened me, even though, when we'd talked about it, Cora had reassured me.

I tried to view it dispassionately. The war was going to be a long and bloody struggle, that much was certain. It was on the cards that a lot of people were going to die, and not just in the Services. In America, Cora would be safe. Against that was my need of her, and that was why, when we next met, I'd got to tell her. She'd got to know about me, and then decide whether or not to stay.

In the darkness, as I walked slowly along Edinburgh Street, I tried to sort out the words I would use to tell her. And then, as I reached the entrance to the barracks, I heard someone talking to the officer of the Day, and recognised the voice of the Chaplain.

I made a decision. I would talk to the Chaplain. Tell him my problem. Ask his advice.

I caught up with him outside his office.

"Chaplain, sir," I said breathlessly. "Can I talk to you please?"

"Of course," he answered readily. "Come along inside. There'll be some coffee in a minute or two."

I followed him inside and sat down whilst he examined various messages on his desk, and after a little while, a rating came in with a flask of coffee.

The Chaplain rummaged under his desk and produced two cups. As he poured out the coffee, I caught the faint smell of rum.

"Helps keep out the cold," he said smilingly as he handed me a cup.

I thanked him gratefully. He held his cup in both hands, contemplating me over the top of it. His eyes very blue. Very kind.

"Let's see. Stevens isn't it?" he said at length.

I nodded.

Now, draining his drink, he leaned back in his chair watching me. Waiting for me to speak.

I mouthed, seeking words.

"I need advice," I jerked out at length.

"What's the problem?" he asked.

"You're a man of God," I said abruptly. "You believe all that about the sins of the fathers passing on to their children, don't you?"

"I don't believe they should," he answered carefully, "but indisputably, in many cases they do affect the lives of the children - and succeeding generations."

"My father was hanged!" I blurted harshly.

The expression in his calm eyes didn't alter.

"Tell me about it," he said simply.

It was easy, once I started. The words came pouring out.

"They shouldn't have hanged him! They shouldn't!" I ended bitterly. "She was rotten all the way! She asked for it! Any man who was a man at all wouldn't have stood for it. He was a good, decent man."

"A good man doesn't take another's life."

"My father was a good man," I repeated quietly.

"There may have been great provocation," he agreed calmly, "but nevertheless, your father broke two laws. The law of our community, and the law of God. The law of God makes no exceptions. He said 'Thou shalt not kill'!"

"They hanged him, didn't they?" I reminded him harshly. "How do you justify that in 'God's law'?"

"I can't," he admitted. "God gave us a set of rules. Standards for us to live by. All of us. No exceptions. He didn't say 'You mustn't kill except for such and such a reason'. We can't blame Him if men defy His laws."

"If God made the lot of us, He must have known how we'd turn out," I muttered. "The good and the bad. The crooked and the straight. The strong and the weak. He's got to take the blame for the lot of us."

"He does, Stevens. He does," the Chaplain assured me earnestly. "But life isn't a rose-strewn path to eternal glory. It's a tough climb. It has to be. We've got to prove ourselves worthy to share Eternity with Him. It's not easy to understand or accept. Believe me, you need faith. We all do. Perhaps you'll find yours through Cora."

"I have to tell her, don't I?"

"You don't need me to tell you that," he replied. "The fact that you're here is proof that you know what you have to do. You know you must tell her, for both your sakes, and what's left afterwards is perhaps the true measure of your faith in God and in your fellow men. There's purpose in everything. God's purpose. Faith gives us the ability to recognise that purpose. All we need is the will to see. I'd like to help you, Stevens, but you've got to help yourself. Talk to Cora and then come and talk to me again."

"Thanks," I said with a sigh, "I'll do that."

He glanced briefly at his watch.

"I don't like to cut this short, Stevens," he said quietly, "but I'm due at the CO's shortly. I ought to be going."

Hastily I stood up.

"Sorry sir," I apologised. "Shouldn't have come barging in on you like this. Keeping you..."

"Nonsense," he interrupted me, "You needed to confide in someone. I'm glad it was me, and I'll be looking forward to seeing you again when you've got it off your chest to Cora."

I murmured my thanks and went out into the cool air. I felt no different. The Chaplain had said what I'd expected him to say. What, in my heart, I'd hoped he wouldn't.

Why couldn't the past stay dead. What right had it to intrude upon the future. A future already in the jeopardy of War! Depression gathered me up as I went back to the mess. Stayed with me, holding me moody and restless. Resentful and frustrated. And the days crept by, leadened by doubts and fears. I'd got to know!

As soon as Cora returned from Bournemouth, I would tell her. I'd got to. The resolve became a fixation. My impatience making the intervening days even longer.

We spoke on the telephone every day and I hungered for her.

And then my training at Whale Island was completed, and eagerly reading the draft chit on the notice board, I found I was to join the crew of the Audax, a destroyer attached to the Local Defence Flotilla, and that Lofty, Mike and Beady would be my shipmates. We had seven days shore leave before joining the ship.

We all went ashore for a drink together. Wondered about the officers, our mess mates and the ship herself which was lying alongside another destroyer at North Slip jetty. Mike and Beady quickly decided they would spend their leave with their respective families. To Lofty it was a heaven sent opportunity to be with Kate.

We were excited. Eager. Ribbing one another, and perhaps our laughter was a shade too loud, for underneath the facade of exuberance, lay the sobering thought that soon we were to play an active part in the war.

When I 'phoned Cora to tell her the news, I sensed the concern in her voice. For the first time, I was going to be on active service and the thought frightened her. Then she told me she was returning to Portsmouth the following day. Train times were uncertain, and she had some business to attend to with the staff at the nursery school. We arranged that we would meet at the flat in the late afternoon.

I looked forward with mixed feelings. Much as I longed to see her, I knew I could no longer delay telling her about my father. Tomorrow would either be the beginning of a new life for me - or the end of a dream. If she turned away from me, what would be left? I shuddered. Maybe fate was marking my card again. Active service! The war at sea... the prospect of a watery grave...

I turned in early. Spent a restless night trying to sort out how I would tell her... How she would react...

Then came the nightmare that was to plague my life. My short bursts of sleep were filled with grotesque visions of my mother. A nightmare as my father, head lolling, eyes bulging, held her in his arms. I wrestled with him, trying to tear her away. Screamed at him. And all the while, she laughed. Mocking me. Shouting obscenities. The protests of my messmates broke the dream.

"Put a sock in it, Stevens!" Muffled curses...

I sat up with a start, bathed in sweat. Hammers pounding at my head. Afraid to let sleep claim me again, I lay wide-eyed staring into the darkness. I had dreamed of my parents before, but never like this. Perhaps my talk with the Chaplain had laid it all bare. How was I to know that the horror of Sandworth would return again and again to haunt my dreams.

The following morning passed on leaden feet, and then, leaving the barracks in the hope of spending an hour or so with Lofty, I saw Arthur Ryan!

Arthur in uniform!

Momentarily, I forgot my problems as we greeted one another.

He told me he'd been called up a couple of weeks previously and was hoping to get into Signals.

"Didn't think you'd make it so soon," I told him.

"Neither did I," he admitted. "The old man's nephew came

down from Crewe. He's taken over. When he started throwing his weight about, I couldn't get out soon enough. Mum's a bit upset, but she knew it was in the offing. She's gone down to Devon to her sister-in-law. She can stay there indefinitely until things settle down. She'll be writing to you anyway. So how are you making out, Stevo?"

"Okay," I assured him. "Yes. Okay."

He smiled, the little wrinkle of concern disappearing from the corners of his eyes as he stared at me.

"You look great," he decided. "I'm glad it's turning out all right for you. How's the gunnery course going?"

"Finished," I told him. "I'm joining a ship after this leave."

"Great! Look - I'm meeting some of the chaps from the mess at the Fisherman's. Come along. We can catch up with the news."

"You've soon found your way around," I laughed, and falling into step along the Hard, we started off towards the town, and suddenly, there was Cora hurrying towards us.

At sight of us she stopped uncertainly, and eagerly I went towards her.

"Cora!" I greeted her in surprise. "What..."

She hastily silenced me.

"I was coming to leave a message for you," she explained. "Oh, Mark, I'm so sorry. I hoped we'd have a little time together but I'd only been here a couple of hours when I got an urgent message to return to Bournemouth immediately. Aunt suffered a stroke soon after I left the house. She's very, very ill."

I held her in my arms, murmuring my sympathy, and then I remembered Arthur.

"Meet Arthur," I said, releasing her. "My best and oldest friend. Arthur meet Cora, the best thing that's happened to me - ever!"

He shot a quick searching glance at me, then turned to shake Cora's hand. It seemed to me he lingered over the gesture a shade too long, and there was an expression in his eyes I'd never seen there before.

Perhaps, like me, he fell at the start. Certainly, he came to love her. Abruptly, that first time they met, he released her fingers and looked away from me. A prickle of misgiving - dismissed as I turned to Cora.

"Have you time for a drink with us?" I asked her.

"I'm so sorry, Mark," she told me. "I'm going straight to the station now."

Her words were cold water. Disappointment roughened my voice.

"We'll come with you then."

Scarcely time to say goodbye. A swift kiss and the train was moving out.

"Hope things turn out all right," I called through the window. "Write to me..."

Her answer was lost in the noise of the train and the milling crowd of servicemen on the platform. Her face seemed very small, pale and anxious as I watched it out of sight.

"Hell!" I muttered.

"Nice girl," Arthur said quietly. "Known her long?"

"Long enough to love her. To want to marry her," I answered almost defensively.

Silently we made our way along the platform and out into the street.

"Have you asked her?" he wanted to know.

Somehow his interest irritated me.

"Not yet," I answered shortly.

Silence again, then,

"Does she know about..." he commenced seriously.

"What happened at Sandworth?" I finished bitterly. "No. She doesn't."

He glanced at me dubiously.

"You'll have to tell her, Stevo," he declared.

I swore.

"Of course I'll bloody tell her," I said savagely. "What sort of a heel d'you take me for? I'm sorry, Arthur. I've been working myself up to be able to tell her. Meant to do it today. Sort of turned sour now! Waiting, wondering, getting in a sweat about it, and now, just when I've psyched myself up to get it off my chest - this happens."

"I can guess how you feel," he assured me solemnly, "but I don't think you need worry. Not with a girl like Cora. Only get it off your chest."

"I'll do that," I muttered, but it was nearly a month later that the opportunity came...

Audax was a destroyer of the 'A' class. A slim, graceful two funnelled vessel gleaming from stem to stern with polished brass and steel. Built for speed, her armament consisting of two forward 4.7s superimposed, one amidship and one aft, two sets of torpedo tubes, and port and starboard depth charge rails projecting clear of her stern. She was also equipped with asdic.

Her peacetime complement had been eighty, but she had recently been modified to take a hundred and twenty men.

During those first hours aboard, jostling shoulders with stokers, engineers, asdic and torpedo men, gun layers and a whole variety of ratings forming part of that one integral unit, the Ship's Company, I felt a surge of spontaneous pride in the knowledge that I was part of it.

I had been detailed to ammunition supply No. 1 gun - Lofty to bridge look-out and Mike and Beady to the fire party.

Throughout the day, other ratings joined us, and we were exercised at Action Stations to give us some idea of what to expect when the alarm bells sounded.

A few dummy runs when we jostled and blundered, and suddenly, we were a unit - a machine. Crews closed up. Confident. Alert!

Our gun layer, a Leading Seaman GL2 was a keen one, working with his sights set on 'the rate' of Petty Officer through a course of gunnery instruction at Whale Island. He eyed us grimly.

"Our ammunition supply will have to be on the ball to get up to our firing rate," he told us. "We're the record holders in the flotilla, and we're not going to lose it!"

His expression dared us to fail him.

All around, torpedo tube and depth charge crews were going through their drill. Liberty men, we learned, were to be granted leave from 16.30 to 23.00 hours only, which didn't suit Mike at all as he'd arranged an all night session ashore.

"Not while we're on the move," a stoker told him. "We flashed through boilers this morning. That means we'll be under way anytime. Number One ordered Cox'un to prepare for sea during the dog watches. We never know the exact time we're going to slip. Could be any time."

And so it was. At 08.30 hours the following morning, a pale sun filtered through the early mist as I scrambled up the ladder to the fo'c'sle and fell in with five other hands under the leadership of Petty Officer Bowering who was in charge of the forward party.

"Stand by wires and ropes," he ordered.

A stocky man with the two and a half rings of a Lieutenant Commander, climbed the ladder to the bridge followed by the Sub-Lieutenant and the Yeoman of Signals.

Over the voice pipe the Cox'un reported,

"Cox'un at the wheel, sir."

I had been detailed to assist with the head wire.

"Watch the splinters in the wire, son," Bowering warned me with mild reproach, and self-consciously, I pulled on my protective leather gloves.

On the bridge, I could see Lofty, a fatuous grin on his face.

"Hold on after spring - let go forward - let go aft!"

The voice of the Captain echoed through the ship.

A hum of activity followed a succession of orders from the bridge. We cast off breast rope and spring and hauled our wires inboard until only the after spring remained. Came another order from the bridge.

"Let go after spring!"

A shout to the waiting hands on the jetty, and the remaining wire ran free and was quickly hauled in, and as we fell in smartly on the fo'c'sle, Audax edged her way from the quay side and swung her bows towards the harbour entrance.

Slowly we steamed past Fort Blockhouse, the ship's company at attention as the Bo'sun's mate piped the 'Still', the traditional salute to the flag of the Admiral commanding submarines, then passing down the buoyed channel into the famous fleet anchorage of Spithead, we turned west into the Solent and the Needles.

My first real encounter with the sea! A strange anticipatory thrill ran through me.

This was to be a routine affair. A rendezvous with three other destroyers off Portland Bill for an asdic sweep of the channel. The first of many in the weeks to follow, and though many were more eventful, more bloody, more soul-destroying, there were none that I remember more vividly.

From a building on the headland, a light flashed, answered by a series of flashing signals from our Yeoman. I learned later that this was a recognition signal which all ships must give before passing through the narrow channel.

It was early March. The wind was strong and biting. Gently at first, as we headed for the open sea, Audax rose and fell, but as her bows cleaved deeper, the deck began to leave my feet, and in those moments of suspension, my stomach was in my throat.

Near me, a young rating turned green. I watched him sag, hang by the rails for a moment, then heave himself upright to grimace at the Petty Officer who gibed him,

"Now then. What's this? Don't go pulling a Nelson on me!"

At his station on the bridge, Lofty seemed glued to his binoculars, unperturbed by the motion of the ship.

Ahead, I could see the high point of land known to sailors as the 'Hump' and the harbour and its breakwaters, and beyond, a slowly moving line of three destroyers.

The leading ship exchanged flashing signals with Audax as the gap between us narrowed.

"Stand fast asdic watch. Remainder fall in amidship," piped the Bo'sun's mate.

The undulating motion of the ship grew more violent as we neared the Bill.

"Rig life lines," came the next pipe.

"Take my tip and grab one when she's rolling," advised an AB with three badges on his sleeve. "One arm for the King. One for yourself!"

Now the wind was razor keen, thrusting the salty tang of its breath in our faces as we took our station astern of the rear ship and with signal flags flying, fanned out beyond the races of the Portland ledge, and headed westward.

The distance between the four destroyers widened until almost a mile separated each one, and so insidious was their motion, each seemed to be standing still.

The sky darkened, completely overcast with low scudding cloud and visibility so bad that the nearest ship seemed a grey ghost, animated only by the intermittent flashing of her light.

From the bridge the order passed to the asdic office,

"Range of reverberation 5,000 yards."

"What's all that about?" I asked a 'Killick Sparker' - the colloquial name for a Leading telegrapher.

"If you listen under the bridge," he explained. "You'll hear a repetitive 'ping-ping' from the small office there. That's the asdic transmission note which gives off an echo from any obstruction the sound wave meets."

"And how do they identify the object?" I questioned him.

"Different objects give off different sounds," he told me. "You get to know them. When I was in the old Portland Flotilla, they used to choose chaps with musical ears for asdic duty. I was in the first ship to be fitted with it, the old four funnelled cruiser 'Antrim', way back in 'twenty-five. We had to lower and raise the dome by western purchase in those..."

He broke off as there came a sudden shout from the bridge and I recognised Lofty's voice,

"Aircraft bearing Red 50!"

Came the clang of alarm bells. Men hurried to their action stations.

At No. 1 gun, I scanned the sky. Away to port, at an angle of about forty-five degrees, I saw a speck in the sky - no more.

I held my breath.

The aircraft was moving towards us. A black, twin-engined machine. Beside me, I heard Harris mutter,

"Bloody Heinkel!"

Already, the guns from one of the destroyers were blazing away. Our own gun crews waited, but Audax's 4.7 were not high altitude guns, and wouldn't bear. We only had a mounting of 5s and Lewis guns.

The 'plane came nearer. It was moving fast, wings dipped. I

stood there gaping at it, nursing a shell like a babe in arms, waiting for an order that couldn't come because of our ineffectual elevation.

I was holding my breath. Fear paralysing me. Then our 5s opened up, their rapid firing stinging my ears as I watched the tracers stretch towards the 'plane.

The Heinkel banked steeply, straightened, and with a roar of defiance streaked towards us.

At last, our 4.7s were able to bear.

"Keep that ammunition moving," shouted our gun layer. "We might hit the bastard. You never know!"

Each time the gun recoiled, I cringed, expecting to feel the impact in my stomach. The spent shell cases splattered on the deck all around me. The machine climbed and turned away to the east, a line of tracers following in its wake.

The silence that followed was uncanny.

Then came an announcement over the loud speaker,

"This is your Captain. That was a German reconnaissance 'plane. He will report our position to his base, and undoubtedly, we will attract the attention of more purposeful opposition. The destruction of U-boats is our objective. That is the purpose of this sweep, so I want every man on deck to keep his eyes open. Carry on with normal duties, but with extra vigilance. AA lookouts will be doubled."

My first encounter with the enemy. Not very spectacular. No heroics, and yet so finely etched in my memory. The men, the ships, the sea gently growling, quietly menacing, her sludge green depths sinister. Frightening, concealing unnameable terrors.

Even the expected U-boats failed to materialize, although on that first sweep we did have a bit of excitement when our asdic officer reported an echo at a distance of 3,000 yards on the port side. We reduced speed, but even as our crews prepared to let go depth charges, a definite whistling sound replaced the 'ping-ping' in the asdic, revealing that our supposed U-boat was nothing more formidable than a tight shoal of fish!

That was the pattern of my first weeks on Audax. It varied little except in the length of time I was away from Portsmouth.

Sometimes three days, sometimes a week. I 'phoned Cora whenever I could. Wrote to her. Received her loving letters, but all the time I ached for her, torturing myself with thoughts of her reaction when at last I could tell her what she had to know.

The war pattern varied little. In those early days of the war at sea, the U-boats were lone hunters, preying on lone ships. Swooping on the unprepared and unarmed. Although during that time Audax never came to grips with one, the anticipation was always there, especially when darkness came. The tension in the air - the uncertainty! It was there in every mans face. In the taut figures of the watch, stiff with expectancy.

And then, returning to Portsmouth after a six day sweep, I found that Cora had returned. Her aunt had died. There was no need of her in Bournemouth.

I rang her flat. Her voice answered me, and half an hour later I was holding her in my arms.

"It's been a long time," I murmured against her lips. "I've missed you."

"I've missed you too," she sighed.

I moved away from her. Gripped her hands.

"I love you, Cora," I told her solemnly. "You know that don't you?"

Her eyes were warm and soft as she looked at me.

"Yes, I know," she answered softly. "I've wanted so much to hear you say it."

"I love you," I said again.

"And I love you too, Mark," she whispered tremulously. "So much!"

She led me into the cosy sitting-room, and we sat together on the settee, the firelight making gold of her hair. My grip on her hand tightened. I resisted the desire to pull her into my arms again. Now! Now was the time to say what had to be said.

"Love's a funny thing," I muttered uncertainly, feeling for words. "Something that happens. Just happens. No rules. No conditions."

"Isn't that the way of all natural impulses?" she smiled. "They come from the heart. No strings attached."

"No strings," I echoed.

"It's only when the mind steps in that we get strings," she said thoughtfully. "When the mind tries to wear down the heart with reasoning."

I held her chin between my fingers, tilting it upwards so that her eyes looked into mine.

"That's just it," I told her earnestly. "Reason! If no one stopped to reason..." I broke off abruptly, then as she looked at me in puzzlement, I murmured shakily. "You don't really know anything about me, do you?"

"It cuts both ways," she reminded me calmly. "Love's an instinct. You don't ask for credentials before you fall in love."

"I know," I answered, "but for what comes afterwards. Marriage. Children..."

Abruptly I released her. All at once afraid. And as I buried my head in my hands, I felt her kneeling beside me. Her fingers caressing my hair.

"What's wrong, darling?" she whispered. "What are you trying to say?"

"I should have told you before," I blurted. "I tried, but I couldn't. I was scared of losing you."

"And now you're not?" she asked.

"Now more than ever," I told her, "but I've got to tell you about myself - about my father..."

I swallowed hard. She went on stroking my hair.

Waited. The silence broken by the crackling of the fire, and the sudden wail of the siren outside. Street noises as wardens went to their posts.

And then the words came tumbling out. She moved closer to me and I felt the beating of her heart. And when the words were drained from me, the story told, I heard her murmur huskily,

"Oh, Mark! How terrible for you! If I can help to make it up to you..."

It was then I dared to look at her, and saw in her shining eyes, the promise of all I'd ever hoped for.

And then she said some magic words.

"Let's get married, darling. As soon as possible. With this

dreadful war on, time is so precious."

CHAPTER FIVE

On the 13th April 1940 Cora and I were married at the local Registry office. The brief ceremony was witnessed by Lofty and Kate. My happiness was complete, and in the days that followed I began to see some kind of reason in what had gone before.

Nothing I had ever known could measure up to what I shared with Cora. Every moment together was precious.

My time at sea aboard Audax went on as usual and between long vigils with the destroyer flotilla, my leave periods were pretty regular. With Kate, Cora still played in the band at the Gladstone Hall, and against a background of sirens and menacing aircraft, with Lofty, Arthur and the others, we danced and sang the nights away until Cora and I returned to the sanctuary of the flat - 'our home'.

The war news was depressing. Hitler had invaded the Low Countries, driving on through the Channel coast, and the British Expeditionary Force together with Belgium and French forces had been forced to withdraw to Dunkirk, the only port not in enemy hands.

Some half a million men were stranded on the beaches at the mercy of waves of Stukka bombers attacking them and the two British destroyers embarking as many men as possible alongside the quay.

Churchill had taken over the reins of government from Chamberlain.

In Portsmouth things were happening. The harbour was a hive of activity. A large number of vessels were mustering. Ships of all sizes. Battle cruisers, down to landing craft, trawlers, hospital ships and countless small craft.

It was obvious something was brewing. Something pretty big. There was a sense of urgency among crewmen, but at that time we knew nothing of the gravity of the situation the other side of the Channel.

Certainly we knew the war wasn't going our way. The myth of the impregnability of the Maginot Line had been exploded with almost farcical ease. Our forces had fallen back to the sea. The

Hun was poised for victory. Confident. Lusting to go in for the kill, and the rest of the world waited for the coup de grace. Was Britain about to be invaded?

From their nice safe perches on the fence, the United States and Russia, still smarting under her ignominious showing against the stout-hearted Finns, decided Britain was finished. Her army about to be annihilated.

Then suddenly, all leave was cancelled and the build up of vessels in the harbour had meaning as Churchill launched Operation Dynamo!

A plan to evacuate as many British troops as possible. Although, as history records, it did not seem possible that more than 45,000 men could be embarked.

And then came Dunkirk!

As long as men write of great deeds and miracles, they will write of Dunkirk, and as long as there are survivors who took part in that great triumphant defeat, they will wonder how survival was possible.

The miracle of Dunkirk! The miracle that saved over three hundred thousand British and French fighting men, and made possible by Operation Dynamo, that audacious, seemingly impossible plan for the evacuation of the British Expeditionary Force from the beaches of Dunkirk!

I'll never forget the night of the 27th May 1940. The night a motley assortment of hundreds of vessels put out to sea from our South Coast ports. Fishing boats, barges, steamers, yachts. Anything that could keep afloat. A silent, purposeful armada converging on the Channel port where, under unceasing enemy air attack, their job would be to ferry nearly half a million men off the beaches to the off-lying cruisers, destroyers and other ships, for transportation back to England.

Audax went with the rest, laying off Dunkirk that night. On the beaches, men lay among the sand dunes. From the decks of the destroyer we could hear them. See their faces in the glare of bursting bombs - for five days. Five days of hell let loose when many of us shared the Fuhrer's belief that escape was impossible.

The sea was dead calm, and lying out there in the darkness,

with all around the harsh whine of Stukkas, the scream of bombs, the muffled explosions and mens cries in the night, many of us waiting aboard the big ships, shuddered, taut with fear, not so much for ourselves, but because we believed we were witnessing the death agonies of a once proud force as it gave its life for a freedom already doomed.

It was much later we learned that the huddled troops had suffered surprisingly few casualties, as the bombs plunged into the soft sand of the beaches, and throughout the long hours, we marvelled at the composure and courage of the men waiting for deliverance.

Hour after hour, Fighter Command patrolled the skies undaunted by the numerically superior enemy. Attacking and scattering and taking heavy toll of the Nazi 'planes, their pilots showing almost superhuman endurance.

But courage on the beaches and valour in the air would have been futile without the rescuers of the sea, and the little boats were magnificent! Moving inshore, they gathered up the weary men as they waded neck deep in the water, plucking them up as they collapsed into the sea.

Amongst men, the small craft and the waiting ships, there were casualties. Many died. It was inevitable. The relentless air bombardment was an inferno of horror that went on and on. Beside Audax, a trawler, packed tight with troops being ferried out to a waiting destroyer, took two bombs amidship, and sank almost immediately. All around, the sea was full of wreckage and men milling about in the water, struggling to haul themselves aboard any vessel available. Somewhere close at hand, a ship was on fire.

Audax had sustained some damage to the bridge and our Yeoman had been seriously injured. Our first Lieutenant went ashore to help marshal the embarking men and was killed by small arms fire from a hidden sniper, and on the third day, filled to capacity with exhausted troops, we nosed our way out to sea and headed for the English coast.

Oh yes, it was something to have been at Dunkirk. The whole dedicated unit, the motley armada was invincible, and those who shared in Operation Dynamo, and survived, felt a sense of glory and achievement that the nightmare of bombs and death and destruction, and all the holocaust of horror, could never erase.

Audax limped back to Poole, the Dorset harbour town, and I remember the lines of rescued men standing to attention on the deck of an old trawler moored alongside as we disembarked. Men standing with the precision of a line of guards. Filthy. Unkempt. Bandaged. Half naked. Bloody. Barefooted and weary. Utterly weary, and yet somehow mustering new strength as they went down on to the quay side, quietly accepting cigarettes, chocolate and mugs of hot tea from the small crowd of bystanders who, during the past few days, had witnessed part of the miracle that had saved the country's fighting force when all seemed lost. Saved them in their thousands under the very nose of the enemy.

None of those who took part in that fantastic adventure, will ever think of it as anything but a triumph, although the cost was enormous in men and ships, but where historians record great deeds of valour and matchless courage, the name of Dunkirk will be written.

We took Audax back to Portsmouth where she was taken out of commission for repairs to be carried out, and thankfully, I went home to Cora to commence ten days leave.

With the news that she was pregnant, it seemed my happiness was complete. When my leave ended, I was drafted to Arras, a sister ship to Audax, and joined the Destroyer Flotilla for asdic sweeps of the Channel once more.

I was able to get home pretty regularly to Cora and despite the war, I was happy. This time, I told myself, it was going to last. Cora was in splendid health and eagerly looking forward to the birth of our child.

France had fallen. In July, vessels of the French fleet put into Portsmouth harbour. Submarines, destroyers and mine sweepers, to be taken under British control.

And in that same month, the war took a different turn. The Germans now had control of the French airfields, and launched their first great air attacks. In what became known as the Battle of Britain, a handful of Spitfires and Hurricanes fought off the might of the German Luftwaffe. But the war in the air was hotting up all the time, and early in September, night after night London became the target for enemy bombs. The Nazi 'planes in increasing numbers, were adding another word to the jargon of war, 'Blitz'. Concentrated aerial attack on one town at a time, leaving a trail of death, destruction and terror.

Inevitably, they came to Portsmouth. On a night in October. A fierce and bloody night that left me desperately afraid. Urgently I pleaded with Cora to leave the town. To go down to friends in the West country, to the comparative safety of North Cornwall.

But she would have none of it. Now, more than ever, she said, there was work to be done among the people she knew.

The German bombers were still ravishing the Capital. Tearing at its guts. In the blazing inferno, the death toll was heavy. People lay crushed under the ruins of the city. The piles of debris rose, obliterating familiar places.

The sirens, the raids, the bombs, the toll. These things became part of the pattern of every day, and every day, somewhere in England, people died. Horribly. Suddenly. Their lives torn away between the wail and the howl of the sirens.

My uneasiness grew, and whilst my fear of losing Cora was an ever present shadow, I drew courage from the deep rooted conviction that what had happened to me once, could never happen again!

God! What a pipe dream that turned out to be! Tragedy doesn't bring exemption from further tragedy. There is no degree of human suffering that guarantees immunity from more. No recognised quota for despair!

But I didn't know that - not then. I couldn't believe that anything could take Cora away from me. How can I describe my life with her? There really aren't any words. It was all too brief. A dream perhaps? If only it had been! But no. Rather an interlude in which my life began and ended. What did we really share? What time did we have together from that April morning when we married, to that nightmarish April night barely twelve months afterwards, when she was torn away from me. Cora and our son!

Perhaps six weeks really together. Certainly no more. Six weeks snatched from eternity.

Our first Christmas passed. Ten more weeks and our child would be born. Cora was so happy I tried not to show how I feared for her safety.

Night after night the bombers came, picking their targets indiscriminately. Coventry - Plymouth - Southampton - Portsmouth... and then, to worsen my fears, in January I was detailed to go up to Rosyth to report for duty with HMS Juniper, an ex-American destroyer, the first of fifty such vessels promised by the Americans for use as escort vessels with the North Atlantic convoys under the Western Approaches Command.

The ship was old, but in those days we needed all the help we could get to keep open the shipping lanes for the merchantmen. Radar was in its infancy, but operating in groups comprising destroyers, corvettes and at least one armed merchant cruiser and an anti-submarine trawler under the command of officers who were master tacticians, these groups were responsible for shepherding the precious cargoes of food and arms vitally necessary for the survival of Britain.

The size of the convoys varied, but during the time I spent on the North Atlantic run I came to know many of the merchantmen. Felt a personal interest in them and their stalwart crews.

Old, ugly, outmoded ships that miraculously rode the temperamental sea. Rolling. Buffeted. Belching smoke. Often falling away from the main convoy when the antiquated engines reduced their speed to a minimum.

In those early months we lost surprisingly few of our charges, but our escort strength was not sufficient to give protection right across the Atlantic, and the U-boats attacked in the western zones, outside the protected area where many a lone merchantman fell prey to the lurking submarines.

After my first spell of duty, Juniper put into dock with engine trouble, and I got an unexpected three day leave. I travelled down to Portsmouth to find the town had taken a pounding since I left. Gaunt blackened walls, piles of rubble, grim-faced people. The aftermath of terror. The signs were all there. I found myself running, but Seaton Flats were still there, and Cora herself opened the door to me, and I held her in my arms and thanked God that it was so.

It was the next night that Beady died. Many others died too. They had no choice, but Beady did.

I met him with Mike in the Fisherman's early in the evening. We had a few drinks together while I waited for Cora who had gone over to the Gladstone Hall to see Kate.

Audax, they told me, had been detached from the flotilla for special duty, and was on her way to Gibraltar with a hand picked crew. Lofty and Arthur had gone with her, but Mike and Beady had been left behind to enjoy a 'twenty-four hours' before reporting for duty with another ship of the flotilla.

When the sirens went, I left the bar and went to meet Cora, and together, at her insistence, we made for the deep air raid shelter at the rear of Gladstone Hall.

It was a long raid. Concentrated and heavy. The earth shuddered and the din was ear-splitting.

Around us, huddled men, women and children - many of them in their night clothes. Faces pale and strained. Ears cocked, listening. Frightened, but managing to smile though there was no laughter in their eyes. Others cursed. Some sang and joked, for in that way they kept their courage alive.

I held Cora close to me. We scarcely spoke, only sometimes she smiled at me, and my grip on her tightened with desperate reassurance. Children were whispering, and a man with a mouth organ played 'Land of Hope and Glory'.

Outside, the guns blasted away. Came the roar of aircraft followed by the ominous crumph of bombs much too close for comfort. A high pitched whine. A sudden cry as the lights in the shelter dimmed momentarily, and then a louder crumph that sent us all reeling, and came the anguished shriek of a child as a shower of debris sprayed from the roof.

Desperately I clung to Cora... Heavy with child, her face strained and puckered with fear, her arms tightened about me, and I heard her whisper a prayer...

But the shelter held, and at last we heard the welcome sound of the 'All Clear'. Those of us who weren't spending the night there, climbed and stumbled our way up to the street.

Outside, the sky was aflame, and a great pall of smoke moved towards the sea. The acrid smell of burning filled the air. There was shouting and a great confusion of sound as firemen, rescue workers, ambulance men and other officials tried to do their jobs. And everywhere, there was blazing rubble. Smouldering masonry. Shambles - just shambles!

The Gladstone Hall had mercifully escaped damage and had become a temporary hospital, and an endless procession of wardens and Civil Defence workers moved in and out of the building carrying, leading, dragging the injured from the debris, leaving them lying on the steps of the hall as they went in search of other victims of the raid.

Broken limbs, burns, shock, the moans of the injured were lost in the crackle of the flame and voices shouting and calling to each other.

Doctors and nurses worked with feverish haste attending to the casualties, directing the helpers as they loaded the wounded into ambulances and other vehicles forcing their way through the ravaged street.

There were many dead. Many died as they lay, but there was no panic. Almost before I realised it, Cora had left my side, and I saw her join Kate who was attending to a child on the pavement.

My first impulse was to follow her, and then I noticed a group of men about fifty yards down the street. Men working frantically with shovels.

The Fisherman's! Mike and Beady!

I started to run.

When I reached the shattered building firemen were trying to get the flames under control whilst rescue men dug desperately at the smoking rubble.

A small hole had been made in the masonry, and a man, lying on his stomach, backed out of it and scrambled breathlessly to his feet. His face was streaked with blood and dirt

"Who's inside?" I demanded hoarsely.

"Only one man so far as we know," he told me. "Small chance of him being alive. Naval rating. It's a bloody shame! They was all out, when this little fellow starts yelling for someone called

'Mike'. Seems this mate of his was down in the cellar when the bomb fell. Before we could stop him, he dashed back inside. Reckon he fell and knocked himself out, then the wall caved in on him. All for nothing. His pal must have managed to crawl out through a hole in the rear wall. Got out with a broken arm. Must have been on his way to hospital before the little fellow went in."

It was Beady all right. I was there five hours later when we brought him out.

Mike was there too. It was he who, despite the handicap of his plastered arm, carried Beady to the mortuary, and all the way, he cursed and swore, but his cheeks were wet and his eyes swollen, and it wasn't the smoke and the dust and the burning that brought the tears.

In the early light of morning, through the stricken city people salvaged what was left of their possessions, piling them in pathetic little heaps in the streets. Standing about uncertain, helpless, weary and begrimed, and it wasn't courage or defiance on the faces of the homeless and the maimed, but bewilderment, shock and despair.

Miraculously, Seaton Flats had come through that night of horror unscathed, but the view from the windows as Cora and I ate a silent breakfast, showed unfamiliar shapes on the skyline, and desolation and destruction in all directions. Burnt and blackened buildings. Ominous gaps. Walls clinging drunkenly together.

Cora looked pale. Her eyes red-rimmed. It was time for me to go, and to leave her then was the hardest thing I ever had to do.

In that last hour we spent together, the very last as it turned out to be, I tried every argument to persuade her to leave the city. I pleaded, begged, demanded, shouted, but it was no use.

She remained calm but adamant. Running away, she told me quietly, wouldn't solve anything. If the war went the wrong way, there would be no hope for any of us under Nazi rule, and if we were to win any sort of peace, every able bodied man, woman and child was needed for some task somewhere. Here in Portsmouth, she said, there would be plenty to do.

Just then I didn't share her patriotism. All I wanted was to know she would be safe. That she would be alive to bear our child when the time came - and that time would be soon, I reminded her. Five weeks perhaps...

I returned to Juniper with a heavy heart, and went back to the business of the war at sea.

It was nearly two months before I saw Portsmouth again. In February America entered the war, two months after the Japan assault on Pearl Harbour which had taken a heavy toll of her warships and men.

Germany was planning an invasion of Greece, and Juniper was deployed to join a British force carrying troops to Crete. Italy had now joined the Hun and her 'planes and warships were proving a formidable hazard.

Juniper together with nine other destroyers and four battleships, engaged ships of the Italian fleet. My first taste of battle and it was hairy. Nevertheless our ships were comparatively unscathed and we had sunk enemy cruisers and two destroyers, and inflicted damage on others. We picked up a load of survivors. They were a rum lot. Undisciplined and ungracious. We were glad to hand them over to the Officer in Charge ashore for internment.

Afterwards, we got an all-night leave, let our hair down and got drunk. Our skipper wasn't very pleased and set about cancelling leave and docking pay, which didn't go down well with the crew.

The worst thing was lack of news from home. I had only had three letters from Cora, and those right at the beginning of the time I had been away. Had our child been born? Surely then... A hundred fears assailed me. National news filtered through of the continued intensity of the Nazi air raids on Britain. Cities being devastated...

And at last came that deceptively beautiful day in April when Juniper put in to Portsmouth Harbour for adjustments to be made to her gun mountings.

Gathering excitement churned me up inside. It seemed providential that soon I would be with Cora again, and this was the anniversary of our marriage.

Just off Spithead, our Captain gave the order to anchor. A group of half a dozen Messerschmits were attacking the city and the ack-ack batteries in the dockyard were making it hot for them.

A barricade of sombre barrage balloons swayed eerily across the blue sky - gargantuan monsters before the warm breeze of Spring. Dull, sickening crumphs echoed across the water.

Our gun crews were at the ready, and as the noise of approaching enemy aircraft warned us that the attacking 'planes were heading for home, the Control Officer barked an order, and our four inch guns went into action.

A great cheer went up as, away to port, we saw a Messerschmit diving seawards with smoke bursting from its tail.

"That bastard won't trouble us again!" muttered a Leading Seaman beside me.

From the mainland, a column of black smoke spiralled upward.

"Looks like they've got the oil tanks," someone said hoarsely. "My old folks live right near by!"

"Christ!" exclaimed another, training his binoculars towards the shore. "What a mess!"

"Bad eh?" I asked quietly.

"You're not kidding," the other muttered. "Looks like a bloody shambles in all directions. Must have taken a pasting and no mistake! D'you know the place?"

"Home port," I said briefly, and turned away.

A strange silence fell over the ship, broken suddenly by the long wail of a siren as it sounded the 'All Clear' Ashore, for a while, it would be safe for people to leave the shelters.

Buildings had crumpled. Almost certainly, people had died. What people? My throat felt dry. Silently I voiced a prayer.

It seemed a long two hours before we moored alongside, and together with other ratings who had homes and families in the town, I went ashore.

There was a peculiar smell in the air. The stench of death and destruction.

Outside the dockyard gates a small crowd waited. Men and women with taut faces and bandaged limbs. Children, grubby and scared, clung to their mothers. In the eyes of them all was an expression of fear and apathy - a frightening silence. Some cried silently, scarcely knowing that the tears came.

I found myself sweating, and then, on the outskirts of the

crowd, I saw Kate and Arthur Ryan.

The sight of Arthur shocked me. He looked so thin, and years older than I last remembered him. And then, as I wondered briefly what part of hell had set its mark on him in so short a time, I looked at Kate.

Her eyes were great dark saucers in the incredible pallor of her cheeks. I pushed my way towards them. They stared at me mutely and I knew what they had come to say.

"Cora..." I grated.

Kate nodded. Reached out her arms to embrace me.

"Two weeks ago," she murmured tremulously. "There was a direct hit on the shelter."

"There was nothing anyone could have done," Arthur put in gently.

"Where is she?" I asked hoarsely.

"They're buried where they died," he answered. "There were forty or fifty of them. We'll never really know how many."

"They couldn't have suffered," Kate's voice was stifled. "It was a direct hit you see."

"Even if they'd stayed in the flat, it wouldn't have saved them," Arthur went on. "A land mine demolished half the street just after the shelter was hit."

"They?" I questioned. "Who was with Cora?"

They glanced fleetingly at each other.

"There was the baby," Kate said brokenly. "He was just ten days old. You'd better come to my place and..."

Like a man in a dream I pushed past her. Started to run. Running as I had never run before - towards the flats. On either side of the road shops and houses had been devastated. Craters in the roadway. Sprawling heaps of rubble. Grotesque distorted woodwork. Broken glass and everywhere, people.

Civil Defence workers. Rescue teams. Demolition workers striving like tortured ants to restore order and maintain morale.

And suddenly, as I came to a breathless halt, there it was. The neatly levelled mound of earth that topped the common grave Cora and our son shared with so many strangers. A mound covered with a profusion of flowers already wilting away, and behind, the ruins of what had been our home.

Disembowelled. Ugly. With streamers of tattered wallpaper flapping from shattered walls, and rafters clutching each other drunkenly to keep the skeleton from complete collapse.

I looked from the fading flowers that covered my love to the bright blue of the April sky.

"Christ"! I burst out. "What kind of a God are you?"

I have no clear recollection of what followed as my grief and anger merged and burst from me. I only know I cursed and screamed aloud, mouthing outrageous blasphemies. I know too, that when reason finally reasserted itself, I felt no remorse for the profanities I had directed towards God.

Despairingly, from the deep abyss of my hurt, I asked, Why? Why... ?

Hadn't I suffered enough when the hangman's noose had choked the life from my father, and torn away everything that mattered once before?

What kind of a God was it who gave, only to snatch away? Who had given me new life and hope and purpose, then ruthlessly destroyed all that mattered to me!

What kind of a deity could let men, women and helpless babes be blown to pieces in the bloody futility of war?

Cora - my lovely Cora and the tiny speck of humanity our love had brought into being. A life too brief for reason!

It was cruel, senseless sacrifice. Murder... Senseless bloody murder!

In the dark bitter weeks that followed, the war grew fiercer and bloodier, and I was glad.

CHAPTER SIX

Russia had come into the war. The marriage of convenience between the Fuhrer and Stalin had been finally dissolved as the Nazi army marched across the Russo-German frontiers.

Whatever private ambitions Stalin had fostered as one after another, the countries of Europe fell to the Germans, had now to be shelved as Russia fought for self-preservation, and for this, help was needed against the vastly superior German forces.

It was obvious to the British Government that if Russia could put up a good show, it would ease the strain on our own sorely stretched forces, but that in order to put up any sort of a fight at all, Russia needed help, particularly in the supply of tanks and 'planes.

Although our own needs were desperate, Britain prepared to send armaments to North Russia, armaments which would go by way of a new shipping lane to the ports of Murmansk and Archangel - to Malotovsk and the Kola Inlet - from Iceland, from the Clyde and Scapa Flow and from Loch Ewe. All routes fraught with danger, passing as they did, under the nose of the enemy for the greater part of the way.

In the early Autumn of 1941, our shipping was already stretched beyond all rational limits, when the Royal Navy, struggling alone with heavy, widespread responsibilities, was given the job of safeguarding the new convoy route to North Russia.

The Russians themselves, phlegmatic and ungracious, did very little to help themselves, nor could they supply sufficient merchant ships to carry the cargoes. British Merchantmen took on the job. A thankless and dangerous one that continued throughout the war, running the gauntlet of lurking U-boats in the North where evasive action was hampered by a barrier of solid ice, and constant shore based air attacks from the East and South-East, all enemy occupied territory.

In addition, there was always the danger of attack by warships of the German Navy which, based in Norway would slip out at will to engage the escort vessels on which the safety of the convoy depended.

And there was always the cold. The freezing Arctic conditions. The long, long watches in the face of icy spray. Past great icebergs. Through blinding snow and blizzards, and fog. Our ships becoming ice covered crystallites, for ice was everywhere, even encasing the ammunition with which we fed our guns.

Among the ships detailed for duty with the Arctic convoys at the end of August 1941, was Juniper.

It seemed right that it should be so. Taking me away from my friends and all familiar things. Things and people that reminded me of Cora.

The first convoys gathered at Hvalfford in Iceland. Inadequate but resolved - and made the run without mishap to arrive at Archangel intact.

It was as though the enemy watched the run with contempt, reluctant to waste effort on a victim presenting so easy a killing.

Harder to take was the attitude of the Russians themselves. Ungrateful, uncooperative, subjecting us to every petty restriction imaginable.

Even the approaches to the Russian ports had to be cleared of mines and submarines by British minesweepers, and often in the months that followed, convoys were attacked in these waters, where U-boasts operated under the very nose of the Russians who seemed quite indifferent to the fate of convoy vessels attacked in there after successfully outwitting the enemy for some two thousand miles.

At that time there were many of us who had more respect for the Germans than for our Russian allies.

At the ports, after sorties with the enemy, we found no welcome - no help with our wounded and no medical attention. Only indifference or open hostility, and often our casualties were left unattended on the quay side at Murmansk for far too long.

By the end of that year, half a dozen conveys had made the run with the loss of only one minesweeper, and this, within the Kola Inlet where, for the first few miles of the journey, local escort vessels came within firing range of German destroyers.

Although the minesweeper was badly hit, together with its

companion, it succeeded in putting up an effective smoke screen to protect the convey, and surprisingly, the Germans made no effort to press the advantage, and the convoy put safely into harbour.

Those were the best days. Long hours of darkness with only brief noon daylight when the enemy failed to locate us, and our most formidable hazards were the weather, the particularly fierce gales, and the strain of waiting for attacks that never came.

The Spring of 1942 brought heavier casualties - still in the area of the Kola Inlet where the U-boats waited to attack the ships as they entered harbour. But here, the greater enemy was the sea itself. A sea so icy cold that whole crews died in the water while rescue ships stood helplessly by.

By this time, the German battleship Tirpitz and three destroyers were reported heading north, following the Fuhrer's orders that all ships should be stationed off Norway to offset the invasion of that country which he believed to be imminent.

The British battleship Duke of York with escorting cruisers, was out searching for her, and the inward and outward bound convoys moved somewhere in the middle of the two protagonists, all of them subservient to the elements of fog, wind and ice which grounded aircraft, and with sportive chicanery, permitted the powerful and the helpless to pass each other again and again, and the convoys, retreating, diverting, ploughing on, backing away from ice packs, all unaware that danger threatened on every side, made port safely.

At this time too, the convoys grew in size and strength and were joined by American ships.

During the whole of that year the convoys sailed every day, save in the months of mid-Summer when the long hours of daylight made survival impossible in the face of the enemy's air might. These were months when the odd letter from Mrs Ryan, Arthur and Lofty, was all the contact I had with the things that had been.

Arthur was still with the Local Defence Flotilla, but Lofty was on the cruiser Powerful, a Portsmouth based ship which I had spotted doing escort duty with an inward bound convoy from

Murmansk.

As the size of the convoys grew, the escort force allocated to them became farcically inadequate. In most cases, two destroyers and two trawlers comprised the total escort strength, just enough to cope with a U-boat attack, or a sortie with surface craft - either, but not both, and certainly insufficient to stave off concentrated air attack.

The British warship of pre-war vintage had gun batteries capable of dealing effectively with low flying aircraft, but their elevation was lamentably inadequate against attack by dive bombers or aerial torpedoes.

Losses became heavier and experience taught its own strategy. Gun crews of destroyers were unprotected against the weather, and the freezing, knife-like wind would lash the icy spray at us so that we were too numb to feel pain as we scraped the ice from the shells to set the fuses.

Refuelling was another problem. The merciless gales often prevented contact with the escorting tankers, and rounding up stragglers and helping lame ducks in the convoy, meant a costly rise in oil consumption. It was a depressing time. The war news on all fronts was grim.

In the Far East, things were as bad as they could be. Singapore, Java and New Guinea had all fallen to the Japanese who had also sunk some of our finest ships.

The Germans were advancing in the Middle East and we had suffered severe losses in the Mediterranean.

In April, the passage of ships and equipment to the Russian Arctic ports, was really getting in the Fuhrer's hair, and with the coming of more hours of daylight, the problem of providing suitable and adequate escorts for the convoys, became more difficult every day.

The weather was terrible. At times, the icy winds from the Pole brought the temperature down to well below zero, but at others, when the wind abated, the ships, blanketed in snow, nosed their way through ice bergs, gliding like silent ghosts, with crews to whom the huge snowflakes were a welcome screen between them and the lurking enemy. But the surrounding ice flows played havoc with the asdics, deflecting tell-tale sounds - cushioning the U-boats.

We continued to lose ships. Through surface attack. Through U-boats, and some were prey to aerial attack. Others were damaged by ice. Some forced to return through bad weather conditions, scattered through gales.

And men died. Suddenly. Horribly, within sight of their comrades. Their life plucked from them by the icy sea. There were deeds of incredible valour. Of supreme seamanship, and moments of fear and pride, and anger and frustration.

The Yanks were screaming for larger and more frequent convoys to be sent to Russia in order to keep the Russians on the right side of the fence, but they, with just a few months experience of the war, were asking the impossible.

Our resources were stretched to the limit, and each time we gathered for the mustering of a convoy, there wasn't a man amongst us who wasn't horribly aware of the significance of Churchill's statement, that if only half a convey got through, the operation would be justified.

The weeks dragged on. The days of endless daylight bringing increased anxieties and depression as we went backwards and forwards under the perpetual threat of air attack, with no real rest from the strident clamour of alarm bells, the noise of gunfire as we dashed to action stations, and the sight of stricken ships ablaze from stem to stern, or heeling helpless, to disappear beneath the relentless waves.

And always there was the cold. Cold and strain that numbed the brain as we huddled in heavy clothing offering scant protection against the keen, rapier-like winds sweeping down from the glaciers.

The pattern of the German attack was monotonously the same. The reconnaissance 'plane, the bombers, the U-boats!

The pandemonium, the nightmare, the fortitude of the merchantmen watching from their small ships. Unable to help themselves. Grimly sticking to the set course of the convoy as long as possible, diverting only when the tracks of torpedoes necessitated emergency turns. For the main hope of salvation for the little ships, lay in keeping close formation, flanked by the escort vessels arraigned to do their fighting for them.

It was a bloody business, and yet in some odd way, I savoured it, feeling a savage satisfaction at the horror of it, because each day I saw men ruthlessly torn away from life, and each tragedy strengthened my belief in the farce of religion. Of the impotence of God!

How could man believe in a God of mercy who permitted the senseless murder of hundreds of innocents? Of brave, helpless men! My bitterness grew, and my loneliness.

There were moments during that black year, when I envied the dead. When I wanted no more of life with its deceitful mirages of a decent future - more soul destroying than the mirages seen by the crews of scattered ships who watched the macabre vision of other vessels being bombed, mirrored in the Arctic sky.

Fear was in every man's heart, but all through those awesome months I wrestled with a more personal enemy - sleep! Sleep that brought torturous images to haunt my dreams. A hideous montage of the dead, dominated always by my mother's mockery. I destroyed her so many times in those dreams, and always it was my poor mutilated father who fought me for her life.

Together they taunted me. Embracing brazenly over the dead forms of Cora and our child. Nightmares! Draining, terrifying nightmares. My nocturnal ravings did little to endear me to my shipmates.

'What's the matter with you, Stevens?" yelled one, as I sat up dazed and shivering, "Reckon you must have something pretty sick on your conscience!"

And from another,

"All that jibbering and jabbering! You need an exorcist mate!"

I mumbled apologies. Sweated with fear that my frenzied cries might betray the secret I guarded so jealously. Cause and effect... After so long?

But as time went on I learned to school myself. To sleep in short bursts. To wake before the nightmares took possession of me. It took its toll. I endured pounding headaches. Lost my strength. Carried on my duties feeling like a zombie.

In May and June of that year, the loss of ships and men was appalling. It was horribly apparent that without escorting carriers, the Arctic convoys were a costly form of heroics we could no longer afford.

Yet they had to go on! Politically, there could be no let up. But the strength of the convoys was to be augmented by the use of auxiliary carriers and more destroyers, and the Russians had at last permitted the establishing of several squadrons of flying boats and torpedo bombers in the Kola Inlet.

But it didn't stop the slaughter, and the toll of men and ships was a costly one, and, of course, always the weather! Merciless gales. Snow and ice packing itself dangerously on the superstructure of the ships, and the unpredictable treachery of the ice pack itself.

Certainly as the months went by, equipment improved. We had steam hoses to clear the guns. Protective shields for the gun crews, and radar techniques were getting better all the time.

And sometimes, the weather became our best ally, keeping the German destroyers holed up. Laying a mantle of snow over the little ships, hiding them from the sight of the reconnaissance 'planes. Yes - an ally! Vicious, spiteful, but an ally!

And then, on the last day of June 1943, it was the turn of Jupiter to die.

Together with four other destroyers, two corvettes, a mine sweeper and two trawlers, we were escorting eighteen merchantmen en route from Loch Ewe to the Kola Inlet, while in touch, but steaming at a discreet distance to the south of the convoy, two cruisers formed a covering force, ready to come to our help at the first sign of any trouble we couldn't handle.

At the end of the first week out, a terrific blizzard succeeded in scattering the convoy, and it was several days before most of them regained contact. Some never did, though these managed to reach Kola themselves - in safety.

When at last the blizzard subsided, the Polar winds breathed ice on everything they touched.

On the tenth day out, we spotted the conning tower of a U-boat and immediately went after it. Although we prevented it attacking the convoy, we knew the news of our positions would be flashed to German headquarters, and it was only a question of time before we were attacked.

Our briefing on tactics in the face of attack, had been short and to the point. U-boats and air attack were the least we had to fear. The rules were simple. The freighters were to stick to their positions and leave the rest to the escort. But if the attack came from German warships, our tactics were more clearly defined. Destroyers would cover the threatened flank and attempt to close with the enemy, while the rest of the escort would concentrate on laying smoke screens to protect the merchantmen, and the cruisers of the covering force would close up with all haste to the assistance of the convoy and take over from the destroyers.

The snag, we all knew, was how long it would take the cruisers to reach us, hampered as they were by the weather, the light, and with no certain knowledge of the convoy's position - for there was strict radio silence in force.

Two days after the appearance of the U-boat, the enemy showed himself again. This time, in the shape of two destroyers heading north in the wake of the convoy.

In company with two other destroyers from the escort, Argosy and Allard, we turned about and steered towards the enemy ships until no more than four miles separated us, and we saw the flash of German guns. Explosive shells flung up great spouts of water in the sea all round us.

Behind us, other ships of the escort, letting out black oily smoke from their funnels, and white smoke from floats on the quarter decks, steamed backwards and forwards, laying a screen between the enemy and the freighters, and then, through the twilight, another ship loomed suddenly ahead of us - large and formidable.

Silhouetted against the background of black smoke, Juniper must have been a gift!

As our guns went into action, came a shout from the bridge,

"Full ahead! Hard 'a' starboard!"

And then it happened! Came a great shuddering crash as a torpedo tore the engine room apart, and Juniper seemed to leap out of the water, writhing in agony.

As the sea rushed in, the hiss of escaping steam was a frightening sound above the rest. Men were shouting and screaming. The wounded lay groaning amongst the dead, and the living desperately turned to the job of shoring up shattered bulkheads, and plugging cavities to keep out the greedy seas.

But the ship was doomed. We all knew it, even before the second torpedo struck home.

The icy waters flooded in. Juniper heeled over, floundering helplessly. Groans and creaks came from the twisted, tormented metal amidships.

Below, but threateningly closer, the sea waited menacingly. Sure of victory - almost at freezing point.

Men struggled to release the remaining boats. Dropping Carley floats over the side. From the limited shelter of the upper deck we waited for the end. There was still gunfire, and away to port, a ship was ablaze.

Juniper's back was breaking. As the wind rose shrieking in triumphant fury, a great rending sound brought terror to our hearts.

I was up forward when the ship broke in two. Officers and men slipping and stumbling, clung on desperately - struggling to remain upright as the bow dipped steeply and the ruptured end of the fore part rose in the air.

And then came the order to abandon ship.

The water was like a naked blade as I struck it. Chilling the breath. Numbing the limbs.

I'm going to die, I thought wildly.

Frantically I summoned strength to strike out for one of the rafts. There were perhaps a dozen of us able to drag ourselves on to it, but not one had the strength to speak or move.

The cold was death itself. We couldn't even think of survival. I had no positive thought. No pain. And then, some deep rooted instinct opened my eyes, and voices penetrated somewhere in the deep recesses of my mind.

Above me, I saw the side of a ship and horror gripped me for I couldn't move!

Around me, on the raft, men struggled to make fast a line. They made no sound. Moved like puppets. Clutching. Grasping at the air, unable to retain a hold with fingers already dead, and gradually, they slipped away and were lost from sight.

Vaguely, I saw the Jacob ladder. Despairingly reached out to it. Came a shout and a confusion of sound. A sudden pain in my head, then no more...

When consciousness returned, the pain in my head was still there, but my first reaction was to the comforting warmth of the blankets which covered me. I lay without moving, savouring the sheer luxury of it, aware of muted voices close at hand.

Someone put a hand on my forehead, and after a while, I opened my eyes. A man was standing beside me. A tall, bearded man wearing on his uniform coat, the red and gold stripes of the ship's doctor.

"That's better," he said quietly. "'fraid you gave your head a crack as we got you aboard. Had to put in a couple of stitches, but you'll do. How d'you feel?"

"Fine, thank you, sir," I murmured. "How did the others make out?"

"We'll talk about that later," he replied. "Better get some sleep now. I'll see you later."

It was not until the following day I learned I was aboard the cruiser Powerful which, with her sister ship, Monarch, had been detailed for stand-off escort duty with our convoy. After sustaining minor damage with the loss of a dozen hands, she had picked up twenty survivors from Jupiter, all that remained of our ship's company.

The British casualties had been one destroyer, a minesweeper and one merchantman. The enemy had lost a destroyer and taken a second in tow.

I stayed with Powerful when she put in to Kola and later returned with her to Portsmouth. And aboard the cruiser, I met up with Lofty again and the chaplain I'd known at the RN Barracks. He recognised me one evening when he'd taken Service on the lower mess deck.

"Stevens, isn't it?" he asked quietly.

"Yes, sir," I told him.

"You're a very lucky man to be alive, Stevens," he said solemnly. "You should give thanks to God!"

"I gave my thanks to the seaman who hauled me up that ladder," I answered tersely. "If you expect me and the handful of survivors from my ship, to give thanks to God for deliverance, what do you say to God about the hundred who didn't make it?"

He looked at me hard.

"Still harbouring the old resentment, Stevens," he said heavily. "I'm sorry for you. It must be almost two years since I last saw you. You didn't come back to tell me how you made out with that girl of yours."

"No. I meant to."

"And how did it turn out?" he questioned.

"Just as you said," I sighed.

"Then it didn't make any difference," he pursued. "I mean - about your father."

"No. No difference," I murmured.

"Well, that's fine," he told me. "I knew it would be all right for you. Most things turn out for the best in the end..."

"I married her," I broke in gratingly. "We had a son, and when he was ten days old, the two of them were blown to hell! I never even saw him! Does that strike you as being for the best?"

He looked shocked.

"I see," he said slowly. "Believe me, I'm sorry. But you can't live out your life carrying that burden of resentment against God."

"God is a word," I told him tautly. "No more. A refuge for fools and the gullible. A doctrine that can be tailored to fit any circumstance. That I can take, but don't ask me to believe that God is a Being, a Supreme Being. A symbol of love and mercy. The Universal Father who accepts all the reverence, all the homage, and yet lets his followers suffer and die in torment."

"You've got it all wrong, Stevens," the padre returned earnestly. "I can understand your bitterness, but believe me, you need faith. We all do. Faith is something we have to hang on to in spite of ourselves. Of necessity, it is an intangible thing. God created Mankind, not as a collection of puppets, but with brain and heart and reasoning. Man himself made creeds and distinctions.

God made the world for all men, and mankind made territories and boundaries, and fought for possession of his world. The impudence! The colossal impudence! We bless the flags as symbols of war. We pray for victory to vanquish our enemies, and our enemies pray for victory over us, and God hears both prayers and weeps, for in the beginning..."

"Save your breath, sir," I interrupted bitterly. "I've heard all the platitudes before. All right. We've got the brains and all the rest of it. We live in co-existence, taking the usual knocks, but if your God, your Supreme Being, is holding a watching brief to see how we acquit ourselves, surely He can step in and work some miracle when things get out of hand."

"The onus is on us, not God," he replied with a sigh. "If I give you fifty pounds and you go and spend a holiday somewhere and the food is bad, the service intolerable, and someone breaks into your room and robs you, do you blame me?"

"I suppose there's a parallel somewhere," I muttered.

"Oh there is, Stevens," he said quietly. "For those who want to see, the Truth is before us. I know it's hard to understand, especially when the going gets tough, but this life is only transitory. A phase, nothing more. You have to believe we are all progressing, one way or another, to the Eternal Glory. Then all things will be made known to us. We all have to carry a cross of some kind. To prove ourselves. You see, it's not this life that's important, it's the next. It's all there in the Scriptures."

"I'll say it is!" I burst out contemptuously. "All of it. A collection of contradictions from beginning to end. Of hope and love thy neighbour - and Hell and Damnation and the fiery pit!"

And then I walked away from him.

He was a good man, the chaplain. In the weeks that followed, as shipmates aboard Powerful, I came to know him as a man. A brave, sincere, selfless man.

A dedicated man, but he died with the rest, and I envied him his faith.

I met up with Lofty the third day after being taken aboard the cruiser. It was the first time I had seen him since Cora's death, but neither of us mentioned it, although he told me he was still going strong with Kate.

There was the business of war to occupy us, and in our particular theatre, there was no let up. Certainly the combined sea and air escort made possible by the use of auxiliary carriers, made the Kola run less of a nightmare, but the shepherding of the convoys was still no picnic.

And then, in the Autumn of 1943, Powerful put in to Portsmouth for minor repairs, and I learned that together with other survivors from Jupiter, I had been drafted to the crew of the cruiser that had picked us up. I broke the news to Lofty as with three other shipmates, Harry Jessop, Douggie Piper and Nobby Clarke, we went ashore.

The Luftwaffe had certainly made a mess of the town. As we made our way out of the barracks to the main thoroughfare, Jessop remarked,

"A few more phallic symbols around and it'd be more like Pompeii than Pompey!"

In the general egress, I lost the others in the crowded street, and inevitably, my footsteps turned in the direction of Seaton Flats.

Half a dozen children played amongst the rubble. Playing by twisted walls that clung together like drunks, leaning one upon the other, distorted, pathetic nothings, oddly drab, with ceiling plaster trailing between them. Naked, lolling beams. Broken electric light fittings.

These had been part of my home. My brief haven. There, had been born my son. From the womb to the tomb. From darkness into light and back to eternal darkness again.

The futility of it all! The bloody futility!

And Cora, her weary, swollen body released at last from its travail, fulfilling the destiny of her sweet womanhood, sweating through the torment of her labour, for what?

Scarcely time to breathe the blessed air of relief. Scarcely time to marvel at the image of the baby she had brought into being, before death reached out and claimed them both.

Now children played, absorbed in make believe. Not understanding the ghastly toll that had been levied for their playground! Their shrill laughter cut across the morning air like a knife across my misery. I wanted to scream aloud, but gritting my teeth, I cursed. Not like I had cursed when I first saw Cora's grave. I had been hysterical then. Now I was cool. Deliberate, and though the words were the same, they meant much more.

Why had Cora to die? Cora, who was good and straight and gentle. And our son who'd never even had a chance to learn what kind of a world he'd been born into?

I knew what the padre's answer would be to that one! I'd heard it all before! All that cant about being too good for this rotten world - and the Higher Life and the Eternal Kingdom!

Crap I say! What about the pain. The anguish. The futile, unnecessary suffering of Cora's last weeks?

I must have been muttering aloud, for suddenly, the children ceased their play and stood in little groups staring at me. Mildly interested, with cocked heads and open mouths.

"S'pect 'e's drunk," hazarded one. "Take no notice. Come on now. It's your turn to be 'itler, Georgie Sykes!"

Abruptly, I fell silent.

There's no tragedy for the very young. The significance of that pile of debris was lost to them. The blackened carcase of Seaton Flats, as full of meaning as the ashes of yesterday's fire that had had its day and served its turn, and passed away into the obscurity of things gone for ever.

And suddenly Lofty was beside me, his thin face expressionless and his mouth, for once, unsmiling.

"Come on, Stevo," he said quietly. "What about a drink."

Mechanically I turned away from the melancholy pile and went with him.

"No use rubbing it in," he muttered tensely. "There's little enough future for any of us. No use brooding about what's gone."

"Are you going to marry Kate?" I asked him.

"Maybe. When this lot's over," he said thoughtfully. "I'm in no hurry. This time I'm not rushing into anything."

"This time?" I echoed in surprise. "You've been married before?"

"Yes, Stevo," he told me, "I was married. First turn of the screw put paid to that. I'd scarcely stowed my kit aboard before she up and hooked it with a gas fitter. I divorced her. I'm not fretting. What's the use? No point in trying to alter what's got to be. You take what comes. That's all there is to it. You weren't married long. That's why you took it so hard. The novelty hadn't worn off. Me - I'd been bashing away for three years!"

"It was the way she went," I burst out bitterly. "Her and the baby. Just got over that, then curtains! Direct hit they said. Not a bloody chance!"

"Tough!" he answered quietly, "but it's a perishin' thin line between life and death. The coming in and the going out! They're inevitable things! We expect them and accept them. Some things are harder to take. Believe me. I know! Deceit. Lies. The things that bust up your faith in people. Take it from me, Stevo. It's better your way. To lose something when it really meant something to you. It's easier than having to live with the knowledge that you've been taken for a sucker by the woman you loved!"

And then I knew that the breaking up of his marriage had wounded him deeply, and whereas my sorrow had left an aching loneliness, Lofty's was like a canker, spreading its tentacles round his every waking thought. A festering foetus of frustration and bitterness which would never leave him and maybe, would cost him any future chance of happiness.

"I left some of the boys at the Stag," he said suddenly.

"Fine," I answered, feeling curiously warmed because I knew he'd left the others to seek me out, and because he'd known where to find me, and I thought what a fine thing was the companionship of man for man. Untainted by the primitive passions and petty jealousies that govern the love of man for woman.

A fine strong thing, the loyalty of brother for brother in a world where loyalty of any kind is a priceless, measureless prize.

CHAPTER SEVEN

The Stag was crowded as we pushed our way through the swing doors. Mostly navy blue uniforms, with a spattering of lighter Air Force blue and sombre khaki.

The first thing we made out was the unmistakable voice of Douggie Piper booming out a chorus of 'Roll out the Barrel' with a crowd of our shipmates, and then a yell of laughter as Nobby Clarke followed it with a parody of his own, drawing a mild rebuke from the grinning barman, and a demand for a repeat from a soldier who, nuzzling the neck of a tiny Wren, had missed the first rendering.

Nobby's encore was interrupted as someone started to bash out a tune on the piano. The cracked notes resounding with titillating discordance above all else.

Lofty shouldered his way to the bar and called for drinks. Then Nobby spotted us, bawling across the room,

"Hi Loft! What's the idea? Think I'm going to nurse this ruddy pint all day! Come on over here."

Lofty emptied his glass, wiped his mouth on the back of his hand, and elbowed a passage to join the others.

I followed him.

Three days leave. Three days to fill in - somehow. Seventy-two hours to kill. Seventy-two unbearable, lonely hours.

I felt very sorry for myself.

I gulped greedily at the whisky someone handed me. Drained it and called for another - and another round with a kind of urgent desperation.

"Take it easy, Stevo," I heard Lofty mutter.

"Go to hell," I told him thickly. "I know what I'm doing."

A pleasant detachment was spreading over me. Settling between me and reason. A befuddlement that brought a welcome feeling of lightheartedness.

Then I heard a rating say,

"Well, so long mates! I'd better go and break the good news to the wife."

A chorus of ribaldry greeted this decision, followed by a wail of dismay as the landlord called 'Time'.

In twos and threes people melted away.

Outside it was raining. I found myself standing on the pavement with Lofty and the three ratings who had left the ship with us.

"What about something to eat," Clarke suggested, and grumbled. "Why the blazes the Old Man didn't give us seven days, beats me. Those bloody dockyard mateys 'll never have the ship ready in time."

"Who cares," growled Douggie Piper. "Let's find some wimmen."

"We'll eat first," Clarke decided. "Can't ride on an empty belly."

Women! Through my bemused head, shapes came crowding, and desire quickened my pulse, sending the blood rushing through my veins.

We piled into Joe's Kitchen.

The swarthy, bald-headed proprietor eyed us dubiously, then evidently approving the fact that we managed to sit down at one of the glass topped tables with no worse mishap than one overturned chair, decided to serve us.

"Well, Douggie, what about the wimmen?" demanded Harry Jessop, his voice thick and slurred as he pushed back his empty plate. "You've been here before. Know your way around. Where you taking us?"

Piper winked.

"Little place I know," he grinned. "I reckon you're all old enough. Come on."

A little thrill of excitement ran through my loins. The feel of soft female flesh again... the transcending oblivion of satiation!

I got to my feet and the rest followed. Joe stood purposefully between us and the door. We haggled a bit about the bill, cursed him for a thieving son of a bitch, paid up and went out into the street.

We moved slowly along the wet pavement, our progress retarded, firstly by Douggie's growing interest in every passing female, and then by Jessop's announcement that he wanted to be sick - an announcement followed almost immediately by the deed.

Watching him, I felt a wave of nausea in my own stomach, then Lofty seized him purposefully by the back of the neck, and jerked him unresisting towards a horse trough. Deliberately, he ducked him again and again, and then apparently satisfied that the dowsing had had the desired effect, solemnly took out a handkerchief and wiped Harry's face and uniform. Then, throwing an arm across the other's shoulders, he led Jessop back to where we waited, Nobby and I determinedly hanging on to Douggie who was cursing us lustily as he watched a brass headed blonde disappear from sight down a side turning.

"Okay. Let's go," Piper conceded, and we followed him at a brisk pace through a labyrinth of narrow passages, past grim, gutted skeletons of bombed buildings, until even Lofty was stung to protest.

"Gawd, Douggie! What's this then? A ruddy route march?"

"Not no more," Piper told him. "'ere y'are mates!"

We came to a halt above a short flight of stone steps leading downwards between two derelict shops, to a shabby doorway.

As we grouped round Piper, a couple of urchins came and gaped at us.

"Giv'us a copper, Jack," said one of them. "We're 'ungry!"

Lofty took some coins from his pocket and pressed them into a grubby palm.

"Now get home to your Mum," he counselled.

"Some 'opes," one of the youngsters told him. "She's in there."

He nodded knowingly towards the dark recess of the doorway, then with his companion, sidled away.

I stared gloomily after them. Inwardly cursing them because their intrusion had cast a shadow over the sensual anticipation that was playing havoc with my senses.

"Come on then, Stevo," said Douggie impatiently, taking the steps in two bounds and shouting back at me from inside the door. "Five steps down. You'll have to mind your head. Lofty just coped a packet! Come on. Five steps to glory, boy!"

I followed him down, ducked into the doorway and joined the others in the ill-lit passage, and suddenly, an inner door opened, and in the thin shaft of light, we saw a woman.

A veritable mountain of flesh with bare arms like sides of ham, and an untidy mass of straw coloured hair.

"Hello, Ma," Douggie greeted her. "Told you I'd bring some of me mates along next trip."

The bloated face broke into a fatuous smile of welcome.

"Come on in then," she said, "and remember - no fighting. I don't want no trouble."

"Don't worry, Ma, we won't get you into trouble," Douggie promised with a grin.

"Ought to be past them worries at your time of life, Missus," Nobby heckled her.

The woman swore good-naturedly as she pushed past us to lead the way along the fusty smelling passage, and as she opened the door at the end, a great roar of sounds greeted us. Raucous, eldritch laughter, the clink of glasses, the slow suspended slither of feet across the floor, and the wail of a gramophone grinding out the latest transatlantic boogie-woogie atrocity.

It was a good sized room with permanent black-outs, and lit by pink wall lights studiedly subdued to give discreet privacy to the couples necking it up on couches lining the walls.

I judged there to be about forty people there. Some dancing, some drinking by the bar, others just sitting around. The air was thick with smoke and a sickly sort of smell that almost took the breath away. As we went in there was a momentary hush. A score of eyes took stock of us.

Finding an empty table near the bar, we sat down. Douggie went up for drinks and immediately started a line with a blonde perched on a stool at the counter. After a while he swaggered back to us, gave us our drinks with an exaggerated flourish, and with a wink, went back to the blonde.

We watched her sink the contents of a glass down her scrawny throat, then slide off the stool with a deliberate leg show, and drape her arms round Douggie's neck. Bestowing on us a languorous look from beneath heavily mascared lashes, she allowed Douggie to steer her purposefully to join the dancers.

Lofty stood up. Casting about hopefully.

"I'm not staying long," he told us. "I told Kate I'd pick her up around five. Don't reckon she'd approve of this place."

Hitching his trousers, he looked hard at me, patted his nose with his forefinger, then crossing the room, asked a girl to dance. After a little while Harry and Nobby drifted off to find partners where dancing was only a means to an end.

Left alone at the table I went on drinking and watched the others. There didn't seem to be any unattached females though they weren't all attached to men!

I began to feel sorry for myself, and then, from somewhere near me, I heard the urgent summons of a telephone. Someone took down the receiver.

"Bloody siren's gone," the barman shouted. "'phone for you, Scottie!"

I saw a man pull himself out of a clinch with a startled looking redhead and go to take the call. He seemed alert, and already far away from the dingy dance floor.

He spoke quietly, remarking as he replaced the receiver,

"I've got to go. See you..." and without a backward glance at the redhead, he went out.

The girl pursed her lips, then catching my eye, smiled and came slowly to where I sat.

"Hello, Jack," she said lightly. "You look kind of lonesome too. Like to buy me a drink?"

I looked at the tight black sheath that was obviously all that covered her.

"Sure," I told her. "What'll it be?"

"Gin and tonic, dear," she answered.

She sat down carefully, pulling the short tight skirt over her rounded thighs. Her heavy make-up couldn't disguise the fact that nature had endowed her with more than a fair share of attraction. Her skin was smooth, her features delicately chiselled, and her wide green eyes the most beautiful I had ever seen.

She smiled before my scrutiny. Her lashes were long and curling. Inviting as they fluttered teasingly.

"You'd better get that drink then," she said.

"Sure." I got up from the table scarcely taking my eyes off her.

Congratulating myself on the good fortune that had brought her there.

"I haven't seen you here before," she said as I put the drinks on the table. "But you're a local boy aren't you?"

"Almost," I acknowledged.

"I've seen you around," she said surprisingly. "But not for some time."

"Maybe," I returned, stifling a yawn.

"You on leave then?" she wanted to know.

"Right," I said. "Seventy-two hours."

"That's nice," she smiled. "Looking for a bit of company?"

"Could be," I replied carelessly. "Another drink?"

"Thanks." She drained her glass and handed it to me. "My name's Rose. What's yours?"

"Steve," I answered shortly and went up to the bar for more drinks.

"Have you got a home in Pompey?" she asked when I went back to the table.

"Not any more," I said harshly. "Ask a lot of questions don't you?"

She shrugged. Leaned back in her chair and stared at me solemnly.

She really was exquisite. The soft titian hair, falling in a tumble of curls to frame her face - those wonderful eyes. Her teeth were small and white - her carmined lips generous. I looked away from her face, to the full curve of her breasts, firm and voluptuous, the nipples thrusting like beads against the taut bodice of her dress.

Already I was hot for her and she knew it.

"Want to come home with me?" she asked abruptly.

I nodded. My throat was suddenly dry. I made a movement to stand up as Douggie pushed his way back to me.

"Got yourself fixed up then, Stevo," he smirked. "Rose'll see you all right. Won't you, me old mucker!"

He draped an arm round Rose's shoulder.

"How goes it then," he asked her. "I 'eard your place was 'it bad."

"So it was," she told him. "Just before Christmas. I've moved into the place next door."

"Good for you. Business as usual eh!" he exclaimed grinning. "Atta girl! Be seeing you then. Look after me mate 'ere won't you."

"You bet," she answered as Douggie disappeared into the crowd. "You a friend of Douggie's then?"

"We're shipmates," I said shortly.

Outside, the drone of aircraft. The staccato stab of flak. I saw her tense. Head slightly cocked. Listening.

"Worry you?" I asked quietly.

"I suppose so," she acknowledged. "Same as everybody. Anyone who says it doesn't, well, they're just lying, aren't they? I mean, you couldn't ever get used to it, could you. Only thing is, you manage to control what you feel."

"True enough," I replied and God knows, at that moment, I was trying to do just that.

More drinks. I scarcely tasted them, and all the time the girl sat watching me. Sizing me up.

"You've had a bad time, sailor," she said suddenly.

"It's no picnic for any of us," I muttered.

"That's not what I meant," she insisted. "It's more personal. There's a sort of look about you. Like you've been through it and..."

"Gipsy Rose," I interrupted roughly. "For Christ's sake let's not be maudlin! Come to that, there's a look about you too!"

She leaned towards me.

"Come back to my place," she coaxed.

"Fancy me do you?" I jeered. "Okay. Maybe later. Let's dance."

As I pulled her into my arms, Lofty appeared.

"I'm pushing off now," he said. "You coming?"

"Later," I told him.

He looked searchingly from me to Rose.

"Well you know where to find me," he said quietly. "Take it easy. Don't forget Kate's expecting us both to stay at her place."

"I won't forget," I promised. "Cheers!"

He gave me a dubious glance and went out. I watched him go, then joined the dancers, holding Rose close to me until her body melted into mine, and I wanted her so bad I could hardly breathe. I felt her tongue moist and gentle at the lobe of my ear, and the prick of her sharp little teeth.

My arms tightened about her, my fingers caressing the soft outline of her, digging deeper into the hollow of her back, pressing her closer to my thighs, one hand cupping her breast. Her face nuzzled into mine. Her tongue teased my lips, and I was hot for her, and panicky in case my longing wouldn't wait until I could lay her.

My arms cradling her, I pushed her through the crowd and out through the door into the corridor, stopping to kiss her hot mouth, thrusting my tongue into its moist depths.

My hand was on the hem of her skirt when she wriggled free, and pulling me by the arm, led me up into the street. The deserted street where fear stalked, and the smell of death and disaster was all around. Polluting the air. Just like it had been when Cora and I stood together in the rubble and the shambles the night Beady died. Only then, darkness had shrouded the full horror of it.

Like the night Cora died. The same smells putrefying the air, the same horror, the same helplessness.

Desire left me. I began to feel bemused and my knees had no strength in them. I stumbled along the narrow streets, Rose supporting me.

A Warden called across to us,

"Better take cover! There's a tidy few of the bastards about!"

At last, Rose stopped at a building that ended abruptly with a great slice of the brickwork torn away. Stark, distorted and ugly.

"Here we are," she said, pushing open a door. "Come on in then and I'll show you my little hidey hole."

The ache in my loins had gone. I felt spent. Back to the dark empty longing that was all that was left of my life with Cora.

In the darkness of the hallway with its echoing hollowness, I stopped suddenly. Outside, the drone of the German 'planes grew louder. Rose tugged urgently at my arm.

"Come on, love," she murmured. "It's nice down here. You'll see."

Still I hesitated, and suddenly the queer echoing silence of the place was broken by the shrill, terrifying whine of a diving 'plane. I heard Rose give a little startled gasp. Felt her hand seek mine to pull me towards an alcoved door under the stairs. Together we stumbled down a steep wooden stairway and the ominous crumph of bursting bombs was mercifully a long way off, and the shuddering walls, a murmur, nothing more.

Now, a hundred hammers pounded at my brain, and my nostrils quivered at the smell of stale sperm and perfume that pervaded the place. Rose switched on a dim light and stood there looking at me, waiting for me to voice my approval of the room.

Brightly coloured rugs and wide low bed with green covers. Bottles of drink on a cupboard, and a marble washstand with bowl and jug of white with scarlet poppies. A dressing table draped elaborately with green material like the bed cover, and covered with bottles and pots.

Rose looked at me eagerly,

"Cosy isn't it?" she said.

"Fine," I muttered, sitting down on the one chair I could see. The reek of the place made me feel sick.

"Don't want Jerry busting in on us, do we?" she said archly. "It's pretty safe down here. 'Cept for a direct hit. I had it specially reinforced."

"Real snug," I told her wearily, my head near to bursting.

"You don't look so good," she said quietly. "I'll get you a drink."

She poured me a stiff whisky, and I drank it neat, holding the glass with shaking fingers. Rose bent over me, kissing the top of my head - soothing my bursting forehead with cool willowy hands.

"There's a toilet behind the curtain," she whispered. "Maybe you'd feel better for a wash."

I stumbled to my feet.

"Christ! My head!" I muttered.

"Lie down a bit, dear. You'll be all right," she said.

Her gentle propelling hands pushed me towards the bed and I stretched out on it, savouring the feel of the soft cool pillows. As I closed my eyes, I felt Rose pulling off my boots.

A brief interval of silence, then a slithering sound. With an effort I opened my eyes.

In the pale lamplight, Rose was standing naked. Her body white and beautiful. Hands cupping her full breasts, her legs long and smooth. Her mouth smiled at me. Her eyes were tender. Hazily, my gaze focussed on the white ring of her navel, defined in talc.

But I had no desire left. The heady smell of the room, the sensation of floating, the pain in my eyeballs. I struggled against sleep.

Now Rose was bending over me. Her breasts brushed my face. Somehow I helped her get my jumper over my head. Groaning - turning away from her. Arching my back as she pulled away my trousers.

"Head hurt bad?" she whispered, her breath warm and moist in my ear.

"Hell!" I muttered, and after a little while, I heard her sigh and move away from me.

Vaguely I saw her pull on a flimsy robe.

"I'll make some coffee."

Her voice sounded far away. And then I must have slept.

When I woke up, Rose was under the covers beside me. Cool, soft as velvet, leg resting carelessly across my own. Her naked shoulders above the sheets, and the dark deep delve between her breasts. Splayed across the pillows, teasing the cream of her flawless skin, the curls of her long red hair, loosened now to fall in soft luxuriant loveliness round her oval face.

Her lashes were long - feathered on cheeks devoid of make-up now, and even in sleep, her wide mouth curved in a smile.

I stroked her leg. Began an exploration of the smooth body, and my loins were alive with desire again. I bent over her, kissing the marble of her gently rising breast, teasing the firm pink nipples, and her arms suddenly encircled me. As I found her mouth, her lips were already parted, her response hot and urgent as she arched towards me.

My body melted into hers. Nothing mattered but the swift, pulsating rhythm of the thrust, the pull and bursting. The transition from the turmoil of desire to the spent exhaustion of satiation. The ultimate extremity of the Universe! The emptiness that follows the driving force of the seed of creation!

These things I knew. And then I fell asleep again. A deep untroubled sleep. Later, when I thought of time, it was already nine in the morning. I stretched and sat up. The room was rank with the smell of sweat and scent and sex.

Beside me, Rose lay watching.

"Hell! Is that the time," I muttered. "I must have slept like the dead!"

"You can say that again," she laughed. "There was enough noise outside!"

"Bad raid?" I asked.

"Not really," she answered. "Though there were plenty of 'planes the second time."

I looked at her questioningly.

"The first 'All Clear' went about ten o'clock last night," she explained. "Just before you turned the heat on! There was another alarm around three-thirty. Didn't finish until nearly eight."

"Never heard a thing," I admitted.

She laughed.

"Don't have to tell me!"

"Sorry," I said ruefully. "Got a cigarette?"

"Help yourself. By the lamp. There's a lighter too. I'll go and make you some breakfast."

"No. No thanks," I said, guiltily thinking of Lofty and Kate. "I must be getting along. The people I'm supposed to be staying with will be sending out a search party."

"Well I'll make you some tea," she decided. She got out of bed and stood there naked in front of me.

"Who wants tea," I muttered, pulling her towards me, my tongue on her navel as her knees rested between my thighs. Their pressure was gentle but it's purpose clear enough.

"Better get that tea," I told her, giving her buttocks a playful nip, and thinking how I'd snubbed Kate's kind invitation, I lied, "I couldn't raise a canter this morning."

"All right," she said, then taking my chin between her hands, "You did enjoy yourself didn't you?" she asked earnestly.

"What do you think!" I answered hoarsely. "It was great."

She smiled happily.

"Look," she said. "You go and have a wash and I'll get us something to eat. Won't take a jiffy. Come on up when you're ready. I'll be in the kitchen. It's on the left at the top of the stairs. You'll find a razor and all that in the cabinet."

"Okay," I agreed. Why not? Might as well be hung for a sheep as a lamb - and I was hungry.

She snatched up a dressing gown, and went upstairs. I pulled on my trousers and went into the curtained recess to clean myself up.

Fifteen minutes later I joined Rose in her kitchen. She was cooking sausages and bacon over a small stove. A check apron covered her dressing gown. Her face was washed and shining. Her hair tied back with a green ribbon.

As I ate the breakfast she cooked for me, Rose munched toast and marmalade, chatting inconsequentially of this and that.

It was as though she had left the siren, the bawd, the strumpet, in the erotic room below. This was another world.

"What are you thinking about?" she demanded suddenly.

"You," I told her. "You seem quite different up here."

"Well, we all look different with our clothes on, don't we?" she laughed. "Straight though. Down there's my job. Up here I can be myself. It's a nice little flat. I'll show you before you go. Down there, well, like I said, it's where I do my job."

And then I remembered.

Taking out my wallet, I drew out five pounds. A sudden look of alarm widened her eyes.

"No," she said quickly. "Please, Steve. I don't want money. Not from you."

"Hey, what's this?" I asked in surprise. "I thought..."

"I know what you thought," she interrupted abruptly. "Only it's not always like that."

She got up from the table and lit a cigarette.

"Sometimes," she went on steadily, "I go with a man just because I like him. See? Because I want to be with him. Does that sound daft to you?"

I shook my head.

"Makes sense," I told her.

"It's the only time I really feel anything," she said. "The rest of the time, it's just a job like any other."

"What made you go on the game?" I wanted to know.

She shrugged.

"I dunno," she answered. "No one 'done me wrong', if that's what you're getting at. I suppose because my body's the only thing I've got to sell. I learnt that when I was a kid."

She fell silent for a while. Her thoughts far away. Her eyes suddenly moist with the mists of memory.

"When I was a kid," she went on quietly, "we lived in London. In the Fulham Palace Road. I used to think my mother was the most beautiful woman in the world. She had hair like mine only redder, and it was so long, she could sit on it. She loved to dance. I can see her now at the wash tub, arms up to the elbows in suds. She'd make bubbles with them and dance about, chasing them all round the kitchen. Singing and laughing all the time - but not when Dad was home.

"We were both scared stiff of him. He was a joiner and drank like a fish. When he'd had a skinful he'd go all religious. Spouting from the Bible. Calling Mum a Jezebel, and making her get down on her knees and repent. Real mad he was. The only thing Mum had to repent was that she'd married him, though I never once heard her complain.

"I remember one day he caught her putting on a bit of lipstick. He dragged her into the kitchen and cut off her beautiful hair with a carving knife. Right close up to her scalp, like a boy. I remember I cried with her, all night long, and the next morning, when he'd sobered up, even Dad was ashamed of what he'd done.

"Mum died a year later. I was nine. I was put into a private school where all the airy-fairy nonsense was to be knocked out of my head. According to Dad, the headmaster was a God-fearing, Christian man who would educate me in the paths of righteousness!

"Only after I'd been there a month, the Head put his hand up my skirt and gave me a couple of bob to keep my mouth shut. It sort of progressed after that. He'd lie on the floor and give me a couple of bob to walk over him - especially you know where. Or I'd come upon him in odd corners, standing with his trousers open, and a few bob in his hand to tempt me to touch it. There was a lot more. I never really thought about the things we did, except that it was a source of pocket money, and that in some odd way, I was getting back at my father.

"And it wasn't only the Head. I had a friend at the school and sometimes I was allowed to go home with her for a weekend. One day, when I kissed him goodbye, her father stuck his tongue down my throat. I got ten bob that time. I suppose I learned early about 'respectable' men. They were all pretty much the same. Your best friend's father. The school master. The milkman. The man on the 'bus who liked to rub up against anything in a skirt. And it was easy money. I never gave anything of myself. Not really. Now, so long as I keep myself clean and give a bit of pleasure, what odds? It's a business like anything else. What about the French girls who go on the game to get a dowry together?

"The way I look at it, anyone who does a job of work gives something of himself to the man who employs him. His brain, his hands. Well, I've not much of a brain, and I never was any good with my hands, so what have I got left to earn money with? Want me to tell you?"

She stopped, arms akimbo, and flinging back her head, roared with laughter, then suddenly, she sat down again.

"No," she said seriously. "I don't give anything of myself. Not often. With you, I felt I wanted to. You know... I like you, Steve."

"Thanks," I grinned at her. "You're all right yourself."

"You haven't anyone here in Pompey, have you?" she asked. "No family or anything?"

"Not any more," I said abruptly.

"I knew it," she declared triumphantly. "Last night you were too far gone to know what was happening, but this morning you'd have been out of here in a flash if there'd been anyone. Well, wouldn't you?"

"I should have been," I told her. "I've a couple of friends who'll be doing their nut wondering what's happened to me but I guess it's too late to worry now. Have you heard any news this morning?"

"Only from the milkman," she returned. "There were no casualties in the town. That's something. An incendiary bomb fell on a garage over at Copnor. A couple of houses were burnt out but no one was hurt, and a Jerry bomber was shot down Southsea way. More tea?"

"Thanks."

I pushed my cup towards her. Handed her a cigarette and lit up myself.

"You married, Steve?" she asked quietly.

"Not any more," I told her. "My wife was killed in a raid in 1941."

"I'm sorry," she sympathised. "Here in Portsmouth?"

I nodded,

"She's buried where she died with about forty others. Less than a hundred yards from here. Our son died with her."

"That's terrible," she murmured. "How old was he?"

"Ten bloody days!" I said bitterly. "I never even saw him - alive or dead! Makes you wonder what it's all about, doesn't it?"

Her eyes pitied me.

"That's life I suppose," she sighed. "We've all got so much to take. No use kicking against it. It's all laid on for us."

"You're a fatalist eh?" I asked.

"I suppose I am," she admitted. "I believe in living one day at a time and being grateful for it."

"Sometimes just being alive's an over-rated blessing," I muttered sourly. "It seems to me that only rottenness endures. Well, I've got to push off and make my apologies to Lofty and Kate."

I got up and stood looking at her.

"Thanks, Rose..." I said awkwardly. "You're sure you don't want anything... ?"

"I've told you - I don't want money from you, Steve," she answered quietly. "But you could come back here - after you've seen your friends."

I hesitated.

"Maybe I will," I said at length. "But I don't want to disrupt your business do I?"

"I'm taking a breather for a couple of days," she said with a laugh. "If you come back this evening, I could have a meal ready - That's another thing I'm good at."

Behind her smile, her expression pleaded with me.

"I'm not sure," I said slowly. "Tell you what. I'll meet you in the Stag at eight o'clock."

"I'll be there," she promised eagerly. "Want to see the flat before you go?"

"You can show me later. I'd better be going."

She followed me to the door and we kissed briefly without passion. I went out into the dull morning, making my way through the tortured streets, past the ugly ruins of gutted buildings, mounds of rubble and charred wood, to the ground floor flat Kate Miller shared with her mother.

Kate had just finished setting her mother's hair, and Lofty was perched on the arm of a chair, drinking coffee.

"Where'd you get to last night then?" he demanded as Kate ushered me in. "Thought you were kipping here."

"I meant to," I apologised lamely. "But I got plastered."

"How did you make out with the redhead?" he wanted to know.

I glanced guiltily at Kate.

"Don't mind me," she grinned. "I'm a big girl now. By the way, Arthur 'phoned about half an hour ago. I told him you were on a seventy-two hours. He's gone to see that everything's all right with the cottage, but said he'll be back tonight to meet us for a drink at the Stag. I thought we might all go to Caswell's for a meal."

"Cora's death hit him hard," Lofty said abruptly. "He spent a lot of time with her during the last couple of months..."

He looked at me searchingly but I made no answer.

"Caswell's then?" asked Kate hurriedly.

"Fine," I murmured, and wondered about Rose.

Maybe I shouldn't have suggested she should meet me like that. It was asking for trouble. Better to have gone round to her place - if I wanted to see her again. Did I? A woman I'd picked up for the oldest reason in the world? In the cold light of morning, exchanging pleasantries with Kate and her mother in the snug respectability of their parlour, I doubted it.

At eleven o'clock a car called to take Mrs Miller to the hospital where she was in charge of the linen.

"No work for you today, Kate?" I asked when her mother had gone.

"I've taken French leave," she explained. "After what happened to you, I can't have Lofty going around on the loose, now can I. Fancy going to Ma Seymour's place!"

"Ma Seymour... ?" I began curiously.

"That club we went to," Lofty enlightened me.

"I don't remember it being there before..." I left the sentence in the air.

"It hasn't been there long," Kate told me, "and somehow I don't think it will last. The police are keeping an eye on it. It's a real rogue's kitchen. Black marketeers and all that. Not to mention all the queers who congregate there!"

Her words pushed me back to Rose again. Maybe it wasn't such a good idea. Me and Rose meeting in the Stag!

I could have done something about it. There was plenty of time during that afternoon. I had only to go back to Rose's place and tell her the arrangement was off - only something stopped me.

Some streak of stubbornness. Some cussed idea that I'd choose my own company, with no strings attached.

Looking at Kate sitting on Lofty's knee, I wondered idly if they slept together - and again I thought of Rose.

What made her kind of woman so different from the scores of others who indulged their sexual appetite with less candour, and for less reward, yet still retained the outward facade of respectability?

Hypocrisy! Bloody hypocrisy that's all!

That evening, we reached the Stag just before eight o'clock, to find Arthur waiting for us. As he ordered drinks, I caught sight of Rose reflected in a mirror as she sat at the counter in the adjoining bar. After a little while, I excused myself, and went to her.

Without giving her a chance to protest, I led her into the saloon to meet the others. It was a mistake of course. Their expressions condemned me out of hand and, for a moment, I thought Kate was going to walk away.

Rose went very pale. Her eyes were luminous.

"Sit down, Rose," I said quietly. "I'll get you a drink," and ignoring the others, I went over to the bar.

And Lofty was up there with me. His face like thunder.

"Christ, Steve!" he fumed. "What the hell d'you think you're doing? Bringing a bloody bawd along to mix with Kate!"

"I'd arranged to meet her before I knew you'd all be here," I said quietly.

"Well, why the hell didn't you say so earlier?" he demanded angrily. "Get rid of her pronto. If you won't tell her to beat it, I bloody well will."

"You stay out of it, Lofty," I told him harshly. "If the company isn't good enough for Mistress Kate, you know what you can do."

He gaped at me incredulously, and Arthur's voice came from behind me,

"Kate was Cora's best friend, Stevo. Doesn't that mean anything to you?"

"Shut up!" I muttered. "Shut up, damn you!"

Angry, tight-lipped, I went back to where Rose was watching me anxiously.

"Let's go," I said stiffly, and together we went out into the street.

We went back to her place in silence, and in the room below the stairs, I took her savagely, satiating my anger and guilt and frustration, in the warm, generous flesh of her.

The next morning, I went round to make my peace with Kate and Lofty...

CHAPTER EIGHT

If Powerful had put to sea at the end of my three day's leave, it might have been the end of the affair, but it didn't turn out like that.

An inspection of the cruiser's stern revealed further damage below the waterline, and it was nearly five weeks before repairs were completed. In that time, whenever I went ashore, I spent the time with Rose.

In the beginning a sort of bravado made me go around with her. Flaunting her around the town. Ignoring the ribaldry of my shipmates. Defiant. Brash. Filled with some inexplicable desire to see what Arthur and Lofty would make of it.

Wisely, they left me alone. No scenes. No recriminations. Somehow, I suppose they realised I was trying to prove something. Perhaps they knew better than I what it was - and maybe they thought it would soon burn itself out.

Almost without realising it, the transition came. The realisation that I really liked being with Rose, not only for the obvious reason, but because I found it easy to relax with her. Learned how to laugh again. To enjoy simple, uncluttered things.

She wasn't always alone when I went ashore. Sometimes there'd be a man with her. Down in that heady place with its tawdry trimmings and the air thick with the smell of sweating bodies and stale desire. And I'd wait. Wait in the gay red and white kitchen where it was clean and warm.

I'd make a cup of tea, and when at last Rose joined me, her great eyes bright and welcoming, we'd never talk of her 'clientele'.

She'd bath, then we'd go into town for a drink and a meal, and when we returned to the flat, we'd lay together in her primly conventional bedroom on the ground floor.

Often I tried to give her money, but she'd never take it.

"It's not like that with you, Steve," she told me earnestly. "I like being with you. I feel something. I enjoy it, and you do too, don't you? I mean you don't just go with me to get rid of that lump in your trousers, do you?"

It was true. I liked her. Enjoyed being with her. She was different from anyone I'd ever known. Uninhibited. Down to earth, and incongruously childlike in her appreciation of simple things. Sucking a stick of candy floss at a local fair. Chasing squirrels when we took a 'bus ride to the New Forest.

Once, she asked me seriously.

"What are you going to do when the war's over."

"Haven't given it a lot of thought," I told her honestly. "Teach the piano perhaps. Do a bit of composing. My father left a heap of unfinished manuscripts we were working on together. Don't think I'd care for an office job again." I broke off abruptly. Dreading a flood of questions about my father. And it struck me, that for the first time since his death, I'd mentioned him calmly and naturally...

Maybe she saw something in my eyes that told her the subject was taboo, for, surprisingly, she asked no more questions.

At those times, when we left the town behind, her face was free of the heavy make-up that was part of her stock-in-trade. The red hair loose. The garish jewellery left at home, but the natural invitation of her swinging hips, hugged tight by her favourite black dress, was always there. When I caught her to me her response to my lips was quick and eager, and the rich clean smelling grass of the forest was a welcome change from the queasy smell of her bedchamber.

One evening when I was alone, I met up with Arthur near the dockyard gates.

"What's got into you, Stevo?" he asked quietly. "If you fancy sleeping with a tart, okay, but why not leave it at that?"

"I like her," I said shortly.

"You're crazy," he snorted. "A floozie who's notorious in every bar in town!"

"I said, I like her," I repeated stubbornly.

He sighed.

"So you like her," he returned calmly. "You don't have to go to extremes to prove it. You've got friends in this town. People who knew Cora."

"Lay off!" I snapped. "I know what I'm doing. Rose is a whore. Everyone knows it. How long d'you think I'd last if all my so-called friends knew about me?"

"So that's it!" he exclaimed. "Well I'm damned! Why don't you grow up, Stevo! Stop flagellating yourself and try squaring up to the past."

"What's that supposed to mean?" I demanded churlishly.

"The world won't judge you by what your father did," he said evenly. "Give it a chance!"

"You must be joking," I declared angrily. "Old Garland bloody soon judged me - and Merrick..."

"They were people caught up in what happened. People with the same complex as you. Afraid of the immediate repercussions."

"Are you trying to tell me I should have stayed in Sandworth after what happened?" I asked incredulously.

"No," he answered. "You had a right to start again, and you proved that the truth didn't make any difference where it mattered most. With Cora..."

"And Cora's dead," I broke in harshly.

"Cora was a lovely woman," he said quietly. "I got to know her very well in the last weeks of her life. To love her, Stevo - I don't mind telling you. I envied you..." His voice trailed off, and then he added abruptly. "You owe it to her memory to straighten up your life..."

In mid-November Powerful left harbour to return to escort duty with the Arctic convoys.

It was the penultimate run for both of us, for although the outward bound convoy reached the Kola Inlet without incident, the return journey was a different story.

At the end of the month, a convoy of fifteen merchantmen set sail for Loch Ewe with a strong escorting force.

The escort vessels, although adequately armed to deal efficiently with attacking U-boats, had no real defence against enemy bombers or warships, but twelve miles ahead of the convoy, Powerful, with her formidable anti-aircraft armaments, kept close cover, ready to protect the returning ships against any attack with which the escort vessels were unable to cope.

The freighters, with empty holds, were having a tough time in the face of a blizzard which buffeted them along with propellers scarcely clearing the water, while ahead, Powerful steamed on a zigzagging course at a steady eighteen knots.

Although a few hours out of Kola, a German reconnaissance 'plane had been sighted, there had been no further sign of trouble. And then, on the third day out, just before noon, without warning, came disaster.

I was stationed by the after pom-poms talking to the crew when the first torpedo hit us. A square hit to port, well up in the bows.

Powerful leapt in the water, threshing from end to end. There was a great tearing sound as the metal ripped apart, and with a roar, the sea flooded in.

Above the awful noise of the stricken ship, the shrieks of men mingled with the wind.

As Powerful reared, a second torpedo tore into her amidships, and a wave of heat rose up as the explosion shattered the engine room. The ship shuddered to a standstill and the frightening hiss of escaping steam added its horror to that dreadful din. Then those of us who waited at our stations, heard yet another sound. A sound that froze our blood. The scream and clamouring of trapped men, helplessly doomed.

"Christ!" muttered one of the gun crew. "We've bought it!"

"Shut up," I said thickly. "Listen!"

Below, as the ship heaved, something crunched and rolled. Men were climbing up from the wardroom - struggling into life jackets - running towards the stricken area while the damage squad got to work shoring up bulkheads and plugging leaks.

Across the loud speakers, came the voice of the CO telling us that the ship had been hit forward and amidships. Calling upon damage control squads to close up. First aid parties to muster at casualty stations, and the rest of us to remain calm.

The ship was a sitting duck. Helpless. Immobilised. Our only hope, that the convoy would see the smoke and realising our plight, detach a ship to take us in tow.

The force of the explosion had carried us right round, and as Powerful settled on the water and the work of shoring up, and making her watertight went on, the wind dropped and the snow came into its own.

Thick. Heavy. Curtaining. Vainly we scanned the horizon for the ship that never came. And suddenly, came the final blow. The death blow that broke the cruiser's back as a third torpedo caught her on the starboard side almost opposite the spot where the second torpedo had struck home.

Powerful seemed to arch. Came a great clanking, grinding sound, and suddenly the deck was steep beneath my feet as the ship heeled over, listing at an angle of fifteen degrees.

It was evident she was doomed. From the bridge, the CO warned all hands to remain on the upper deck.

Rescue parties worked frantically among the dead and wounded. Laying them side by side on the deck as we waited for the inevitable order to abandon ship.

With the rest of the gun crew, I stayed where I was. Stunned. Helpless. Frustrated. At the mercy of an invisible enemy who had killed our ship, the moaning and groaning of her mangled majesty masking the cries of the men who had died with her.

Lofty was one of them.

When at last the order came, the last order, releasing us from our posts, I made my way to the crowd of survivors watching the launching of the Carley floats.

I passed shrouded figures already covered with snow. Snow stained crimson as their life blood drained away.

And then I saw Lofty. It was over for him. I stared in horror at the gaping wound where his head was almost severed from his body. At the mass of bloody pulp that was his arm. He lay among the scraps of men. Horribly alone. His staring eyes wide to the leaden sky. Tears almost blinded me. I retched. My mind raced back to Cora... and I cursed the God that allowed such bloody carnage.

All around me, men concerned themselves with the living. Marshalling the wounded on to stretchers. Getting them on the rafts.

The burn cases were the worst. Scorched travesties of faces. Flayed, tormented bodies writhing in agony. Eyes alive with indescribable pain, and the moans and groans of the wounded rose despairingly to mingle with the soft scurry of the shrouding snow like the wailing of souls already lost.

I fell in with the living. Men streaked with blood and dirt waiting to outwit the threat of the steeply canting deck of the dying ship. Struggling to remain upright. Desperately seeking hand holds.

There was no confusion.

The men themselves, standing by the rails, waiting for the CO's final order, were strangely quiet. Below, the sea, licking its lips round the Carley floats and the one lifeboat it had been possible to launch.

Powerful gave a great lurch. Impatient to be rid of us. And at last we heard it,

"Abandon ship! Abandon ship!"

The order had a hollow ring. For an instant, no one moved, and then some jumped into the icy water, striking out for the rafts.

Instinctively, I cowered away from the rails. Afraid, and seeing my fear reflected in the eyes of some of my shipmates. More jumped. Some hung for a moment then dropped, tearing themselves against the unyielding hull. Yelling with pain. Others shouted obscene quips, calling on friends to join them as they jumped.

I looked once more at Lofty, now almost obliterated by the snow, snow that hid the cruel wounds, the mangled limbs. Only his eyes were visible, the fringe of his long lashes holding back the soft shroud.

Someone called to me,

"Come on, mate! She's going!"

Powerful seemed quiet now. Spent.

I looked round wildly. Leaned over the rails. Below, men crowded the Carleys, buffeting for position... Some clung to the rope nets. And I knew, as they did, that in that icy water, survival would be impossible unless help came quickly.

Despairingly I stared at the white curtain of snow. Only a miracle could pierce it in time to save some of us.

One moment it seemed that Powerful was gently surrendering herself to the sea, then, as I stood poised to jump, she erupted again. Came explosion after explosion, sending great chunks of metal spewing through the air.

As I leapt, a huge fragment of debris hurtled against my legs. An instant of sheer agony, then the water closed over me, and all I felt was the frantic necessity to strike out. To put a safe distance between me and the dying ship. To reach a ratline, and to make contact with other human beings.

And somehow, I made it. Clutching with fingers already numbed, at the line. When I turned to look at the ship once more, she was quiet again, and when at last she heeled over and disappeared into the water, her going was almost too quiet. Like a ghost.

For a while, no one spoke. We all felt the need to retain our strength until the uneasy silence was broken by the sound of men praying, while others sobbed. Some cursed their comrades as they grappled together for the best places.

Soon, beside me, men began to lose their slim hold on life and drift away, silently, to disappear forever.

Men slipped off the Carleys, or were pushed and jostled, and in an agony of desperation, I pulled myself up, bracing myself against clawing hands as weak and bloody as my own, to fall exhausted, flat on my back, staring at the sky.

All around me men were dying. Clinging to each other. Some trying to help weaker comrades. Some gibbering and afraid, but mostly, they died quietly, as though loath to break the awful silence of death's wooing.

I closed my eyes. Resigned to death. A strange drowsiness crept over me. It was as though I was disembodied. A vague sensation of pain. An impression, nothing more. I tried to open my eyes but the icy breath of the blizzard sealed my lids. It was easier to relax. To slip away.

I lost consciousness without knowing that help was no more than a ladder's breadth away!

The destroyers Dorian and Doughty had been detached from the convoy after the flag ship's radar office had reported an explosion in the vicinity of Powerful's last known position.

They came upon the handful of survivors and by feats of superb seamanship plucked us from the hungry sea.

I came to with a thousand knives tearing at my body. Someone was pouring neat whisky down my throat. My head was on fire and lead weights were on my eyeballs. With an effort, I got them open. Closing them again as the sudden glare of electric light sent spearheads of agony through my head.

"Take it easy now," a quiet voice warned.

After a while, I opened my eyes again. A tall man in a white coat stood between me and the naked light. As my vision focussed, he smiled at me.

"Welcome aboard," he said.

I mouthed my thanks but no sound came. Vaguely I noticed the cradle over my legs - the bandages on my hands. A moment of panic as I struggled to sit up. A gentle, restraining hand, then oblivion again.

The next few weeks were a confusion of pain. Of hazy hospital faces. Of operating theatres and more pain. Of long wards, and then, when I came to after what proved to be the last operation, miraculously, I found myself in Haslar Hospital, Portsmouth, my ward mates all survivors of naval disasters... and I learned that of Powerful's ship's company of nearly six hundred men, only twelve ratings had been saved.

One of my legs had been badly shattered - I'd lost all the fingers on my left hand, and one from the right. The skill of the surgeon had saved my leg, but there would be little mobility in it. The news filled me with fear. What would the future hold... without hands... A deep feeling of depression and loneliness enveloped me.

My family, my wife, my child, my friend and the great Company which had formed the background of my everyday life - all had been torn away from me.

I was twenty-four. Alone. Crippled and helpless. I wept. In those first weary days of realisation, I cried the hours away. Wishing that I had died with the others in the icy waters of the Barents Sea. My loneliness was like a canker. Each visiting time when friends and relations flocked in to see my ward mates, my bitterness increased.

I was alone. Alone like Smithy, the man who lay in the bed

beside mine. A rating whose ship had been sunk by torpedo bombers off Spithead, and now, shrouded in bandages, waited for death that had already held off too long.

From time to time I caught a glimpse of him when the screens around him were moved by one or other of the nursing staff who hovered around him in endless procession, futilely prolonging the unequal struggle for his life.

But I heard him all the time! God! How I heard him! The long piteous moaning. The awful shrieking paroxysms of his dementia, and the thin shuddering wail in the night when, endlessly he called his wife's name.

But she never came. A shipmate of the dying man told me she never would. But Smithy never knew of the 'Dear John' letter she sent him. It was the one mercy of his oblivion.

Then one morning when I woke up, the screens round Smithy's bed had gone. So had Smithy, and a gloomy silence settled over the ward. We looked at each other without speaking, studiously avoiding the immaculate tidiness of the empty bed.

Poor devil! Anyway, he'd gone before he learned about his wife and the Yank. Maybe he knew now, and maybe there were compensations for that sort of betrayal in Paradise - or wherever else he'd gone!

We hadn't long to wait for Smithy's successor. They wheeled him in on a trolley after the surgeons had finished with him. He was in a bad way too. We caught a glimpse of his bandaged face as they pulled the screens around him, and we heard his low fretful moaning as he struggled back to consciousness.

The morning dragged by. Lunch then the visitors began to crowd in, and the hum of voices rose through the ward as though a hundred bees had settled there. There was laughter too. A welcome sound.

I wasn't expecting anyone, and the novelty of watching those who came to see my ward mates, soon wore off. I closed my eyes and dozed.

And suddenly, a whistle startled me from the brink of sleep. A long low note which came from Rackham and was immediately echoed all round the ward.

I sat up, leaning forward to see who they were all looking at and there, standing just inside the swing doors, I saw Rose!

She wore the dress she always wore. The black figure-hugging sheath with white fringe outlining the shoulders like epaulettes.

The dress left nothing to the imagination. Accentuated her high full breasts. Outlined the soft curve of her rounded hips. Thoughtfully she had discarded her coat to give us the full eyeful.

Her hat was a cluster of black and white flowers held together on a band of velvet with a wisp of white billowy veiling. I remembered how she loved to wear it and how, when she'd asked me what I thought of it, I'd told her it looked absurd!

She was coming towards me now. Swaying provocatively, and enjoying every minute of the ribald whistling that accompanied her.

Through the open fronts of her white high heeled shoes, her toenails showed crimson under the sheer stockings, matching her wide painted mouth and the tips of her fingers under her white mesh gloves.

Her profession couldn't have been more clearly defined, and in that moment I wanted to crawl away and hide.

And then she was beside me. A smile on her lips and a provocative swing of her hips.

"Hello, sailor," she greeted me.

"Rose," I muttered embarrassed, aware that many eyes were watching me. "How did you know I was here?"

She arranged herself on a bedside chair, sent a fluttering glance round the grinning audience from under heavily mascared eyelashes, and told me.

"Charlie told me. You know. The barman at the Stag. Told me about your legs and that..."

Her glance rested momentarily on the outline of my legs beneath the sheets.

"Still got them then," she said. "I wondered. I'd have come sooner, but I thought you were dead. A chap I know said he'd seen your ship go down, and he didn't think there were any survivors."

"Twelve," I said shortly. "Just twelve."

The sudden recollection of those last ghastly moments on the raft, sent a involuntary shudder through me. I closed my eyes.

"Well," she asked. "Are you glad to see me?"

"Did you have to come dressed like that?" I asked quietly.

Her eyes hardened.

"Like a whore? That's what I am, Steve. Take it or leave it." As I made no answer, she went on. "What's going to happen to you when you get out of here? I mean, you won't be going back will you?"

"To the Service you mean? You're joking! What use is a man with no hands and a gammy leg!" I waved my bandaged hands at her. "Four out of ten!" I said bitterly. "That's all they've left me!"

"Oh, Steve," she murmured. "I'm so sorry!"

"Maybe I'll find myself an easy pitch on the Black Market," I said lightly. "Or a rich wife to keep me. Seriously, Rose, I don't know. It's not going to be easy."

"What were you doing before?" she wanted to know.

"Before the War? Pen-pushing. No more of that thank you. Even if I had my hands..."

"Didn't you tell me you might try teaching the piano... ?"

"You're joking! Though I suppose I could manage four finger exercises with one hand!" I told her with a dry laugh. "You don't have to worry about me. I'll get by."

She fidgeted. Looked at me anxiously.

"I like you, Steve. You know that, don't you?"

"Yes I know," I acknowledged. "I like you too."

Again she hesitated.

"When are you coming out?" she asked at length.

"Can't say for certain. I daresay it'll be pretty soon so long as I've some place to go to. Then I'll have to have therapy somewhere. They need all the beds they can get."

"Haven't you anyone at all then?" she asked. "No family?"

"No," I said shortly. "They're all dead. I suppose I'll have to stay put until I'm able to look after myself, but the doctors say I'm doing fine. Be on my feet in no time."

She looked at me hard. Reached out and took one of my bandaged hands in her own.

"I could do it, Steve," she said earnestly.

"Do what?" I asked curiously.

"Look after you," she told me solemnly.

"You?" I said incredulously.

Her eyes narrowed.

"Why not?" she demanded harshly. "I've a nice place now. I've given up the flat in Cloth Row. Bought a little house in Bursledon. It's nice. On the main road. You'll like it."

"Sounds fine," I murmured.

"And you meant what you said about liking me?" she persisted.

"Of course I do," I assured her. "But I couldn't just come out of here and park myself on you. I'm a bloody cripple. Useless and practically broke. Besides, you've got a lot of friends... and that... haven't you?"

"You don't have to worry about that," she said carefully. "I'd pack all that in. Settle down."

"I don't get it," I shook my head. "What's all this got..."

"It's simple," she interrupted me. "We could get married!"

I gaped at her in astonishment.

"Married!" I echoed incredulously.

She stiffened. Stood up and stared down at me. Her expression hard and unsmiling.

"That's what I said," she told me levelly. "And what's wrong with that? I was good enough for the other, wasn't I?"

"Oh hell, Rose," I said exasperated. "That has nothing to do with it. You're okay. We've had fun, but marriage... You know how I felt about Cora. I couldn't feel that way about another woman."

"I'm not asking you to," she retorted. "I'm fed up with being pushed around, that's all. You've had a rotten deal. You've got no one, and just now you've nowhere else to go. We get on all right. I've got a bit of money saved, and it seems to me we could help each other. Think it over, Steve. I'll be back tomorrow for your answer. Bye now."

She bent down and kissed me lightly on the lips, and for an instant I savoured the soft seductive warmth of her, and the familiar perfume teased my nostrils.

"You know how I feel about you, Steve," she murmured,"

"What's happened to you doesn't make any difference."

And then she was on her way down the ward, preening herself like a favourite cat. Smilingly exchanging airy witticisms all the way. Turning at the door, she waved with a gesture that embraced us all. Offered Rackham the victory sign, and was gone.

An instant of silence broken by Rackham's raucous voice.

"There y'are mates! That's what you find behind the red light! What you been up to, Steve?"

"I know her," put in Morgan from the bed opposite. "She had a place in Cloth Row. I heard Jerry dropped a pill on it!"

"Yes, he tried his best," Rackham told him. "She moved into the place next door though. Business as usual!"

"You can say that again," grinned Morgan.

"How the hell do you know so much about her?" I demanded incautiously.

Morgan raised himself up on an elbow and grinned at me.

"I've been with her that's how," he said cockily, "and I'm not the only one here."

A suppressed murmur ran round the room. A chorus of assent. A snigger. A muted epithet. Suspended derision.

"Well that's all finished now," I burst out defensively. "Rose is all right."

"Don't tell me you've fallen for that, you poor bloody fool," Rackham scoffed. "They never change. Once a tart..."

"Shut up," I shouted furiously. "She's straight now I tell you, and if you want some more to snigger about, I... I'm going to marry her!"

The words seemed torn from me. It was as though someone else had spoken them.

An instant of silence, then came Morgan's voice,

"Christ, Stevens! I thought it was only your limbs that bought it, not your bleedin' head!"

"Too true," Rackham put in solemnly. "Thought you was a sensible bloke! You must be kidding. You don't marry that kind of..."

"No kidding," I broke in harshly. "I've made up my mind, and I don't want any more cracks about it, see?"

"You keep on telling me, mate," Rackham said dryly. "Maybe I'll get used to the idea..."

Then we heard the rumble of the tea wagons along the corridor. The rattle of urns and a confusion of sound that drowned the rest of Rackham's words.

The ward waited patiently to see if the new little Irish nurse was on duty, and for the moment, Rose was forgotten. My nightmare returned that night. I was walking through a forest of naked trees when I came to a clearing where my mother was standing beside a newly dug grave. She was laughing. Laughing with her head thrown back, her mouth wide open and her eyes screwed up with mirth.

I tried to call out to her, but no sound came, and as I watched, up through the grave crawled my father. His head lolled from side to side and a deep red weal was round his neck.

I wanted to go to him, but my feet were like lead weights and I couldn't lift them. Legs astride, hands on hips, my mother taunted him as he struggled to crawl to her, and all the while, she laughed and went on laughing as he cursed and reviled her.

And then, as I watched in horror, with a mighty effort he staggered to his feet, reached out and gripped her by the throat. Helplessly I stood there. Watched his hands slide down to her shoulders, drawing her close to him. Embracing her. And I knew why she laughed. Knew, as she did, that he loved her even as he cursed her.

As the sound of her laughter reached crescendo, he let her go and sank to the dark earth again, burying his head in his hands, covering his swollen eyes, racked by great shuddering sobs.

The pain of watching him was more than I could bear. Anguished, I turned away, and then I saw Cora. She was standing a little way off. Shadowy. Wraithlike, and between us, stark and terrifying, stood the grim outline of gallows. Fear gripped me. I began to shake. A small body of men approached, moving with slow, unmistakable menace. Sombrely attired. Heads bowed. The first carried an open book. His lips moved silently, and the solemn words of the burial service hammered in my brain.

I could still hear my mother laughing, but when I looked at her again, it was Rose's face I saw. Bold and brazen, and my father still crouched sobbing and wouldn't look at me.

Cora's shade had gone. Swallowed up in the shadowy background from which she had emerged. As the men drew nearer, two of them detached themselves from the rest, paused for a moment, staring at me with cold, hostile eyes, then with a great shout, rushed towards me.

Stark fear enmeshed me. Like a hunted beast I stared around me, and then as hands reached out to clutch me, movement returned to my imprisoned limbs, and with a scream of terror, I plunged into the open grave...

I awoke clammy and shivering to find the night nurse leaning over me with obvious concern.

"My word, you gave me a scare!" she admonished me. "Dreaming were you?"

I stared at her wild eyed, my body still trembling. I felt weak and my legs were giving me hell.

"Dreaming," I muttered thickly.

She looked at me curiously.

"Only natural after what you've been through," she said soothingly. "I'll get you a nice cup of tea. That'll calm you down."

Throughout the day, the dream troubled me. Was it a warning of some kind? A foreboding of my life with Rose, drawing a parallel between that and my father's... ?

I was still brooding about it when Arthur came.

"Steve!" he greeted me, his eyes wide with concern. "I came as soon as I knew you were here. We only got in last night."

"It's good to see you," I said quietly. "How's Mum?"

"She's okay," he told me. "I spoke to her on the 'phone this morning. She sends her love and will be writing to you. She says she'll go back to the cottage as soon as you're ready to come home."

"Thanks. She's very kind..." the words dried up.

Arthur was looking me over. His glance rested on the tell-tale cradle. His voice was cautious.

"How are you feeling?" he asked.

"I'm doing all right," I told him, and managed a grin as I

added. "Bit battered about the extremities, but the rest of me's still in one piece."

He looked relieved. Fell silent for a moment as he sat down.

"Bad luck about Lofty," he said suddenly. "I suppose there's not much chance that he was picked up?"

"He was dead before we took to the water," I said heavily. "I saw him."

"I didn't know," he started awkwardly. "I'm sorry, Steve. He was all right."

I nodded. Silence again, then,

"I heard there were twelve survivors," he went on suddenly. "But it's not always final is it? Some of the others may have been picked up."

"Not a chance," I said tonelessly. "Most of them were dead before I passed out."

"What happened to your legs?" he wanted to know.

"There was an explosion just as I jumped. Flying metal got me."

"Bad?"

"Oh I'll walk again," I told him. "With a stick. One leg was pretty bad. They've pinned it together, but it's a bit shorter than the other."

"Tough," he sympathised.

"I'm alive," I said tersely. "Though I don't mind telling you, I wanted to go with the rest. I didn't feel anything. The cold you see. After the first few minutes nothing really mattered. I just sort of drifted. The Doughty must have got me just in time."

"Well, it's over for you now," he observed. "Pity. We're just beginning to make it hot for the bastards."

"What are you doing then?" I asked.

"I've been across to the other side, covering the landings," he explained. "No picnic, but we've got 'em going now."

"Have you seen Kate?" I enquired.

He shook his head.

"She's gone."

"Gone?" I echoed curiously. "What d'you mean?"

"Just that, Steve. She's gone," he repeated.

"Where?" I demanded.

"Don't know. I went round to her place before I came here. The flat was empty."

"D'you think she knew about Lofty?"

"Maybe. Perhaps that's why she went," he returned. "It's a bloody shame."

"I could have gone with Lofty," I muttered. "There's no future in what keeps happening to me."

"What's that supposed to mean?"

I shrugged.

"Being the sole survivor has its problems," I said bitterly. "My life at Sandworth caved in, and I was the only one left. Cora and the baby died, and there was only me. Now the ship. A handful of salvage. See what I mean? There were some good mates. There was the chaplain..." I broke off, thinking of the chaplain.

"Had any other visitors?" Arthur asked.

"Only one," I said quietly. "Rose came in."

He frowned.

"That floozie you brought to the Stag?" he exclaimed in surprise.

"That's right," I agreed tersely. "She's coming again..."

"Christ, Stevo!" he objected. "You're not going to encourage that tart?"

"Rose is all right," I declared defiantly. "She heard I was here and she came to see me. What's wrong with that. Believe me, in my place, you'd be glad to see anyone."

"I know that. But don't encourage her, Stevo. You'll never get rid of her!"

"I know what I'm doing," I said. "So she's not out of the top drawer. She's a harpy who earns a few quid on her back. Immoral. Loose. Damned. You can throw the book at her. The Good Book! Maybe in this lousy rat-race her type has a better chance of survival than the others. Yes, Arthur, she's a whore, but she's alive and Cora's dead! My father's dead! Lofty's dead! The Chaplain's dead! Maybe it's true that the good die young, and maybe I'll be allowed to hang on to a cheap little strumpet because she's beneath the contempt of a bloody choosy God!"

"Cut it out," he muttered uncomfortably. "You don't really mean all that. It's only natural you should feel pretty low after what's happened, but it's no use giving way. When you get back home, you'll feel different. Any idea what you're going to do? Workwise I mean?"

"Too early to say what I'll be able to do," I told him. "I'll be having therapeutic treatment, ready for rehabilitation. They'll even try to fix me up with a job."

"There's always the piano, and that stuff of your Dad's to work on..."

I held up my bandaged hands and shook my head. Explained about my fingers.

"Hell, Stevo," he muttered, his eyes pitying me. "I didn't know..."

He stood up, prepared to leave.

"I'll try and get in again before we sail," he promised.

"How long's the war going on?" I asked wearily.

"God knows!" he answered, "but the worst must be behind us now. We've got them on the run in Africa, and in France they're really falling back now. The tide's turned all right, but there's still a way to go. These doodle bugs are doing some damage. London's really taking a thrashing!"

"I've been reading about them," I told him. "Robot machines won't achieve what the cream of the Luftwaffe failed to do. It's a war of nerves. Things that go bang in the night. How can you have any respect for an enemy who launches robots to do his killing?"

"Got to admire the technology," he replied. "Sign of the times. This is the machine age and you've got to hand it to the Hun! He's really come up with something! Well, Stevo, is there anything you need? I could come in tomorrow. We don't sail until evening."

"Thanks, but I'm okay It's good to see you again. Take care."

"I'll be back," he promised.

I felt his firm grip on my shoulder, then he was off, striding down the ward.

As I watched him go, I thought he was the only one left for me now - except Rose.

Arthur Ryan who had been there to stand by me when I stood alone in Lawson Street. At hand to solace me when I learned of

Cora's death, and who had come again to commiserate with me on the loss of my shipmates.

His words had jolted me into a full realisation of my position.

I had no one and nowhere - save the Ryans and Rose. The one would alienate the other. I could imagine his disgust when he learned what I was contemplating.

And he would learn. Rose had offered to marry me.

Well - Why not!

CHAPTER NINE

The next day, the sky was dark and the rain was pelting down as though it would never stop.

It was two o'clock before Rose appeared wearing a long shiny green coat with a matching hood covering her hair and most of her face.

"You look like a garden gnome," I told her laughingly.

"D'you like it?" she asked eagerly. "It's a new material. Plastic. A Yank gave it to me. It's all the rage in the States. Waterproof, and can be folded up and put in your handbag."

"Very convenient," I murmured.

"He's going to bring me some new kind of stockings," she went on eagerly. "Nylon. He says they'll soon be in the shops here and women won't want to wear any other kind."

"A Yank?" I said questioningly.

She looked at me hard and nodded.

"They're very generous, and it's no use getting your knickers in a twist. Nothing's changed - yet!"

She threw back the hood, undid the coat, leaned over to plant a kiss on my cheek, and sat down.

"So how are you today?" she asked.

"Pretty much the same as yesterday."

"Have you thought about what I said?" she wanted to know.

"Thought about nothing else," I lied.

So I told her I would marry her. By and large it seemed a good day. The consultant had been round to tell me that when the healing process was more advanced, I'd be fitted with a gadget to help me utilise my left hand. My right hand, minus the little finger, would be distorted but quite usable after therapeutic treatment.

And the War news was good. The full scale assault by the Americans and British Forces on the Nazi stronghold of Europe, had taken the German defenders by surprise, and the Allies had taken the port of Cherbourg.

A plot by senior officers to assassinate their Fuhrer, had revealed significant cracks in the German war machine which had had its nose bloodied at Stalingrad. The writing was on the wall!

At that time, the sky over most of Britain was free of Nazi raiders, and the continuous drone of aircraft was the battle cry of our own and American bombers converging in hundreds over German cities, dealing out death and annihilation as they avenged the victims of the blitz.

Not that the Hun was finished. Earlier that month, a new weapon had been launched across the Channel. A robot 'plane carrying an explosive packed warhead, and directed mostly against London.

The 'plane, the V1, was dubbed 'doodle bug' and in addition to the casualties it claimed, there was something uncanny about it. Something that brought a different kind of fear to the hearts of Londoners. An enemy shorn of personality. A 'thing' meting out death. A nasty little weapon which, if developed earlier, when the tide of the German advance was in full flood, might easily have altered the course of the war.

I told Arthur about Rose when he came in to see me that evening. He took it hard. I saw it in the firm set of his jaw and the expression in his eyes. Condemning me for letting Rose stand in Cora's place.

"All right. I know what you're thinking," I burst out bitterly. "You're not being fair!"

"Come off it, Stevo," he countered. "Your life's your own affair, but this isn't the time to make up your mind about anything. You've scarcely had time to lick your wounds. To take stock of yourself. To consider tying yourself to a woman like Rose..." Words failed him. He broke off abruptly.

"'A woman like Rose'!" I repeated harshly. "You don't even know what kind of a woman she is. Why don't you give her a chance?"

"Give yourself a chance, Stevo," he returned quietly. "Wait until you're on your feet again. You'll see things differently."

"What she was doesn't matter," I said doggedly. "That's all over. She's on the level. Ready to settle down. You don't understand. We suit each other. She's had a rotten deal from when she was a kid. She's got a right to a fresh start. The only way to help people like Rose is to make them forget they were ever different, or worse than the rest of us. Give them back self-respect. Help them to integrate into society."

He sighed, glanced at his watch and stood up ready to leave.

"Fine words," he said quietly. "Stop kidding yourself. You've got problems you haven't even faced yet. You don't have to try and justify yourself to me. I'm telling you again. It won't work. It's not the fact that you want to marry her that's wrong. It's the reason. Steve the 'do-gooder', salvaging a lost soul! Giving a chance to the underdog! It's maudlin! Sick thinking! All you really need to tell me is that you love her. Do you, Steve?"

I looked away from him. Caught Ramsden's eye as he winked at me across the room. Glanced at Morgan, surrounded by a crowd of relations.

"I don't know," I muttered. "But she's all right. She's all right I tell you."

He drew in a deep breath.

"Try thinking about your father and mother. That should tell you something," and turning, he left me. He didn't look back.

I lay thinking about what he had said.

Think about my parents! The analogy was clear, I wondered, would I seriously have considered Rose's proposal if the taunts of my ward mates hadn't needled me into the idea? I began to doubt it.

Like Arthur said, there were problems. I was practically broke. No more than a hundred pounds to my name, and whatever disability pension I could claim, wouldn't amount to much.

And what kind of a job could I hope to get. Dragging around a useless leg. Able to write labouriously. There would be a long hard slog before I learned to rehabilitate myself.

Rose could give me a home. She'd got, as she put it, 'a long stocking' to keep us going until I was fit enough to work again.

Optimistic!

I looked at my hands. Eased my legs. What else did the future hold for me?

God knows, I wanted Rose. The sight and touch of her fired my senses as no one had ever done. The soft femininity of her. The thrill of her full yielding mouth. The laughing promise in her green eyes, and the heady lusty smell of her.

Oh, it was all physical, my feeling for her. Sheer animalism. I knew it well enough.

As the days passed, I became obsessed with wanting her. With sharing all my days and nights with her - forgetting.

And wrapped in it all, was the thought that since God had taken all the good things from my life, maybe He would let me keep Rose who, according to the moral code of our society, was bad.

She came to the hospital every day, and after that first visit, she came more soberly attired, and the taunts and the sniggers and the bawdy witticisms stopped.

She was with me when I took my first faltering steps round the hospital. Patient, coaxing, encouraging. Invigorating me with her lighthearted gaiety.

Sometimes, she'd take me out in my wheelchair. Attentive. Tender. Teasing, and I basked in it like a man drugged. Allowing her to take possession of me until all apprehension faded, and the past grew misty and the future full as my mind and body centred on her.

Oh she was something, Rose was!

Once, she took me across the ferry to the Hard, wheeling me through the town, and as we passed the sad ruin of Seaton Flats, depression gripped me. I looked away, unable to bear the sight of that broken twisted pile, and Rose said gently,

"I shouldn't have brought you this way. You loved her a lot, didn't you?"

I nodded dumbly.

I hadn't thought much about Cora lately. It was as though I avoided her in my mind because somehow I couldn't think about her without feeling guilty about Rose.

"She'd want you to be happy, wouldn't she?" Rose persisted.

"Yes," I agreed eagerly. "That's true, Rose. That's true!"

I wrestled silently with my conscience. I'd loved Cora. I'd always love her, but she'd gone, and Rose was beside me. Vital. Alive. Stirring my blood as Cora had never done.

There's no disloyalty in that. Cora had been a pure flame and

I'd have cherished it, but Rose was a maddening tempestuous fire, consuming me.

"Take me back," I muttered thickly, and with a shrug, Rose swung the chair round and set off back towards the ferry.

From the grey eloquent stones where Cora and our child had been destroyed, the gentle wraith of my dead wife watched us go.

I felt her pity, and longed to go to her as a recalcitrant child longs for the reassurance of its mother's arms.

I should have been with her that night, so that the brief interlude of our happiness might have ended there and then, with no regrets, no recriminations, no memories.

But that wasn't the way the cards were stacked. It would have been too easy for me!

"Steve," Rose said urgently over my shoulder. "You want to go through with it, don't you? I mean you and me... ?"

I reached up and caught one of her hands.

"You bet," I told her, and she seemed satisfied.

Towards the end of July, they moved me to Greenleas, a convalescent home at Lyndhurst, in the heart of the New Forest.

A tall, rambling building, with whispering insects animating the creeper covered walls, and acres of grounds heavy with the scent of roses. They gave me a room to myself. A dormer room overlooking the neat spire of the little chapel separating the main building from the annex which housed the 'chronics'.

I had been there three days, when a small car drove slowly into the grounds, and passed me as I stood on one of the lower terraces.

I turned and watched it. Saw it stop a few yards ahead of me, and suddenly the door was flung open and a voice called to me,

"Stevo! By all that's holy!"

And the next moment a man came running towards me. A tall man with thinning tousled hair and wild blue eyes sunk deep in the gaunt cadaver of his face.

For an instant I stared at him without recognition, and then as he reached out and gripped my gloved hand, I knew.

"Mike!" I exclaimed incredulously. "Mike Doyle!"

"The same," he acknowledged cheerfully. "For Jesus's sake! It's good to see you again. What's been happening to you, man?"

"It's a long story," I told him. "What about you? How come you're here?"

"Come on up to the house," he answered. "It's just about time they'll be bringing the tea round. We can talk up there."

He helped me into the car and drove up to the entrance to the annex.

I followed him on to the balcony and we sat at one of the small tables where a nurse brought us a tray of tea.

And I learned that Mike had been at Greenleas since the beginning of the year and despite exhaustive tests, no one seemed to know exactly what was wrong with him.

"It's the ache in my guts see," he explained. "Like me belly's on fire. This place is fine mind, but what kind of life is it for a man? No beer, no smokes, no wimmen! Sure I might as well be in me grave. Not that I'd be much use to a hot-blooded woman in me present state of health. You've eyes in your head, Stevo. You can see for yourself. I'm not the man I was, by half!"

"You've lost a lot of weight," I told him guardedly.

"And that's not all," he said with a sigh. "Me sparks's gone. Tell me the truth now. You didn't know me, did you?"

His blue eyes challenged me.

"Of course I did," I lied. "It was you coming on me suddenly like that."

He shook his head.

"Well," he said. "Never mind about me. Tell me about yourself, and Cora, Lofty and the others. What's been happening to you all?"

I brought him up to date.

"Holy Mother of God!" he exclaimed when I told him about Cora. "That lovely girl! It's a terrible shame so it is! And Lofty. I didn't know. War's a bloody business all right!"

"And it's a long way from over," I reminded him.

"You may be right at that," he agreed. "One thing's certain. The end's already too late for some of us."

His eyes grew darker, sombre, and I heard the ghost of a sigh.

"So you're thinking of getting married again," he went on at last. "Do I know her?"

Remembering his amorous adventures in the town, I thought it quite possible.

Quietly, I told him about Rose.

"Good luck to you, man," he applauded. "I've known a few floosies in me time. If they take a shine to you, they're as loyal as they come. Generous too. Give me a woman who knows more ways of keeping a bed warm than by putting on an extra blanket!"

"She'll be coming here," I told him. "You'll meet her."

"I'll be looking forward to it," he smiled. "Wish we could drink to it in something stronger than tea."

With a flourish, he tipped his cup against mine.

"How long will you be staying here," I asked him. "They reckon I'll be here about six weeks."

"No one mentions time to me," he answered. "I ask all the right questions, but I can't get any sense out of anyone. Just keep telling me to relax and take things quietly. Mother of God! What else can a man do in a place like this? It's so bloody quiet. You know, Stevo, there's many a time I wish I'd bought it on active service, like so many of me mates. Living like this..."

"You're still in one piece," I interrupted him ruefully. "Look at me! Hobbling around on a gammy leg for the rest of me natural - A crazy looking contraption to serve as a hand..."

I held out my left arm with its newly attached gadget of wood and steel and the spring loaded thumb which helped me get a grip on cutlery items and the like. Extended the deformed fingers of my other hand for his inspection.

"That's tough, Stevo," he sympathised. "Though I reckon they'll fix you up with something better than that before long. I was reading about the advances being made in the production of artificial limbs. What are you aiming to do when they've finished with you here?"

"Depends on my mobility," I told him. "I suppose they'll patch me up for something. They tell me I'll learn to adjust when I've conditioned my mind to accept my handicap."

"I guess that's right enough," he agreed. "You got any money, Stevo?"

"Few pounds. And I suppose they'll dole out some sort of

disability pension."

"And small enough that'll be to be sure," he answered. "Is Rose going to work?"

I looked at him hard.

"We haven't talked about it," I replied. "But don't get the idea that I'm going to live off her..."

"The thought never entered my head," he interrupted earnestly. "But one of you's going to do the earning, and that's a fact. Here! Do you drive?"

I shook my head.

"Not really," I told him. "Though I played around with a few cars before I joined the Service."

"Good enough. I'll teach you!" he decided eagerly. "Give me something to do. We'll have a word with the medico, and if he says it's okay, we're off and running. Maybe it'll help strengthen your legs an' all, and like as not, you'll be getting a little runabout from the Ministry later on."

"That's a great idea, Mike," I enthused. "I'd like that..."

There was no medical objection. The doctors endorsed Mike's opinion that learning to drive would help me to control and strengthen my legs and fingers. Psychologically it helped a lot. To be able to move around on four good wheels instead of two reluctant legs, was sheer luxury.

For the next few weeks Mike applied himself wholeheartedly to his self-appointed task.

Rose came down to Greenleas every other day. The first time Mike joined us, I introduced them tongue-in-cheek, and was relieved to find they met as strangers.

The three of us would sit and talk together. Drive round in the old car. Play cards. Rose was over the moon when Mike insisted on teaching her to drive.

Everyday I was feeling stronger. And every day, Mike seemed to look more frail.

Once, coming upon him unawares as, staring into space, he sat in shorts and sports shirt on the balcony, I was appalled at the sight of his wasted limbs.

My presence there obviously embarrassed him. He muttered

something and went into the building. Through the window, I saw him pull on a dressing gown and stretch out on top of his bed, not wanting to talk.

"Stevo," he said one morning, "I suppose you'll be leaving here soon?"

"About a couple of weeks they tell me," I replied.

"That's what I thought," he returned. "Steve, I'd like you to do something for me."

"Name it," I said promptly.

"You and Rose are planning to get married soon aren't you?" he went on.

"As soon as I leave here," I told him. "I've been meaning to ask you. What about coming along to the Registry Office to give me moral support?"

"I've got a better idea," he answered quietly. "I've had a word with Matron, and it's okay if you say the word. How about you and Rose getting married in the chapel here? I could be best man..."

He broke off, his voice faltering.

"That's a great idea!" I exclaimed enthusiastically. "Will they really let us do that?"

"No trouble at all," he assured me. "Matron thought it was the berries!"

"Rose'll love the idea," I said warmly.

"It's settled then," he said. "You'll have to fix things up pretty soon."

"I'll go across and see Matron now," I promised.

Unaccountably, I went down on to the terrace feeling troubled and uneasy. That Mike's condition was worsening was obvious, but the sudden deterioration was frightening.

Suddenly, I heard him call to me, and turning, I saw him coming down to join me.

"Stevo," he said. "The car's yours. A wedding present." He thrust a Log Book and some crumpled petrol coupons into my hand.

"Don't be a chump. I couldn't take it! You'll be lost without it!" I tried to pass the Log Book and coupons back to him, but he waved them aside.

"I want you to have it," he said doggedly. "You and Rose. You don't have to thank me. I won't be needing it anymore."

"What kind of talk is that?" I demanded roughly, avoiding his eyes now blurred with tears.

"They told me this morning," he murmured almost inaudibly. "I'm on my way out. A couple of months - maybe less."

He paused. Swallowed hard, then burst out passionately,

"Mother of Christ! It's a stinking way to go! To feel your manhood draining away. Your flesh rot!"

He stopped again, anguished. Stared at me for a moment, then added calmly,

"It's cancer you see. I had to know. Now we won't talk about it anymore."

I felt his fleshless hand grip my shoulder. Tried to find words to comfort him, but no sound came from my constricted throat, and turning he went back up the steps to his room.

I watched him go inside, then went down to where the little car stood gleaming, wax polished in the sun. Leaned against it. Cried a little, and after a while, I went to see Matron...

Rose and I were married in the middle of August. Married in the chapel at Greenleas where Rose, in a big black picture hat adorned with multi-coloured flowers, and wearing a simple white dress, was given away by the senior physician, and Mike, pale and drawn but smiling, was best man.

Afterwards, a buffet, prepared by the kitchen staff, was shared by everyone at Greenleas, staff and patients really entering into the spirit of the occasion.

And when it was over, we drove away in the little green car, dragging streamers and tins and goodwill messages, to the house in Bursledon which was to be our home.

As I glanced back at the well-wishers waving from the terraces. I had eyes for only one. The tall figure with death in his eyes. At Mike from whom life was slowly and relentlessly ebbing away.

The house at Bursledon was a trim semi-detached villa on the main Portsmouth road. Rose had filled it with flowers, and on that mid-summer afternoon, when jostling, struggling and laughing, we carried each other over the threshold, it seemed that life was really good.

Rose was radiant and happy, and I was content.

It was two days later that Arthur Ryan called. Rose was out shopping.

"Nice to see you, Arthur," I greeted him. "Come on in."

"I got this address from Greenleas," he explained as I took him into the sitting room. "Seems you're getting along okay."

"I'm doing fine," I told him. "Sit down and I'll fix you a drink."

"No thanks," he returned. "I can't stay long. Got to report back to the ship at three-thirty. I just came to tell you I was in Sandworth at the week-end. I met my old boss. He can give you a job. Stock records clerk. The money's good. How about it?"

"There's one obvious snag," I told him quietly.

"I told him about your hands, and he knows you can't move around very fast..." he commenced.

"I don't mean that," I interrupted him. "I'd learn to cope - but not in Sandworth."

"Before you start digging up the past," he returned urgently, "let me tell you. Garwood has cleared out. Moved up North. Your old house has gone too. Incendiaries put paid to half a dozen houses in Lawson Street. Those that weren't burnt out had to be demolished. Most of the old faces have gone. It's not the same any more. Besides, you'd be based at Lilac Cottage with Mum."

"And I'm not the same," I said quietly. "I burned my bridges as thoroughly as any Jerry bombers. I don't believe in going back - and there's Rose."

"You can't go on living in her house," he frowned.

"*Our* house," I corrected him. "Didn't they tell you at Greenleas? Rose and I were married there a couple of days ago."

I watched the deep furrows pucker his forehead.

"I didn't know," he muttered. "So you really went through with it!"

"Rose and I understand each other," I told him. "We've both got a past to overcome. I've got the advantage really. She doesn't know about me. She doesn't have to."

"There's a difference, Stevo," he said earnestly. "You're still the man you always were. What happened at Sandworth didn't change you, only the way you have to live your life. But to accept the protection of..."

"Don't say it, Arthur," I cut in harshly. "Rose is my wife. Whatever she's been, it's over."

"Don't kid yourself," he ground out contemptuously. "They never change. D'you think you're going to be able to compete with her earning capacity? They tell me tarts make up to a hundred quid a week."

"Shut up!" I shouted at him. "There's nothing more to say."

"Every brick in this house," he went on relentlessly. "Paid for on her back. Are you going to be able to live with that?"

"Get out!" I muttered. "Get out, damn you!"

His face was pale as he opened the front door and turned to look at me.

"I'm sorry for you, Stevo. Watch your direction," he said quietly. "Seems to me you're going round in circles. If you look hard at your wife you'll recognise a lot of your mother there. I'll get your stuff sent over to you the next time I get home."

And then he was gone, and as I stared at the closed door, I thought of the nightmares that plagued me and robbed me of sleep, and vague feelings of misgiving gripped me.

I poured myself a stiff whisky and drank it moodily, and after a while, Rose came back.

"Hello, love," she greeted me breathlessly, depositing parcels on the table. "Sorry I've been so long. I stopped to have my hair fixed. D'you like it?"

She pivoted around, showing me the upswept style that emphasised the slender arch of her long white neck.

"Nice," I slurred thickly.

She looked at me searchingly.

"What's got into you?" she asked. "Knocking it back a bit aren't you? Just on teatime too."

"Rose," I said solemnly. "How much did you pay for this place?"

"Why? I told you," she replied with a frown. "Fourteen

hundred."

"And all weighed and paid for eh?" I murmured.

"You know it is," she answered impatiently. "What are you on about?"

"If they'd paid you in bricks, you could have built your own!" I sniggered.

She looked away from me, to the ashtray on the table.

"Who's been here?" she asked, her eyes narrowing.

"Arthur," I said shortly.

"I see," her voice was tight. "He's been getting at you. He doesn't like me."

I toyed with my empty glass.

"He thinks you'll make a pimp of me," I told her.

"Bloody nerve!" she exclaimed angrily. "I hope you gave him an earful!" And as I remained silent, she said quietly. "Did you tell him about Mike being up at Greenleas?"

"No. It slipped my mind. Anyway, he wasn't here very long..."

"Well, I'm going to have a bath," she decided. "My feet are killing me. Put the kettle on, love, and we'll have tea as soon as I come down. I've bought some kippers."

I watched her run lightly up the stairs, heard her singing as she turned on the bath.

It was stupid to let Arthur needle me. I knew well enough how Rose earned the money for the house, and the six hundred pounds of her savings.

But that was all over. We hadn't talked much about money, or me getting a job, though we both knew my disability pension wouldn't keep us. Like Rose said. It was early days. I'd got to get used to going around. Time to look for something in a month or two.

It was good of Arthur to find me a job. All the same, I wished he hadn't taken that stand about Rose. Reminding me of my mother like that too... but I ought to have told him about Mike. His words kept reverberating through my mind, and then Rose called to me,

"Throw up my talc, love. There's a new tin in my shopping bag."

She stood at the top of the stairs, a bath towel draped carelessly around her. Clutched wildly at the tin as I threw it. Revealing for a moment her full naked glory. I watched her spray the powder in the hollows under her armpits and into the delve between her breasts, then she ran down to me and put her arms round my neck.

"No regrets, eh, love?" she whispered. "We'll be all right. You'll see."

"Yes," I murmured into her hair, savouring the velvety touch of her skin as she clung to me.

And for a while as we made love, Arthur's visit was forgotten until.

"I wish I'd been here when he came," she said suddenly as she lay in my arms. "I'd have given him a mouthful. Who does he think he is?"

"Arthur's all right," I told her. "He just doesn't understand. Now go and put some clothes on. I'm starving."

Her lips were close to mine.

"I love you, Steve," she said quietly.

I kissed her, and she clung to me, sensing the awkward, nameless thing that stopped me saying the words she wanted to hear.

At last, with a sigh, she drew away from me and went upstairs.

Oh yes, we were happy enough to start with. Through the summer and September, when Paris was liberated and the German armies reeled back across the Seine.

We spent our days quietly. Sunning ourselves in the small garden. Hoarding our petrol coupons for the occasional drive into the West country. Calling in at the local for a drink.

Spending an afternoon with Mike. Listening to his cheerful anecdotes of his childhood in Ireland - trying to pretend that his physical appearance didn't deteriorate with every visit.

I was due to start at the rehabilitation centre later that month, but somehow I jibed at the idea, convinced that once I knew which way I was going, I could land some kind of job myself.

But what? I talked it over with Rose.

"You don't have to rush into anything," she told me. "Just have a look round for something nice and light to start with. There's plenty of office work about, and you being good at figures..."

"Yes. I'll find something," I interrupted her.

What use telling her that was the last thing I wanted? True, I had no qualifications for anything else. Only my head had been giving me a bit of trouble for the last month, and the idea of being cooped up in an office, frankly appalled me. Maybe it was too soon.

"Don't worry about it, love," Rose consoled me when I voiced my thoughts to her. "We'll manage. If you don't find something to suit you, you can always go to the Centre and see what they suggest."

"We'll see what they have to say when I go for my check-up in a couple of weeks. They're going to make some modification to this hand of mine," I told her.

But I didn't tell her about my head, and as the days passed I became more and more dependent on pills and drink to ease the nauseating pain that distorted my vision and nagged persistently at my throbbing temples.

Most mornings I'd get up about ten o'clock and make my way to the Legion Hall, where I'd spend an hour or so yarning with the regulars about the war. Raking it over. Like the failure of our parachute regiments to hold the enemy at Arnhem, where in a fierce and bloody battle, even the weather had allied itself to the Germans, grounding our aircraft at a time when their support was most needed.

Like the epic battle of Stalingrad which almost certainly changed the course of the war.

And the V2 rocket bombs, bursting down on London from heights of sixty feet, from launching sites in Holland and Northern France. Vicious, frightening weapons against which neither the RAF nor the ack-ack batteries had any effective reply.

In the club, I soon found my disability was always good for a drink. Not that I sponged deliberately, but rationing myself to weekly pocket money of a couple of pounds from my meagre post office savings so that I could hand Rose my pension, I wasn't exactly flush.

"I've been thinking," Rose said one morning. "What about me

getting a job for the time being?"

"Something in mind?" I asked, trying to sound casual.

"Mr Mason asked me if I'd like to work in the café," she explained.

"Mason? Who's he?" I questioned.

"You know. Where I get the bread," she returned. "He can never get enough staff in the restaurant. We were talking about it the other day. He asked if I knew anyone who'd be interested. Not bad money. Three pounds a week and tips - and lunches. I'd be home just after four. Start at ten in the morning and give a hand in the kitchen,"

"D'you think you'd like that?"

"Wouldn't mind," she admitted. "Be a change, and I like talking to people. Besides, the money would be useful and you wouldn't have to worry for a bit."

I pulled her to me, kissing her lightly on the forehead.

"You're all right, Rose," I told her. "Didn't pick yourself much of a specimen for a husband, did you?"

"Don't talk daft," she protested, hugging me. "I'm not complaining. We've got to be practical that's all. Besides, I'll enjoy getting out of the house for a while. I like meeting people, and the hours will be just right for us."

"Means you'll have to cook a meal at night," I reminded her.

"No, love," she said. "Mr Mason says you can come down to the café for a mid-day meal, and I'll be having mine there of course. That's worth a bit, isn't it? And it'll help with our rations."

She drew away from me, leaned back, looking hard at me.

"I told him I'd start on Monday," she said simply.

"All cut and dried," I laughed. "All right. If that's what you want."

"That's settled then," she declared. "You off out now then? Bring me back some fags will you..."

That was the morning she learned about me.

The big plain van was pulling away from the kerb as I drew up outside the house shortly after noon.

I didn't pay much attention to it, and then, as I let myself in and went to where Rose waited in the sitting room, I saw the piano.

Rose was standing behind it, resting her arms on the shining wood that had been my father's special pride. I stared at her speechlessly, choked with memories.

"Arthur sent it over with the rest of your belongings."

Her voice was oddly stilted, but it didn't register, not then. My thoughts were with Arthur. How was I to construe the arrival of the piano? Was it an acknowledgment of my right to live my own life as I chose, or was it intended as a final act of renunciation of all that had been between us?

"Was there any message for me?" I asked cautiously.

Her laugh was harsh.

"There was a message all right," she said, "but not for you. Why didn't you tell me about your father?"

I felt myself go cold. Mouthed for words.

"So Arthur told you," I whispered hoarsely.

"Not Arthur. One of the chaps on the van," she answered accusingly. "He lived in Lawson Street. Knew all about the Stevens!"

"I see," I muttered. "Well, I suppose it had to come out sooner or later."

"You should have told me," her voice accused me.

"I know," I confessed heavily. "Oh God! What a mess! I'm sorry..."

"I should bloody well think so!" she said angrily. "A right fool I looked when that chap came out with it, and me gaping at him as if he was barmy!"

"I've said I'm sorry," I muttered. "What d'you want me to do about it?"

Silence for a moment. She eyed me steadily.

"Did she know - Cora?" she asked shortly.

"Yes, she knew. I couldn't have married her without telling her!"

"Thanks very much!" she ground out bitterly. "That puts me in my place all right! What about me? You married me didn't you?"

"You're different," I said awkwardly.

"Yes! I'm nothing I suppose!" Her voice rose shrilly. "Your precious Cora was a saint! Everything to you. You've made that pretty clear. Maybe I'm dumb but it doesn't make sense to me. You didn't mind taking a chance on losing her. Did you think having a murderer in the family wouldn't matter to a whore like me?"

"That's not fair," I floundered feebly. "It was a long time ago. A lot's happened. All right. I should have told you, but I thought you'd taken me for what I am..."

"And what are you, Steve?" she demanded raspingly. "You're the son of a murderer. Christ! I had a right to know that. I haven't asked for much!"

I sat down, suddenly desperately weary.

"Tell me the truth," I asked quietly. "Would it have made any difference?"

"I don't know. Perhaps it would."

"I see," I drew in a deep breath. "D'you want me to clear out?"

"Oh don't talk like a fool," she retorted impatiently, coming round the piano, padding across the room with bare feet and lighting a cigarette. "What would that solve? I've had a shock. I need time to think about it."

"Of course." Words came hard. I tried to choose them carefully. "A man can live with his past just so long," I jerked out.

"That's got nothing to do with it," she declared. "Past, present, future. It makes no difference. It happened. You can't outlive it or pretend it didn't happen. Your father was hanged. You've just got to accept that. But you had no right to involve me in a thing like that without giving me a choice."

"How the hell can you be involved in something that happened before you ever knew me?" I demanded churlishly.

"Oh, be your age! Don't you count your wife as one of the family then? Whether I like it or not, I've got to share the shame of it. My father-in-law was a murderer. Condemned and hanged! It's horrible!"

"You don't know about him," I muttered.

"I don't have to," she said quickly. "I know what he did and what happened to him. That's all I need to know. And it's not so long ago that people don't talk about it. Like that van driver."

"A chance in a million," I reminded her. "Made a proper mess of things, haven't I? What do you want me to do?"

"What the hell can you do now?" she demanded hotly. "Nothing that can do me any good! I'll just have to learn to live with it, but don't expect me to pretend nothing's happened."

"I don't expect anything," I assured her heavily. "It's up to you. I shan't blame you, whatever you decide. If you want me to go..."

"Talk sense, Steve," she sighed wearily. "Where could you go?"

"I could go to the Ryan's place," I said without conviction. "At least I've nothing to hide there, and they wouldn't expect me to keep on making excuses for something I couldn't help anyway."

"Oh stop feeling sorry for yourself," she cried irritably. "No one's said anything about wanting you to go."

She stood looking at me uncertainly for a moment, then impulsively, crossed the room to kneel beside me.

"I'll get used to it," she went on quietly. "It was finding out unexpectedly like that. Turned my stomach up. I just couldn't believe it."

"Must have been a shock," I muttered. "I'm so sorry, Rose. I really am."

"I know. It doesn't really make any difference to what I feel for you. Deep down I mean. I love you. Can't just turn it off like a tap when things go wrong, can you? Only, like I said, I've got to get used to it."

I mumbled my thanks.

"If you'd let me tell you about it. The truth. It would help. I know it would. You see, I'm not ashamed of what Dad did, I..." Truth! I shuddered. The impossible truth that in nightmarish guise would never let me free!

"Not now," she broke in quietly, getting to her feet. She stood looking down at me. Hesitated, then said solemnly, "You know, Steve, you've never once told me you love me."

Curiously embarrassed, I searched for words.

"I married you, didn't I?" I tried to sound flippant, but the words fell flat. Fleetingly, the light went out of her eyes. She sighed deeply, shrugged, and turned away.

"I'd better get on with the lunch," she murmured.

Perhaps that was the moment things began to change between us. Or later that day when, despite her reluctance to listen, I told her about my father. Justifying him. The loneliness of a decade of frustrated, adolescent years, hammering home the full impact of my mother's treachery.

Perhaps more clearly than I, she saw her own reflection in my mother's image. Sensed the danger. The frightening parallel. Reading in my vicious denunciation of what my mother had been, an indictment against herself.

I couldn't pin-point it. Yet quite certainly, I sensed a subtle change in her attitude towards me. Or was it mine towards her?

Some subconscious feeling of guilt that made me tense. Suspicious. Reading into her every mood, hidden meanings. Deliberate barbs!

Perhaps, for the first time, she began to question why I had married her. Became afraid that some perverted mental quirk, some latent masochism, had compelled me into marriage with a strumpet like the mother whose memory was the suppurating canker on which my bitterness, shame and frustration thrived.

CHAPTER TEN

The following week, Rose started her job at the café.

She went off eagerly. Excited even. Taking special care with her appearance. Brushing and coiling her lovely hair. Swinging out of the house, her short skirt a shade too tight, too revealing.

I stood by the window watching her but she didn't look round, and when at last I turned back into the room, depression caught me by the throat, and the house was suddenly unbearably empty. I sat down. Tried to read the morning paper, but my thoughts were restless, grass-hopping from one thing to another with no continuity.

I should have told Rose about my life in Sandworth. Told her before I married her. I knew that. Just as I'd told Cora. Why hadn't I then?

As Rose had been quick to point out I had more to lose with Cora, loving her as I did. Was it the measure of what I really felt for Rose that I hadn't thought it necessary to fill her in with background details of my life. The background from which I had emerged marked forever as the son of a murderer?

Sort of silent contempt. I'd thought about it. Oh yes! Used it to weigh in the balance against the wanton commercialization of lust that formed the sordid purpose of Rose's life. Used it to level things up. To make Arthur see I was doing Rose no favour.

But I hadn't told her. She'd found out the hard way. From the lips of a stranger. Unexpected. No punches pulled. Hard, deliberate, basic facts!

'Good morning Madam. I've brought the piano. Museum piece really. Belonged to a murderer. Should have thought they'd have put it in the waxworks after they strung him up! Fancy you being married to his son! We wondered what had happened to him after he cleared out of Sandworth. I heard he'd copped a packet in the Navy!'

Bland. Garrulous! Must have felt ten feet tall! What a bloody mess!

I got up and went to the window again. Stared out across the sunlit pavements. Of course she'd had a shock. Only reasonable that she'd take a bit of time to get over it. Only she'd been so quiet for the last few days. Sort of remote. And I felt uneasy.

I tried to analyse the feeling. Admitted to myself that I'd married Rose for a number of reasons, but love wasn't one of them. Mostly, I think, because I was lonely and we got on well together - and because she excited me and I could bed her any time of day.

And she'd offered me a home when I most needed one, and once she'd planted the seed in my mind, and the bawdy ribbing of my ward mates had goaded me into accepting it, it seemed the solution to many of my problems.

Only since our marriage there'd been a change in our relationship. I needed her. Felt incomplete without her. Disturbing! Inexplicably, the realisation irked me.

Like the morning soon after we were married, when I'd come down to find Ralph Allcott drinking tea in the kitchen with Rose perched on a stool beside him, her flimsy dressing gown draped much too carelessly for my peace of mind.

Allcott was an electrician who lived with his mother a few doors further up the road. A rugged, good-looking type.

"So you're the lucky man," he greeted me breezily as Rose introduced us. "You know, when your missus first moved in here, I thought I was on to a good thing. Best looker I've set my eyes on for a long time, I can tell you."

"Don't take any notice of him, Steve," Rose laughed. "He's a proper one for kidding."

"How'd you two get together?" I asked, trying to sound casual.

"Ralph's the one who fixed up all the power points for me," Rose explained.

I registered the use of his first name.

"I see," I said formally, odd feelings of resentment nagging at me.

"Ha-ha!" Allcott exclaimed with an exaggerated wink. "The old green monster's on the move! You're wondering why I'm here cavorting with your wife over a cuppa. Right?"

"Oh don't be silly," Rose said hurriedly, a little frown creasing her smooth forehead. "I told Ralph about you, Steven, and he said if you needed any help - you know, getting about - he'd be glad to take you in his car when he was home."

"We've got a car of our own," I reminded her ungraciously.

"Well Ralph didn't know that," she returned. "He's been away on a job up North for the past six weeks."

"That's right," Allcott put in seriously. "I don't want to butt in, but Rose told me..."

"I was a bloody cripple eh?" I interrupted bitterly. "Well, thanks for the offer, Allcott, I'll know where to come, won't I. Now, if you don't mind, I'd like to get on with my breakfast."

I sat down stiffly not looking at either of them. Rose flounced off the stool, went with Allcott out through the back door to the gate. Her voice came to me clearly.

"Don't mind him, Ralph. He doesn't mean it. He never feels so good first thing in the morning."

"Who does?" Allcott answered. "That's all right, girl. I understand. You know where I am if you want me. Believe me, it's you I'm sorry for. He's sorry enough for himself."

She came back quietly. Busied herself at the stove.

"You could have been decent to him," she said. "He was only trying to help."

"Sorry if I put the damper on some nice cosy relationship," I told her caustically. "But I don't exactly feel at my best when I find my half-naked wife entertaining some stray male she's picked up."

"Oh, for heaven's sake!" she cried, her cheeks flushed as she turned to look at me. "What are you trying to make of it? I told you, Ralph came here to fix the points when I bought the house. I told him about you. How you couldn't get about very well, and he said he'd be pleased to help."

"Must have spent a lot of time on those points," I jeered.

"He spent a lot of time here, yes," she admitted calmly. "A lot of things needed doing. Someone had to do them."

"Sure he didn't do you?"

Her eyes were luminous as she stared at me, and the colour died out of her cheeks.

"That's a rotten thing to say," she whispered. "A filthy rotten thing..."

"Is it?" I demanded harshly, getting up from the table. "You were here alone together, weren't you. On first name terms in no time at all. He admits he fancied you. How did you pay for the jobs he did? With a particular job of your own."

"Do you really believe that?" she asked chokingly. "Do you?"

"What do you expect?" I said truculently. "We've been married for no time at all, and a chap turns up, calling you by your first name. Making himself at home..."

"All the same, you shouldn't have said what you did," she broke in. "If you must know, it was his mother I met first. She ran up the curtains for me, and I popped in for an odd cup of tea with the old lady. Felt sorry for her, being there by herself most of the time. One day, when I went in, Ralph was there. She introduced us, using our Christian names. Seemed natural enough. I was looking for a handy man to do a few jobs here, and Mrs Allcott suggested Ralph. It was as simple as that."

"I'm a bastard," I muttered, reaching for her.

We kissed, then she pushed me away, looked at me hard, then said earnestly,

"D'you know, love, I'm glad it happened. D'you know why?" and as I shook my head, she finished with a chuckle. "It shows you're really jealous of me!"

Jealous? Perhaps I was, though at that moment I hadn't recognised it. Seeing her there with Allcott, had angered me. Reminding me of her whore's past - of my own indeterminate position.

Allcott never came to the house again. Like Rose said, his work took him a long way from Bursledon most of the time, and although, on the odd occasions he returned for a day or two, I saw him chatting to Rose at the kerb's edge, we never spoke of him.

One day, she persuaded me to go with her to meet Mrs Allcott. Perhaps to drive home the truth of what she'd told me, and as we drank tea and ate home-made scones, with the disconcerting candour of her generation, the old lady said,

"As soon as I clapped eyes on Rosie, I said to myself, 'Here's just the girl for my Ralph. Bright, pretty little thing. Just what he needs'. He's thirty-four, and it's about time he settled down in a home of his own. I don't mind telling you, Mr Stevens, I was quite disappointed when she told me about you. You're a lucky man having someone like Rose to stand by you."

"The law of compensating returns," I told her quietly. "There has to be something to even up the score."

I remembered that as I watched Rose walk up to the bus stop on the morning she started work at the café.

Feeling restless, insecure and strangely alone, I went into the sitting room. Stared at the piano. Sat on the stool, my maimed fingers caressing the yellowing keyboard. Then opening the stool, I took out the bundles of manuscript papers. The unfinished compositions on which my father and I had worked together. Fingered out the melodies on the instrument. Nostalgia! Tears filled my eyes. My throat constricted, and with a sudden curse, I threw the manuscripts back in the stool and slammed the lid on them.

My father! Naturally, learning about him had startled Rose. I could understand that. And maybe, when I told her about it, I should have painted a different picture. She wanted the truth. Truth? What was the truth? My father had died at the end of a noose, but he was no murderer. He was a martyr! But it was as a murderer posterity would recall him. His story related again and again in the pages of true crime.

Memories set the hammers pounding in my head again. It was like throwing a brick into a pool. It got fussed up. The ripples had to sort themselves out before the surface got back to normal.

Only the surface didn't really matter when you came to people. It was what went on underneath.

With Rose, for the first time in our relationship, I wasn't sure, and it worried me.

Oh, she was warm enough in my arms. Attentive. But her sparkle had gone. We shared long bouts of silence, and often I'd look up to find her staring at me, and though she'd smile, the smile was only a mask that disguised the concentration in her brooding eyes.

She seemed happy enough in her job. That much was apparent

when I saw her laughing and joking with the customers as I sat alone at a small table reserved for me each lunchtime. But at home she was different. Withdrawn. Quiet, and when I protested, she said she was too tired to talk. Only it went deeper than that. I sensed it.

"Rose," I said one evening, "if you'd rather I cleared off altogether, say so!"

She looked at me over the top of the magazine she was reading.

"What brought that on?" she sighed.

"You tell me," I told her testily. "Something's eating you. All right. I'd rather have it straight. It's because you found out about me being the... about my father, isn't it?"

"I told you it was a shock," she answered quietly. "Surely you can see that."

"I suppose so," I muttered, then burst out angrily. "It's so bloody unfair. All my life I'm supposed to carry the can for what he did! It would be a damned sight more humane if they exterminated the whole family of a murderer..."

"Don't talk daft," she broke in impatiently. "You don't understand. You're too busy being the injured party to care about other people's feelings. Let me tell you something. What your Dad did makes no difference to me. I love you. That's why I married you. I thought you felt something for me too, although I knew I was only second best to your Cora..."

"But I did, Rose," I said earnestly.

She shook her head.

"What you felt, I could have had from any randy Jack with a couple of pounds to spare." Her tone was contemptuous. "You didn't even level with me. Tell me about yourself. Give me a chance to decide for myself, and then, when it all came out, you made it pretty clear what you thought of me, didn't you? Why did you do it, Steve? Was it some kind of guilt complex. You were close to your father I know, but what are you trying to prove by making your life a pattern of his?"

I looked at her appalled.

"For God's sake," I whispered. "That's not true. I never thought of you being like her. She was rotten..."

"She was immoral," she corrected me. "Could be it was the only way she could put food into her belly - and yours."

"She was rotten I tell you!" I said fiercely. "She destroyed him."

For a moment I could have sworn there was pity in her eyes.

"Face it, Steve," she went on, suddenly as old as wisdom. "It's hard to admit faults in those we love. A kid can never judge the relationship of its parents. It makes much of little, and little of much, and never really knows how to look at them as man and woman, instead of father and mother."

"Are you saying he was to blame?" I asked harshly.

"I'm saying there must have been faults on both sides. They just never came to terms with each other."

"How the hell do you know?" I muttered churlishly.

She shrugged.

"Your parents unique or something? They all have their rows. A kid takes sides. Sometimes one, sometimes the other. Only with you, it was different. You were looking one way all the time."

"That's bloody rich coming from you," I sneered. "You're the one who was scared stiff of your father."

"So I was," she acknowledged calmly. "He was strict while Mum was free and easy. Stands to reason I favoured her, but when they had rows, though they scared the living daylights out of me, I never questioned the rights and wrongs of it. As I grew older I learned, that bad as he seemed at times, he meant well. It was the way he saw things, and Mum knew what he was when she married him. I don't think we should judge one another. You told me yourself. Whatever your mother did, your father loved her. And it's time you faced up to something else. Your Dad was weak. If he'd asserted himself as a man instead of taking to the bottle, it might never have worked out the way it did."

That was the first time I hit Rose. Full across the face with the flat of my hand. Jerking her head back. And as I stood there, staring angrily down at her, and the red weals of my fingers showed scarlet on her pale cheeks, her lips trembled, tears rose in her eyes, and she murmured huskily.

"I know, Steve. The truth hurts. Go on then - hit me again if it makes you feel better."

Contrition gripped me. I knelt beside her, cradling her to me.

"I'm sorry, Rose," I said brokenly. "I didn't mean it. I'm all on edge. Get fed up on my own all day, and you not talking much when you come home. I keep wondering what goes on in your mind. Whether you're sorry you married me. I'm no good to you, Rose. No bloody good at all."

"You're the one who's complaining," she whispered, stroking my hair. "Oh, Steve! Stop feeling sorry for yourself. We'll be all right. You've got to find something to occupy yourself."

"A job," I said. "I've got to find a job, then you wouldn't have to sweat it out at Mason's place."

"But I like working there," she protested. "Besides. Be sensible. It's no use you thinking about a job until you get the okay from Greenleas. You'll be going there at the end of the month. See what they can suggest."

I nodded dumbly, pressing my head into the warmth of her neck.

"Rose," I murmured huskily. "About my father. D'you think you can learn to live with it - like me?"

For a while she didn't answer, then pushing me away from her, she took my face between her hands.

"I'll learn to live with it, Steve," she told me quietly. "But not like you. Look, Steve. We needn't ever talk about it again. But you've got to face up to things properly. Stop propping yourself up on the past."

"You must be joking!" I exclaimed. "Christ! That's the last thing I..."

She put a hand over my mouth.

"No. Don't carry on. Don't you see? You're making your father an excuse every time anything goes wrong. You're an individual. You've got to take the knocks on your own account - not his. You can't keep looking back."

"Oh, turn it up, Rose," I mumbled wearily. "I can't just pretend it didn't happen."

"You don't have to," she persisted, her voice hardening. "But you can't change anything either. It's time to stop making a martyr of yourself. I knew there was something eating you when we met. At first I thought it was the war and losing Cora and the baby, but as soon as that driver told me about your Dad, I tell you straight, I understood a lot more about you than I'd done before."

"Quite the little psycho-analyst!" I murmured.

"Perhaps I am. One of us has to be. It's not hard when you love someone. You sense their hurts, and if they won't confide in you, you worry about their every mood. Look for reasons. Wonder if you're to blame. I've always felt there was a part of you that closed itself against me. When I heard what happened at Sandworth, it shattered me, but at least I knew what was bugging you, and in a way, I was glad. It was only when you told me how you felt about your mother that I began to feel scared. Oh, Steve, I know you don't feel the way I do, but don't despise me!"

"Now who's talking daft!" I soothed her. "You're okay, Rose. Don't worry. Things'll sort themselves out. I was having a look at the music this morning. There's a lot there for me to work on. I'll try to get interested again, until I get a proper job and..."

I broke off lamely leaving the words in the air, and we fell silent again, and after a little while, Rose sighed, got up and went into the kitchen, and I sat tense and brooding, prey to my own melancholy thoughts.

It was the pattern of the days that followed. Days that dragged, from summer into autumn and the chill sombreness of late November.

Rose was spending more time at the café, often not getting home until late in the evening.

At the clinic, I had been fitted with a more permanent artificial arm. It was ugly and I hated it. The metal hook that caused derision among children who pretended to flee from me, shouting 'Here comes Captain Hook!' But it, and the spring loaded thumb made it possible for me to feed myself and pick things up without calling attention to myself.

Once or twice, I'd tried to get interested in the music, but my mind wasn't clear enough. I couldn't give it the concentration necessary. I was beginning to resent Mason.

I mistrusted him, though he always treated me well when I

went to the café for my mid-day meal. Often sat next to me, chewing one of his interminable cigars, yarning about this and that, and always, at some time during the conventional chit-chat, he'd steer the conversation over to Rose. Telling me how fortunate I was to have a wife like her. Vivacious. Beautiful. Hard-working.

And as he spoke, his eyes sucked her in. Devouring her. Then, almost deliberately, he'd look at me, and I knew he was taking stock. Wondering how a broken down cripple like me, could measure up to such a woman. Measuring the waste!

And I hated his free and easy manner. The way he put an arm round Rose's shoulder, or catch her round the waist, his fingers playing there. Brief, sensual messengers.

Sometimes, out of sight behind the serving hatch, I'd hear Rose laughing and skylarking with him, and my food almost choked me as I contrasted the sound with the taut silence that set my nerves tingling when, night after night, Rose and I sat together scarcely communicating.

Physically she was mine willingly enough, but otherwise I couldn't reach her. It was nothing specific, and therefore nothing I could purge, and so it festered inside of me. When I took her in my arms, I did so savagely, drowning myself in her, and in that at least, we were attuned. Giving and taking without stint, only when that was spent, she seemed more remote than ever.

The evening before I went back to Greenleas for my routine check-up, I sat watching her doing her hair. Pushing it this way and that, cocking her head to study the effect in the long wall mirror.

"D'you think it suits me up on top?" she asked casually. "I'm supposed to have pretty ears."

"Who says so? Mason?"

"Well, what if he did," she retorted. "No harm in paying me a compliment, is there? If I ever got one from you, I'd die of shock!"

"I don't like the way he paws you around!" I burst out angrily.

"Oh, for God's sake! Not again!" she exclaimed. "Just because the man's friendly and likes a bit of fun."

"He's a damned sight too friendly for my liking," I shouted. "I'm not blind. I've watched him. Never loses a chance to creep up and do a bit of mauling. Quicker you're out of there, the better."

She swung round and faced me, hands on hips, looking more angry than I'd ever seen her.

"Hark at Rothschild!" she mocked me. "Who's going to pay the bills and keep things going then if I stay at home?"

"You don't have to work for Mason," I said doggedly.

"What odds," she returned bitterly. "If not Mason, somebody else for you to find some rotten, warped objection to! God knows why you get so rattled. You don't go short of what you want of me! The only bloody thing so far as I can see!"

Her voice grew tight, curiously muffled, then died away.

For a moment we glowered at each other, then she snatched up the tray of things she'd been using on her hair, and went upstairs. What she said, wasn't true, I told myself angrily. I wanted a helluva sight more from our marriage than a bed mate, only it wasn't working out right and I didn't know why.

I poured myself a drink. Noticed a couple of bottles of whisky in the cupboard. Whisky was scarce and expensive. I thought about it for a bit. That bastard Mason! It was him I had to thank, just as I had to thank him for a well filled larder that made rationing a farce.

Why the hell was he doing us favours? Did he treat all his staff alike, or was it only Rose? He fancied her all right. I knew all the signs. Only I wasn't sure about Rose.

For most of her life, what Mason wanted had been as much a part of her daily routine as eating and drinking. 'A job', she called it, and I had to admit, it was one she did well.

I went on drinking.

Much later, warmed and mellowed by the neat spirit, my last conscious thought as I staggered up to bed, was that Mason was a damned good fellow to keep us so well supplied when the stuff was so bloody short!

Returning to Greenleas the following day, my head was like a ton weight and my mood as grey and melancholy as the bleak November day.

"Well, how are things working out for you, Stevens?" Doctor

Reynolds asked as he finished examining me.

"I'll be all right when I get a job," I told him.

"Anything in mind?" he wanted to know.

"Not really," I confessed. "Haven't really got down to it yet."

"Well it shouldn't be too difficult," he said brightly. "Should be easy for you to get back into local government offices - especially with a reference from Sandworth."

"I don't want to ask for one," I said. "There was a bit of a row when I left. I needn't have joined up when I did."

"That's nonsense, Stevens!" he declared. "They can't refuse you a reference because..."

"I don't fancy working in an office again," I put in quickly. "It's too confined - and not being able to write properly."

"You'll be able to manage that all right in time. I'm giving you a letter for the rehabilitation centre in your district. They'll help you. Believe me, Stevens, men are overcoming far greater handicaps than yours. You've got to persevere. Help yourself. If you can drive, you can write."

"It's not only my hands," I muttered. "I've been getting headaches. Bad ones."

"How long has this been?" he enquired, pushing my head back to shine a light in my eyes.

"Month or two," I told him.

"Certain amount of anxiety neurosis," he said thoughtfully. "You're a married man with responsibilities. Until you can see some kind of future security, you're going to worry. It's only natural. Get yourself fixed up in a job you can handle and you'll feel a new man."

His fingers were on my head, working over my spine, then the light was there again, he was drawing up my eyelids, his face close to mine.

"Been hitting the bottle pretty hard eh?" he said quietly.

"I like a drink. Yes," I admitted shortly.

"Too much never solved anything," he replied. "Don't be a fool, Stevens. You're making good progress. There's no reason why you shouldn't enjoy a near normal life. Saturate yourself with the hard stuff and, believe me, you'll really be a sick man."

He handed me an envelope.

"Here you are," he said. "Take this to the Centre and let them help you. I'll want to see you again in three months. Get nurse to make an appointment for you as you go out."

"Thanks," I answered, and as he turned to go, I asked him "How's Mike? Mike Doyle?"

He hesitated, trying to find some medical platitude with which to answer me, and I said quietly,

"I know about him. He told me. He's had it, hasn't he?"

"That's right," he confessed. "There's no hope now I'm afraid. No hope at all."

"I haven't seen him for a few weeks," I told him. "Can I see him now?"

He shook his head.

"I'm sorry," he answered. "It wouldn't do any good. He hasn't long now. For the past week or so, his only visitor has been the priest. He wants it that way."

"That's what they told me when I 'phoned," I said. "But I thought that while I was here... He's my friend..."

"I'm sorry," he said again, and left me.

Dressing myself, I registered my next appointment in the records office, and went outside. Walked slowly across the terrace to the annexe and out on to the balcony where Mike had his room.

An old man sat there, muffled in a blanket, gazing into space.

"If you're looking for the Irishman," he said, recognising me. "They've moved him into that small room just inside the entrance. Very ill he is. They won't let anyone in to see him except Father Doughty."

"They told me," I replied heavily. "They say he doesn't want any visitors, but I don't believe it. They're treating him as though he was already dead. Cutting him off from his friends."

"I think you've got it wrong, laddie," the old man said, shaking his head. "Man lives most of his life in the public eye, I reckon he's a right to die in private."

Perhaps he was right, but at that moment, the loneliness of death seemed a terrible thing, and the silence unbearably awesome. It was as though all life hung suspended - in jeopardy until the dark angel made his choice and withdrew once more into the shadows.

The loneliness of death had been my father's. How long had he hung and suffered in the lonely darkness of that shameful pit?

Poor Mike! He had been so proud of his physique! Now wasted and emaciated by that loathsome disease... Perhaps it wasn't hard to understand why he didn't want visitors!

Morose and dejected, I went down to the car and drove back to Bursledon.

Rose was sitting stretched out on the couch by the fire as I went in, a dressing gown pulled round her, her hair tied up in a coloured scarf.

"Hello, dear. You're early aren't you?" she greeted me in surprise. "I didn't expect you back until evening."

"Nothing to hang about there for," I told her wearily.

"Thought you might have spent a couple of hours with Mike."

"They won't let him have visitors," I told her. "It's a bloody shame! Treating him like he was dead already!"

"Well, they did warn you when you 'phoned," she reminded me. "I suppose they're keeping him drugged or something. And anyway, perhaps he doesn't want anyone to see him. He'll be so changed."

"A priest goes in every day."

"Well, they do, don't they. Him being RC. Got to be there to give him Absolution."

"Something like that," I sighed, sitting down.

"Well, what did they say about you then?" she wanted to know.

"Nothing much really. I've got a letter for the Rehabilitation Centre. According to Doctor Reynolds, they can work miracles."

"Oh, it won't be bad, love," she declared. "Some of the boys down there haven't any hands at all, but they soon learn to manage..."

"Then what?" I demanded bitterly. "Some lousy desk job, sitting on my arse all day."

"There you go again! Why don't you give yourself a chance!" she said impatiently. "Go down to the Centre in the proper spirit. Let them help you. Once you begin to feel independent, everything will look different. Would you like a cup of tea?"

"I'd rather have a tot," I answered. "I'm cold. Think I've got a chill or something."

"That stuff won't do you much good in the middle of the afternoon," she chided. "Come and sit by the fire. You'll soon get warm."

"The whisky's by kind permission of Mr Bloody Mason, I suppose," I muttered churlishly.

"Oh don't be stupid!" she retorted. "Drink the lot for all I care!"

"Thanks," I returned caustically, and went across to the sideboard. She sat watching me as I poured out a generous tot and drank the neat spirit.

"If it comes to things being out of place in the afternoon," I said laconically. "What's the idea of sitting around in your dressing gown? Nostalgia?"

She looked puzzled.

"I told you," she explained. "I didn't expect you home so early. I had a bath and washed my hair. I've got a steak and kidney pudding on, and it won't be ready until six o'clock."

She got up suddenly, and put her arms round my neck.

"You're tired, love," she murmured, "and upset about Mike. Come and sit down."

I held her to me. Warm, soft, satisfying.

A current of feeling surged through me. A strange sweet fusion, and all at once, there were a hundred things I wanted to say to her. Thrilling, tender things.

Perhaps if I had told her then what she meant to me, simply and quietly, while the words hammered in my brain, we might have made a go of it. I was on the brink. Gripped by an emotion I thought had died with Cora, only at that moment, as I held her to my heart, I caught sight of something on the mantlepiece.

Something that jolted me cold.

Came an instant of almost stupefied silence. Then I stiffened, releasing Rose with a suddenness that sent her reeling away from me. A couple of strides, and I snatched up the stub of the cigar from the ashtray. The end was still wet. Chewed almost flat.

"So he's been here!" I shouted accusingly. "I go away for a couple of hours and that bastard's here with you! You cow! You dirty cow!"

"Steve!" she cried in dismay. "For God's sake! Mr Mason was here, yes. There's nothing wrong in that. I got my shopping today, the same as I always do on Fridays, and he offered to bring it home for me. Well, you weren't here with the car, were you? And what's wrong with giving him a cup of tea?"

"Is that why you took your clothes off?" I demanded furiously.

She glared at me. Angry now.

"If that's what you think, to hell with you!" she stormed. "Going off at the deep end like that..."

"Mason fancies you all right," I interrupted her. "He knew I was out of the way, and he couldn't get here quick enough!"

"Okay. So he fancies me!" Her voice was shrill, ugly. "So do a lot of others! That's how we got this house. Remember? When are you going to accept the fact that I'm the same woman - only I don't live the same sort of life!"

"Who're you kidding?" I said savagely. "You've been at it too long. D'you think Mason doesn't know that? Any man can recognise a bit of spare when he sees it!"

"You rotter! You bloody rotter!" she whispered. "You know what? It's not your legs and hands you've got to worry about. It's your mind. It's nasty, and mean and warped. You've got nothing to do all day but twist everything decent into something dirty. You can't forget your own past, and you're not going to let me forget mine. You won't let me be different! You get a lousy, perverted sort of pleasure in believing I'm the same as your mother. Well, let me tell you something. I'm not hanging around to end up the way she did!"

The intensity of her anger drained me of mine.

"Rose..." I faltered. "I'm sorry..."

"Sorry!" she flared. "You make me sick! You think you've only got to say 'sorry' to square everything."

"It's Mason," I muttered. "Like red rag to a bull..."

"Mason or any other man who behaves like a human being," she scoffed. "You're a freak, Steve. If anyone's sorry, it's me!

Sorry I was fool enough to marry you! Sorry you hadn't guts enough to tell me about your father - and sorrier still that I didn't realise you'd be too obsessed with the past to try and make a decent future for us."

She went out into the hall. Started to go upstairs.

"Rose," I called to her. "You've got to be patient with me. Give me a chance to adjust..."

She looked back at me.

"I don't know," she said wearily. "I just don't know."

"You said you liked me to be jealous of you," I reminded her, trying a smile.

"There's nothing wrong with a little healthy jealousy," she said. "But possessiveness, suspicion, abuse - I just can't live with those. You flying off the handle every few minutes, accusing me of Christ know's what! I bet you didn't treat Cora like that!"

"Cora," I echoed, disconcerted. "That's crazy! Cora wasn't like..."

"Say it," she broke in bitterly. "Cora wasn't a whore before you married her!"

"That's not fair," I protested feebly. "Cora was different. I've never tried to compare you with her."

"Oh, what's the use," she answered, and went on upstairs to the bedroom.

I went back into the lounge. Sat there, listening to her moving about in the room above, and after a while, she came down, wearing her black overcoat with its big lynx collar.

"I'm going out," she said stiffly. "This place stifles me."

The front door banged behind her before I could answer.

I don't know what I felt then. Just empty. Drained and desperately lonely. Perhaps a little afraid.

Where had she gone? To Mason? If she had, I'd pushed her into it.

I shivered, cold right through. Heaped coal on the fire, crouching before the flames. My thoughts muddled, my aching head pressed against the arm of the couch.

It was past seven when the smell of burning cloth set me scrambling to my feet, into the kitchen.

On the stove, the saucepan had boiled dry. The cloth on the pudding basin was singed muddy brown. I turned off the gas. Beside the stove, pans of uncooked vegetables. On the table, a bowl of fruit salad. A jug of creme. A gay pot pourri of variegated sea fern set in the centre of the bright checked cloth Rose had prepared for our evening meal.

Beside the boiler, my slippers warming. All prepared with care. With love.

Guiltily, I returned to the lounge. Sat down. Turned on the radio.

The V2 rocket bombs were still giving Londoners a bad time, but everywhere else, the war news was good, and the Allies, despite heavy fighting, were advancing on all sides.

I reached for the whisky bottle, and after a little while, the voice of the announcer grew blurred and far away, until I couldn't hear it at all.

I awoke with a start some three hours later, and now I was really cold. Painfully I eased my cramped limbs, massaging them into life and mobility. Stiffly made my way into the kitchen again. Rinsed my throbbing head under the cold tap.

The house was strangely silent. I shuddered. Put on the kettle and mixed a hot whisky. Sat by the boiler, hugging the glass to me between my palms.

The silence got on my nerves. It was nearly midnight when I went up to bed. Lay in the darkness wondering about Rose. Where was she? What was she doing? Suppose she didn't come back? The thought brought a feeling of panic, and darkness was suddenly unbearable. Suffocating.

I groped for the bedside lamp, suffusing the room in pink light. Closed my eyes, trying to sleep. Alerted by every creak - every footstep in the street below - every car that passed and slowed down to take the corner.

I kept looking at the clock on the dressing table, and then, just before one, Rose came home.

The sound of her high heels, clipped and deliberate on the still air. I held my breath. Exhaled with relief as I heard the front door open and close - Rose moving around.

After a little while, she came upstairs.

She was singing to herself. Went on singing as she undressed without even looking at me.

Perching on the dressing stool, she combed her hair and creamed her face, her expression betraying nothing as she caught my eye in the looking glass.

When at last she was ready for bed, she climbed in beside me, lying with her knees up, pulling the sheets up to her chin. Stared at me quizzically. Daring me to ask where she'd been.

"Hello," I said quietly.

"Hello," she returned. "Feel better then?"

"Better now," I told her huskily, reaching out for her. "Oh, Rose! I'm sorry! I'm a louse."

"I won't argue with that," she whispered, but her hand gripped mine.

This was no time for words. I moved closer to her, felt her straighten down in the bed, her body turning towards mine. The warmth of her was electrifying. Re-assuring.

I lost myself in her, and afterwards, as I settled down to sleep, I heard her whisper close to my ear,

"About tonight. I was only down at Nora Page's place. You know. She helps cook at the café. I told her I'd do her hair some evening. It seemed a good time..."

Gently, I put a hand over her mouth.

"It doesn't matter," I murmured.

Three days later, Mike died.

Matron gave me the news over the telephone when I put through my daily call to Greenleas from the newsagents across the street.

I put down the receiver and went back to the house. I felt odd. Sort of isolated. Empty, and in a strange way, guilty. As though something was expected of me. Some personal requiem. Some demonstration of deep grief. Only I wallowed in a vacuum. Inventing things for my mind to cling to.

I stood by the fire, savouring its warmth. Started thinking about cancer. The word had a strange sound. A fearsome mysticism. A word that inspired so much naked fear that people were afraid to say it aloud. A word with more impact than the dirtiest epithet. Synonymous with death and yet more deadly.

I said it aloud. Repeated it. How long before medical science expurgated that destroyer from the world? I moved about restlessly. Time to be going down to the café, but I didn't feel like food.

A drink! Of course! A drink to absent friends. Solemnly I gathered up a bottle of whisky and went into the kitchen. Reached for a glass and sat down at the table.

Absent friends! Too many absent friends!

The drink released the tension inside of me. Pictures crowded into my mind. Mike as I first knew him. The good times we'd shared with Lofty, Beady and the others. All gone now. All but me.

Why had death rejected me, leaving me maimed and broken to struggle on?

I brooded on it. Resentful. Dark with bitterness. Hadn't I died a little with each one of them? A long protracted dying. Why me?

I went on drinking, huddled over the table.

What was it the Chaplain was on about? Life being transitory - the path to a better place somewhere beyond death. Was it true? Did Cora wait in some Great Beyond? Cora and the others?

Suddenly I thought I knew what the Chaplain meant. Eternal Glory was in the limitless space, beyond the meagre range of this bloodied globe where man struggles through his allotted span. The world's a cesspool of man's corruption, and he wallows in it. Helpless.

Life is Man's travail. The price he must pay in blood and tears and turmoil and tribulation, for the merciful surcease of oblivion. The everlasting glory was freedom from thought and feeling. Nothing.

The Divine Theorem - QED - Paradise was nothing!

Sweet Fanny Adams!

That was a laugh!

Solemnly, I drank to nothing.

And according to the Chaplain, I was lucky to be alive. He had to be joking!

You wound up with nothing. Broken. Disillusioned. Drained. And that was lucky! Christ! How could you take the bad luck, with good luck like that!

Well, at least I'd got Rose. By kind permission of the bloody Almighty!

Mockingly, I drank to the divine magnanimity!

Already I was feeling better. A glance at the clock told me it was two-thirty. Rose would be wondering why I hadn't shown up at the café. Well, it wouldn't do any harm to break the daily routine. For once, Mason could stuff his lunch.

Must toast absent friends. All of them! A communal toast then.

I fumbled for the half empty bottle, the stumps of my fingers closing over it, urging it towards the glass. Felt it slip away from me. Grabbed at it urgently with both arms. Clasping it to me as the glass crashed to the floor. Tipped the bottle neck to my lips. Felt the raw spirit flood into my mouth. Gasped for breath. Sat panting. Glowing with an unwelcome warmth. Tilted the bottle again, leaning back in the chair, and the drink was slopping over my chin, sweeping down behind my collar.

Then Rose came in.

I heard her in the hall

"Steve!" she called urgently. "Where... ?"

Her voice stopped abruptly as she reached the kitchen, and the timbre changed as she rasped at me,

"God! What a mess! What the hell d'you think you're doing?"

I looked at her through half closed eyes, finding it hard to focus.

"Mike's dead," I said, churning out the words with difficulty.

"I know," she answered. "They told me at the shop. You forgot to pick up the papers."

"Bloody shame!" I muttered thickly.

"It's a bloody shame that you should get yourself in this condition!" she said angrily. "Of course it's sad about Mike, but it's not unexpected, is it?"

"So what's wrong in drinking to the memory of the poor devil?" I asked solemnly.

"With more than half a bottle of whisky," she fumed. "Don't

make me laugh! All it means to you is a chance to get sloshed!"

"It's a lie!" I mumbled hazily. "Anyone'd think I was tight."

"Well, if you're not, you damned well ought to be," she returned angrily. "You're sodden with the stuff. If you don't watch out, you're wind up an alcoholic! If only you'd use your hands for other things with the same enthusiasm as knocking back booze, who knows, you might even cope with a job of work one of these days!"

"Bitch!" I muttered.

"Maybe," she answered harshly. "But I'm no fool, Steve. I'll tell you straight. I'll take just so much of this bloody father image. What he did was one thing, and I'm not blaming you for it, but they say what's bred in the bone is bound to come out somewhere, and it strikes me you've got a lot more of your Dad in you than's healthy."

Her voice was hard. Metallic. Alien. Disembodied. Echoing through my brain. A meaningless confusion of words.

The noise hurt.

I felt sweat running from my forehead. A tightness in my throat. A throbbing in my head.

"Shut up! I groaned. "For Christ's sake, shut up!"

"You're too much like him," the voice pounded on. "Need a skinful of booze where your guts ought to be..."

Now the words melted into one another. Became an unbearable cacophony of sound.

Releasing the bottle, I made an effort to push back my chair. Something crashed around me. A great roar in my ears. A confused impression of furniture buckling around me. Of shattered glass. Of Rose's shrill cry. Of her clutching at me as I hit the floor.

Then I passed out.

CHAPTER ELEVEN

I woke up with a throat like a rasp and a head that weighed a ton. Managed to open my eyes.

I was lying on the settee. Rose was sitting by the fire, reading.

"What time is it?" I asked.

"Nearly nine."

"Christ! Have I got the father and mother of all headaches!" I muttered.

"What d'you expect," she retorted. "Drinking yourself silly. Passing out on the kitchen floor!"

"Kitchen? D'you mean you got me in here?"

"Me and the man from the paper shop," she told me. "Made me feel a proper fool I can tell you!"

"It was hearing about Mike," I said. "Shook me. Got me down."

"That's no excuse. You knew he could go at any time and..."

"Cut it out will you," I interrupted her. "So I had a drop too much of your boy friend's whisky. What d'you want me to do about it?"

"That's up to you," she said calmly. "You remember me coming in this afternoon?"

"Vaguely," I confessed.

A sort of uneasy silence, and I sat up staring at her.

"Oh I see," I said slowly. "I've been speaking out of turn again have I?"

"No. It wasn't anything *you* said," she replied with quiet emphasis. "Do you remember what I said to you?"

I shook my head - carefully.

"I thought as much," she sighed. "All right. I'd better say it all again."

And she did. With an intensity that defied interruption.

"It's no use getting sore at me," she finished seriously. "If there's going to be any decent sort of life for us together, we've got to start being honest with each other. You may as well know what I feel. Seeing you sitting around feeling sorry for yourself - hitting the bottle - bawling me out every time a man comes near me - I don't like it, Steve. It scares me."

Her words scared me too. Robbing me of anger.

"You're the one who's finding parallels," I muttered. "You're expecting too much of me, too soon. There's nothing wrong with liking a drink. What else d'you bring it home for? Today I admit, I went over the top. It wasn't only Mike. It was a whole chain of things that got me down. Mike just triggered it off. I got to thinking about Lofty and Cora and all the others who've gone west in this lousy war. And the others, like me, uprooted from the things we had. Crippled and chucked back on the rubbish heap to start again."

"You don't believe that any more than I do," she said scornfully. "What did you have when the war started? Damn all! If you ask me, it was a blessing in disguise for you. You escaped into the Navy! At most, you've lost a few years."

"What about these?" I demanded, holding out my arms.

"What about them?" she snapped impatiently. "As I told you this afternoon, if they can cope with a bottle, they can cope with a pen, and the quicker you get working on it, the better. Now - would you like some black coffee?"

"Thanks," I said bitterly. "That should solve everything!"

"It's a start," she told me wryly. "Are you going to the service?"

"I'd rather not."

"All right. I'll send a wreath tomorrow. You know they're sending the body back to Ireland for burial."

"Yes," I said. "They told me."

"Rotten for his parents," she observed thoughtfully. "I mean - it's not as though he was killed in action or anything. You sort of expect those things when there's a war going on, don't you? But to go away from your family and die from some rotten disease without even a chance to fight back..."

She left the words on the air and sighed, then,

"I'll go and make the coffee," she murmured...

The days up to Christmas were a mixture of good and bad. I went regularly to the Centre where they made adjustments to my artificial hand, teaching me to manipulate it like pincers.

At first, the thing was repugnant to me. More unbearable than the sight of my useless stump. Wretchedly struggling to overcome my revulsion, I became more awkward in my efforts to accustom myself to it, and each failure drew a rebuke from Carlyle, my therapist.

"Of course you can't manage it and it's your own fault," he said impatiently. "You're psychologically opposed to the idea. That's what's holding you back. You'd better learn to accept it fast, because it's your only chance of leading a normal life - of integrating..."

Somehow I got the impression he didn't go for me. Sort of sneered. Maybe I wasn't maimed enough for him. He went for the serious stuff. No arms - No legs - No limbs at all.

After an exchange I'd clear out in a dark mood. Head bursting, and maybe I'd go to the Club and sink a couple of pints and a glass or two of whisky. When the cash ran low and there was no one to stand me a drink, I'd move on to the local and try my luck there.

I didn't realise how much I depended on it until the night I went to the sideboard cupboard and found the bottle empty.

Rose sat watching me, though she didn't let on, and I asked casually,

"All the Scotch gone then?"

"That's right," she answered quietly. "All gone, and that's how it's going to be from now on."

"Signed the pledge have you?" I gibed lightly.

"Doesn't make any difference to me, one way or the other," she returned. "I can take it or leave it alone."

"Sort of 'I'm all right Jack'," I grumbled.

She looked at me solemnly.

"You know better than that," she said. "It's no use beating about the bush. You're drinking too much."

"I see," I said tersely. "Not paying my corner I suppose."

"It's nothing to do with money," she told me patiently. "Mr Carlyle says it's not doing you any good."

"Mr Bloody Carlyle! What the hell's it got to do with him?"

"Now you're being silly," she chided. "After all, it's his job to..."

"It's his job to play Frankenstein to a lot of bloody monsters!" I shouted angrily. "Teach us to use these pretty little things!"

I flung out my arm. Waving the pincers at her. Feeling like some ridiculous lobster clawing the air.

"Carlyle doesn't have to tell me how to run my life!" I stormed. "And anyway, when did you two have this little heart to heart?"

"I met him coming out of the post office," she explained. "For heaven's sake be reasonable! Isn't it natural I should ask him how you're getting on? It's on your last report from Greenleas - about the drink..."

"And I suppose you told him I couldn't leave the stuff alone!" I sneered. "Christ! Anyone would think I'm a bloody alcoholic!"

She laughed.

"And they wouldn't be far wrong, would they? You've got rid of a couple of bottles this week, and I can't keep forking out for them on my pay."

"So it is the money!" I said harshly. "Why the..."

"Oh, for God's sake," she interrupted shrilly. "One of us has got to think about the money! I can't afford to keep digging into my savings just to keep you in booze. You'll never be good for anything the way you're going on. God knows I'm doing my best, but it's about time you got a grip on yourself. I'm not going to be able to keep both of us for ever..."

"I wondered when you'd start rubbing that in," I silenced her. "Well, you can stick your whisky!"

I turned and slammed out of the house. Went down to the Rose and Crown and bought myself a double.

That was when Fraser and a crowd of other chaps from the Club turned up.

Fraser was getting married the following day. This was his stag night, and he was making the most of his last day of freedom. I joined in with them and went the rounds, drinking and skylarking until well after midnight when, divesting him of his trousers and tying him to a lamp-post, we wished Fraser all the best, and went our separate ways.

It was one o'clock when I put the car away and made my way somewhat unsteadily towards the house.

The night was dark and almost uncannily quiet, and despite the fact that I'd had a skinful, I felt sober enough. Sober enough to feel guilty as I fumbled for my key, hoping I wouldn't have to face up to another row with Rose until morning.

Only as I opened the door, she was standing there in the hall. Ran to meet me. Clinging. Her wet cheeks pressed against mine, and I heard her murmur,

"I've been so worried about you, Steve. All the pubs closed. I didn't know where to look. I was so frightened something had happened to you."

I stroked her hair, floored by the anti-climax. No grumbles. Nor recriminations. Just concern. Worry.

"I got caught up with Alf Fraser's stag party," I explained. "I'm sorry. I didn't mean to be so late, but you know how it is. Things get a little bit out of hand and..."

"So long as you're all right," she whispered. "I went to bed, but I couldn't sleep. Then when it got so late, I just couldn't stay up there imagining what might have happened. I got dressed again. If you hadn't come when you did, I was going down to the police station to see if there'd been an accident. Can I get you anything before we go up?"

"No thanks," I told her. "I'm ready for bed." And holding her round the waist, we went upstairs together.

I felt warmed. Glad to be home, but later, when I pressed her close to me, wanting her, I couldn't do anything about it. It just wasn't there.

It was a frightening humiliation, and long after Rose had turned away from me, hurt and frustrated, I lay in the darkness cursing the hovering spectre of impotence.

It was different in the morning, though the experience had shaken me. I said as much to Rose after I'd proved to her that a good night's sleep had been enough to recharge my batteries!

"I know you were tired, and I don't want another row," she said seriously, "but no kidding, Steve, you"ll have to cut down on the booze."

"That's a laugh," I told her. "Don't you know that alcohol stimulates sexual desire?"

"I wasn't thinking about that," she returned. "The doctor says you should go easy on it."

"What, on drink, or on the other?" I bantered. "You know what's the matter with you? You worry too much."

"And you're spending too much," she countered. "We can't do it, Steve..."

That was the theme that generally started all our rows, and I suppose she was right.

After she stopped bringing home the drink, I started to buy a few tots when I drew my pension. Took to carrying a flask around with me, cadging the odd tot to top it up, and when Rose didn't bitch at me for holding back some of my pension, I stopped a bit more and more - until I got to blowing the lot before I got home.

So there were rows and more rows, and shouting and slanging and tears and remorse, and at those times, it was as though I stood outside myself - cowering on the stairs. A child again, listening once more to the frightening, bitter words that echoed through my childhood.

The quarrels became harder to mend. Too bitter to dissolve in the fleshy pleasures that until then had drained us of all other passions.

There were nights when Rose turned away from me. Throwing off my groping arms, and in anger and frustration I would rage at her,

"What the hell's the matter with you? Anyone would think I had the pox or something!"

"The pox would be better than what you've got!" she flung at me. "At least we'd know how to treat it! You know what? I don't think you're right in the head!"

"I won't argue with that," I rasped. "Why else would I have hitched up with a cow like you? Bloody funny! Spend your life opening your legs to Christ knows how many men, and turn your back on your husband!"

"You're forgetting something," she reminded me bitterly. "They could pay for it!"

Silently, I acknowledged the truth of that. Fumbled guiltily for her hand.

"Why do we have to quarrel all the time, Rose," I murmured contritely. "I know it's not easy for you being married to a helpless..."

"Oh my God! Spare me that old record! It's nearly worn out. You're not helpless, Steve. Just gutless. Let me tell you something. Nothing that's ever happened to you, is an excuse for what you are now. Nothing! D'you hear? And I'll tell you something else you may understand. I'm not sticking it much longer! Either you pull yourself together, lay off the booze and get yourself a job, or I'm clearing out!"

I knew she meant it.

I lay there in the silence brooding over her words, and the pain was there in my head again. An iron band round which snatches of thought surged and receded with no real meaning. Distorted visions came crowding. Clamouring in my brain. I buried my face in the pillow, pressing my hand on my head so hard that it hurt, but the hurt on the outside was more bearable than the anguish inside.

It was the first quarrel which didn't end with Rose in my arms. She got out of bed, pulled on a dressing gown and went downstairs. She didn't come up again that night, and in the morning, she left home before I was up.

I thought about it all morning and then, ignoring the obvious reasons, I began to look deeper for reasons to explain the change in her attitude towards me.

She was leaving the house earlier in the mornings. Often going off before I went downstairs. I'd lay in bed working it over in my mind. Thinking about her and Mason. Remembering the way he looked at her. The time she took with her make-up. The way she spruced herself up to go to the café.

The little luxuries she brought home. Extra rations. Chocolates. How she was never short of nylons and perfume.

Mason and Rose! The thought grew.

Sometimes I'd spend an hour or so at the piano. Torturing myself with memories and regrets. Trying to pick out a favourite melody with fingers that reacted like chunks of wood.

It hurt! It hurt like hell! I remembered my father telling me music was inside of me, but it never reached my fingers. Wondered if he knew what had happened to me. Perhaps it was some sick kind of joke!

Savagely I banged down the lid of the piano.

That was the time I started going down to the café half an hour before they expected me. Going in through the back entrance where I could see into the kitchen and Mason's office.

Sometimes I'd see them together. Talking. Laughing. Close together. Intimate. Watching how he made a meal of it every time she handed him anything. The easy way his arm rested round her shoulders. The way he never missed a chance of passing close to her. Touching her.

At home, the warmth was missing. The place untidy. Uncared for. Rose would potter around in her dressing gown. Hair in curlers. Grease on her face. Submitting to my embrace almost contemptuously.

Once, just before Christmas, when my head was giving me hell, she said quietly,

"Don't you think you ought to see someone about it? Old Doctor Simpson down the road. He'd give you something for it I'm sure."

"I might just do that," I told her wearily. "It's stinking rotten, I can tell you."

"Perhaps it's something to do with that knock you had when they picked you up," she went on thoughtfully. "You know. Where that scar is?"

I shrugged.

"Should have thought someone would have spotted it by now - if something's wrong. I've had enough treatment for one thing and another."

"Have you complained to Doctor Carlyle about it?"

"You know what he'd say! Too much booze!"

"Maybe," she agreed. "But sometimes the effect of a head injury doesn't show up for ages, then something sort of starts it off, like illness, or worry - or drink or something"

"Never miss a chance to harp on it, do you!" I sneered.

"I'm not going to quarrel with you, Steve," she said quietly. "If you're content with things as they are, that's up to you. You just won't let anyone help you..."

"I know. I'm a louse!" I sighed. "You've got to stick by me, Rose. Let's get Christmas over and things'll be different I promise you. I'll look for a job and..."

My voice faltered. The words stuck in my throat, and suddenly, as I buried my head in my hands, she was beside me, kneeling there, cradling me to her.

"It's all right, love," she murmured, her hands cool on my throbbing forehead. "You'll be fine. You've just got to stop punishing yourself. Give yourself a chance. And please, promise you'll see the doctor?"

"I will. First thing in the morning," I told her. "You're so good to me, Rose. Give me time. Just give me time. I'll make it up to you."

"Of course you will," she whispered.

That was one of the good nights. Close, tender and warm.

An island. An island that was to seem a long way off before many hours had passed.

True to my word, I did go to see Dr Simpson. He prescribed some tablets. Gave me a cursory examination, and advised me to consult the doctor at the clinic who had access to my medical history.

I made up my mind to do as he suggested but decided it could wait until after Christmas.

Rose seemed happy. Chattered excitedly about the Christmas Eve party Mason was laying on for his staff. Their relations and a few personal friends.

"It'll be a change for you, Steve," she told me. "From what I've seen it's going to be a right merry do. Give you a chance to unwind..."

I didn't share her enthusiasm. My mistrust of Mason went too deep, but of one thing I was sure. She wasn't going to that party without me!

On Christmas Eve the café closed early. Rose went in soon after lunch to help with the catering, and when I got there at eight o'clock the party was in full swing.

About a dozen couples danced to the music from a radiogram, and a score or so of men and women crowded round the buffet bar, drinking, laughing and bawling together.

I couldn't see Rose, and after a little while, it was Mason who came to greet me.

"Welcome aboard," he said cheerfully. "Come on in and join the gang."

His arm rested easy across my shoulder, piloting me to the bar.

"Where's Rose?" I asked.

He looked around.

"Must have gone to powder her nose," he said. "She was here a minute ago."

Vaguely he introduced me to one or two people standing around, then called to the ginger haired man behind the counter.

"Here Fred. Fix Mr Stevens a drink. He's a whisky man. Look after him, won't you."

"Trust me, Mr Mason," the man promised solemnly, and gave me a wink.

I caught sight of Jennie, the young waitress who usually served my lunch, and she came over to me.

"Wouldn't you rather sit down, Mr Stevens?" she asked.

"Thanks, Jennie," I answered. "See if you can find Rose will you?"

"Over here," she replied, leading me to an empty table near the radiogram. "Make yourself comfortable. I'll tell Rose you're here."

She went away, and it was Rose who brought me a tray of sandwiches and party savouries.

Her eyes looked luminous. Her cheeks flushed, and in the green velvet, figure-hugging dress she wore, I thought she had never looked so lovely.

"I see you've got a drink," she said, eyeing the generous tot of whisky beside me. "Are you all right?"

"Fine," I assured her. "Quite a spread isn't it."

"Oh yes. Mr Mason's spared no expense. Got everything you want then?" Her eyes were casting around, beyond me - and it irritated me.

"Don't worry about me," I said. "What have you been doing?"

"Me?" The intonation was false. "Oh... nothing really. Helping get things ready. Had a couple of dances..."

The words seemed vague. The smile in her eyes not for me but for the crowd lining up to play Musical Chairs.

"They're going to start the game," she said eagerly. "Maybe you could join in something..."

"No thanks. I'll just watch. Catch me making a bloody fool of myself for the amusement of this mob!"

Now her expression was all mine as it reproached me.

"Oh, Steve! It's Christmas! Why do you always twist things. There's no harm in a bit of fun."

"Okay," I agreed calmly. "But not at my expense. Just leave me alone."

Mason joined us, reaching out for Rose.

"Come on, Rosie," he said. "Can't have you dodging the column now, can we?"

His arm was round her waist.

"All right then, Stevens?" he asked. "They looking after you?"

"I'm doing all right," I told him, stifling the desire to smash a plate of trifle into his bloated face. "Sorry I can't join in the fun and games, but Rose has enough enthusiasm for both of us."

"You can say that again," he applauded. "Still, we've got to keep the old man happy eh? What about this then?"

With the air of a conjuror he produced a bottle of scotch from behind his back, and with a flourish, set it on the table in front of me.

I looked at Rose derisively.

"See what the nasty Santa Claus has given me!" I said mockingly.

Rose looked uncertainly at Mason and he gave a deep throated laugh.

"What's this then, Rosie?" he demanded. "You been getting on to him? Go on! Drink up man! It's Christmas!"

And he whirled Rose away to join the others, grabbing a paper hat as one of the women pushed in a trolley loaded with balloons and party novelties.

I sat there feeling better with every mouthful of the raw spirit. Joined in the choruses. Exchanged banter with some of the dancers, but as the evening wore on and the air was thick with tobacco smoke, and the shrill babble of voices mingled with the blare of the music into a deafening cacophony of sound, my head started pounding away again, and I felt sick.

Grating back my chair, I stood up, reaching for my stick to steady myself, and made for the toilet.

A woman called out to me.

"Anything I can do for you, Mr Stevens."

I managed a dry laugh.

"No thanks. This is one thing I have to do for myself!" I heard her laughing as I carefully edged my way round the counter. Stood leaning against it for a moment, looking round for Rose.

No one else took any notice of me. In the centre of a group of shouting men and women, two men, stripped to the waist, were playing around doing balancing tricks. I couldn't see what was going on beyond them, though here and there some couples were doing some pretty heavy petting.

My head weighed a ton and any feeling of well-being was beginning to slip away from me. Standing there, on the edge of things with no one caring a damn - and where the hell was Rose?

I pushed my way into the toilet, relieved myself, then put my head under the tap. Savoured the ice cold water, and after a little while, I felt better. But I'd got to get out into the fresh air - away from the noise... I wanted Rose.

And then, as I went out into the passage again, I saw them. Rose and Mason. Reflected in the big mirror on the opposite wall.

Standing there in a clinch, his hands working overtime! I went stone cold. Started to tremble, then I moved, treading light and soundless on the red carpet so that they didn't know I was there until I was within a yard of them.

Deliberately, I let my stick fall. Heard Rose's startled cry as she pulled herself from Mason, and he stood there panting, eyes glazed, grinning at me, his face smeared with her lipstick.

"Take it easy, old man," he said thickly. "All part of the merriment you know. Nothing like a good old fashioned game of

Postman's Knock!"

"You bloody liar!" I ground out furiously. "What kind of a fool d'you take me for? This was the one time you had to ask me along, so you thought a bottle of scotch would keep me out of the way while you and that dirty cow went through your daily routine!"

"That's not true, Steve," Rose said urgently. "You've got it..."

"Shut up, Rosie," Mason silenced her. "It's time someone told this husband of yours some facts about himself. Either you're a nut case, Stevens, or you're a snivelling little runt. No spunk in you! If Rosie fancies a man sometimes, who'd blame her? I tell you straight, I wish it was me!"

"Who d'you think you're kidding?" I spat at him. "I know what's been going on..."

"So you know!" he taunted me. "And as long as it wasn't under your nose, it suited you fine. You rotten bastard! You dirty rotten pimp!"

That was when I hit him. Deliberately tearing at his sneering face with the metal claw that made my hand a fearsome weapon.

Rose was screaming. People came out, shouting.

The blood was gushing from Mason's torn mouth, and I saw him square up to me. And then, as I raised my arm for another blow at him, he flung out a vicious right to my jaw and brought his knee up hard to my crotch. I crumpled as he struck me again. Felt a sharp pain as I hit the ground...

That was the end of Rose's job at the café. When I came round, I learned that someone had helped Rose bring me home, and Mason had been taken to hospital needing twelve stitches in the wound on his face. Suppose I was lucky he didn't bring charges against me. Maybe he was satisfied that he'd put me on my back for a few weeks with severe bruising and a couple of cracked ribs. Perhaps he kept quiet for Rose's sake. Or did he feel guilty knowing I was the injured party?

Rose didn't reproach me. In fact, we hardly spoke. There was nothing to say that hadn't been said before over and over...

She brought in Doctor Simpson because I was running a temperature, and my body felt as though I'd been poleaxed. She told him we'd been to a party and I'd had too much to drink and fallen down.

He strapped up my ribs and wrote out a prescription while Rose told him about my headaches, my moods, my irrational tempers, my jealousy and my drinking. I closed my eyes and listened to her churning it out.

"I've seen such cases before, Mrs Stevens," Simpson told her. "He's been through a great deal of course. The memory of his ordeal. The knowledge of disability - these things have undoubtedly made a serious impact on his mind."

My eyes were heavy. I lay back feigning sleep.

"D'you mean he may be insane?" I heard Rose whisper fearfully.

"Certainly not," He sounded shocked. "But the mind is a complex and unpredictable thing. We've only explored the threshold. There's no prescribed pattern. Each case is individual. All kinds of strains and stresses build up, and in any case of anxiety neurosis, alcohol only aggravates things."

"He's certainly been worse since he started drinking heavily," she said quietly, "What can we do, Doctor?"

"For the time being, just let him take things easy," he advised. "Keep him on a light diet and see that he takes the tablets regularly. They should help, though he's going to feel some discomfort until those ribs settle down. When he's able to get around again, I'll arrange an appointment for him to see Doctor Eddison at the Neurological Clinic. He's a psychiatrist. Had a lot of experience with war disabled. I'll be in tomorrow to have another look at your husband, Mrs Stevens. Just keep him quiet..."

Rose went with him to the front door, and I opened my eyes as she came back into the bedroom.

"Trying to get me certified eh?" I ribbed, trying to grin. "Well, I can't say I blame you."

"Don't talk so daft," she said, buffing up my pillows.

I caught her hand.

"I'm sorry, Rose," I told her contritely. "For everything. Mason was right. I'm a bastard! A proper bastard!"

She pulled her hand away.

"The doctor says you've got to rest," she answered. "I'm going down to the chemist now to get your tablets,"

"You filled the doctor in pretty well," I told her. "Thank you for not telling him about Sandworth."

"Time enough for that when you see Doctor Eddison."

"I don't go much on this psychiatry caper," I muttered peevishly.

"Anything's worth a try," she insisted earnestly. "You'll have to tell him everything. Oh, Steve, you've got to beat this thing once and for all - for both our sakes."

I avoided her eyes.

"Don't know what all the fuss is about," I yawned. What's wrong with a man being jealous of his wife?"

"If only that's all it was," she sighed.

She was right. It was Mason I was jealous of. Mason and all the others like him who were big and strong and *whole*.

"Suppose I see this Eddison," I burst out lamely. "What will it prove? I know I'm a funny sort of cuss. Not easy to live with, but you knew what you were taking on..."

"Oh I know I made all the advances," she cut in swiftly. "But I didn't know about Sandworth, did I?"

"Well, answering bloody fool questions to a quack isn't going to wipe that out, is it?"

"Maybe not. But it'll help you bury it. Perhaps it'll stop you treating me like I was her. Give us a chance together."

I tried to look at her then, but my eyes weren't focussing properly. I was tired. Utterly weary...

"You've got it all wrong," I muttered. "We'll be all right, and d'you know why? Just because you *are* like my mother! It's the Almighty's special brand of humour, and the joke's been on me too many times. One by one, all the decent things swept away. Only rottenness endures..."

"I'm not going to listen to that rubbish," she said tightly, going to the bedroom door and looking back at me. "You're all twisted up inside. You're not the only one who's lost somebody..."

"Somebody!" I echoed feebly. "I've lost everybody!"

"Thanks! What does that make me?"

"All the decent things," I lurched on solemnly, struggling

against the desire to sleep. Desperately wanting her to understand. "You're like her..."

"Have it your way. I'm like your mother, and she's dead!"

"S'right," I said thickly. "She got what she deserved. She was rubbish. Dad was a sensitive man. She was destroying him. He loved her too much you see, but she drove him to breaking point and... and she ended up dead... ."

Maybe I went on talking aloud to Rose, and maybe the words were only in my mind. I don't know. I wanted desperately to justify my father, and I seemed to hear someone sobbing in the background, and I was very hot, and very tired.

Most days went like that. The row that came from nowhere, erupting over a word, a memory.

Rose was so vulnerable. So easy to hurt, and in some odd perverted way, I enjoyed doing it.

Sometimes she'd bite back and we'd bawl at each other. A bitter slanging match. But more often than that, she'd take it. Confounding me with her patience. Shaming me into contrition, and at those times, in wild exaggeration, I'd promise her the moon.

For the four weeks I spent most of the time in bed, Rose slept in the spare room. We never discussed it. It just happened. And I missed her warmth. Her nearness, but I didn't let her know. I noticed she was losing weight. That her face looked unusually pale with black hollows beneath her eyes.

The first morning the doctor said I was well enough to go out, I dressed myself with extra care and went downstairs.

Rose looked me up and down.

"You look fine," she said quietly. "Are you going to make that appointment at the clinic? I've got the letter from Doctor Simpson."

"It'll keep," I told her. "Sure I look okay?"

She nodded.

"Where are you going then?" she wanted to know.

"I'm going down to see old Cleaver at the club," I explained. "Just before Christmas he told me he knew of a job that might suit me if I could hang on 'til the end of January. Well, it's nice timing isn't it?"

"What kind of a job?" she asked dubiously.

"I don't know much about it," I confessed. "Something in an office. It's a boat building firm at Hamble. No harm in trying is there? It would be nice and handy."

"If you're sure you feel up to it."

"I'm sure," I said, and drew her close. The smell of her hair warm and sweet in my nostrils. I kissed her tenderly, but she didn't respond.

Releasing her, I looked hard into her eyes.

"Everything's going to be all right. You'll see," I said. "I'll make it on my own, without the help of any trick cyclist."

There were tears in her eyes.

"Take care of yourself won't you," she whispered huskily.

"You mean, lay off the booze," I smiled. "I'll take it easy, I promise you. It's all part of the new Mark Stevens."

"Mark," she repeated solemnly. "Funny, I never think of you by that name. It's nice. Sort of different."

"I'm telling you, I'm a nice, different, decent sort of chap," I grinned. "Well, I'd better get going."

"Good luck then," she murmured, and reaching up, kissed me solemnly on the cheek.

Well, I got the job. Storekeeper at Daley's, a shipbuilding firm on the Hamble river, making lifeboats under Admiralty contract.

I didn't like the incessant noise of the saw outside the small, dingy office behind the timber store where I spent most of the day, but the money wasn't bad, and the job not too exacting, and I had no one breathing down my neck.

Most important, I had a weekly pay packet to take home to Rose, receiving back from her a small amount of pocket money that left little margin for more than an occasional drink at the club.

I felt good, and after a couple of months, I began to believe we would make it.

CHAPTER TWELVE

The war in Europe was in its final stage. The leaders of the allied nations had met at Yalta to discus the coup de grace, and now the British and American forces were advancing across France into Germany, while on the eastern front the Russians were fighting their way into Berlin. On the way, they had already overrun the notorious Auschwitz concentration camp where thousands of Jews had been murdered as part of the Fuhrer's plan to annihilate all Europe's Jews. As it turned out, there were many such camps, each bearing witness to the obscene crimes carried out by German guards.

Soon the war would end. It would be time for the licking of wounds. For rebuilding. Streets. Cities. Nations. Lives! My life. My life with Rose.

My head still gave me hell at times but Simpson's tablets seemed to be keeping things under control and the letter for Doctor Eddison remained behind the clock on the sitting room mantelshelf.

Rose was happy again, and so was I. The early months of 1945 were amongst the most contented I shared with her. I began to work on the music. Writing bits in here and there. Fingering out the simple melodies.

I remember one evening as I played around with the notes, I heard her humming the melody.

"That's pretty," she said. "Did you write it?"

She came over to the piano. Stood behind me with her arm round my shoulders.

"It's one of a dozen or more we were compiling for a tutor for beginners," I told her. "This is only the air. The left hand accompaniment has to be written in. I can do that, but I can't play it..."

I held up my left arm.

"If you can write it, we can always get someone else to play it, can't we?" she said.

"I suppose so. It's not the same though."

"Well, at least you can hear it," she reminded me. "That man who wrote the V-sign music was deaf."

I laughed.

"That's part of Beethoven's Fifth Symphony," I told her. "And you're right. In his later life he was deaf."

"Well then..."

Yes, the first months of 1945 were good ones. I was happy enough in my job. Rose was always there when I got home. Glad to see me. Warm. Welcoming.

I wondered sometimes how she spent her days. Ribbed her about it. Asked her one day if she ever thought of getting another job.

"Why should I?" she questioned. "When we're managing all right off your pay. Besides, you're such a jealous old thing..." She broke off suddenly, her eyes dark and troubled. "Oh, Steve," she added tremulously. "Don't let's have all that ugliness again. Ever! No more harping back. From now on it's just you and me."

I was content. Began to look forward instead of back. And I thought a lot about Arthur and Mrs Ryan. Felt guilty about losing touch. They had been there for me when I most needed someone. I could understand what he thought about Rose - especially after knowing Cora - but Rose was my choice, and surely not a reason for breaking a friendship which had been so close?

And Mrs Ryan - Mum. I should have answered her letters. Let her know what was happening to me and that whatever Arthur had told her, things were turning out all right for Rose and me. The Ryans were the only people I could remember without bitterness when recollection took me back to that other April day at Sandworth.

Procrastination! April! How the weeks were rolling by! Momentous things were happening in the world. The end of the war in sight. The death of President Roosevelt. Tito became the leader of Yugoslavia. Italian partisans captured and killed Mussolini, who had been Hitler's chief ally.

Soon, everything would settle down. The Americans had only to bring the Japs into line, and we could all concentrate on making a success of the peace that would follow.

One day soon, I decided, I would write to Arthur. Let him

know that sometimes the crumbs from the table could provide a Byzantine feast for a man who had known starvation!

Perhaps we could get together to celebrate when the war ended. And I WAS happy with Rose. I wanted him to know that. Where was he now I wondered and what were his future plans. Would he stay in the Service? Make it his career?

And then as if my very thoughts triggered into action my own particular malevolent nemesis, three weeks later, just before lunch on a Friday when I had handed the men their pay packets, an Admiralty van drove into the yard, and I recognised the man sitting next to the driver, as a rating I'd known in the barracks.

We stood yarning together for a while, and then he said,

"Here. You were a mate of Arthur Ryan's weren't you?"

"That's right," I told him eagerly. "Is he still with the LDF?"

His face clouded.

"You haven't heard then," he said. "He was with the Audax when she went down. Struck a floating mine off Spithead, Sunday before last. All hands lost. Poor devils never knew what hit them. I saw Ryan just before she sailed. Real chuffed he was. Just got his hook up. A good mate."

I tried to speak but the words stuck in my throat. I just stood there staring sat him. Shattered. Feeling sick.

"Here - you all right?" he asked anxiously, gripping my arm. "Take it easy now. Sorry I opened my big mouth. D'you want to sit down or something?"

I shook my head. Pulled myself free of him and went back into the office. Shut the door and stood leaning against it, my body a dead weight, and my mind a vast echo chamber, repeating and repeating,

"Arthur's dead! Arthur's dead!"

Then the trembling began and my head was bursting, and I wanted a drink, desperately.

Freeman, the Manager, called to me.

"You okay, Stevens?"

I pulled open the door.

"They tell me you've had some bad news," he said quietly. "Anything I can do?"

I shook my head dumbly, muttered my thanks and went across the yard to my car. Drove over to the 'Swan'.

In the bar, half a dozen yard hands were drinking with Bill Potter the Foreman. Eating hot pies. Exchanging bawdy stories, their laughter filling the small room.

"Come on over, Steve," Potter called, catching sight of me. "Don't just stand there. It's my birthday. I'm in the chair and you're wasting good drinking time.

Maybe company was what I needed then. A buffer between me and my thoughts.

I sat there drinking until closing time. Drank until my grief turned to anger, and the numbness passed, and I seethed. Wanting to hit back. To destroy!

My mood was black when I returned to the office, and when, a little later, one of the yard hands came in with a bottle of black market scotch, I gave him what was left in my wage packet.

A small enough price for oblivion! Only the clamour in my brain wouldn't be silenced. I couldn't shut it out. The whining of the saw, the noise and the hurt!

They say I went berserk. I remember shouting. The shriek of my own voice above everything. I remember rushing at the shelves. Sweeping them clean. Sending the bins of shackles and thimbles crashing to the floor. Treading them. Tearing at chains and wire ropes. Hurling them in all directions. Falling over them, and just vaguely, I remember the instant the whole metal framework supporting the bins, caved in on top of me, pinning me to the ground, but I felt nothing.

They dragged me from the wreckage and took me to the hospital. I was lucky they said. Nothing broken, but they kept me in over night, and the next morning Rose brought a taxi and took me home. No recriminations. Just silence even when I told her about Arthur.

At what point of strain does a heart break? Perhaps mine broke then, or did I just give up the struggle? Maybe, as Rose said, there never was any real struggle in me. Just that festering sore of discontent and bitterness round which the pattern of my life was woven.

A memory of grief and pain to which I clung, not because it had torn my heart out, but because it had become a whipping block for all that followed. An excuse. A refuge. A chosen masochism round which I whimpered when things got tough.

Well, reasons don't matter now. What's done is over, and in the way of things, it's too late to see things straight.

Too late for Rose. No chance to tell her that at last I see myself as I really am. A heel. A prinking hypocrite. A pimp not worthy to lick her shoes. What right had I to condemn her? At least she was honest, and what she was, well, I was to blame for that! Pulled her out of her whoredom with high sounding phrases. Sanctimoniously had the nerve to make her think I was doing her a favour by marrying her, and then, when she'd proved she could rise above it, I kicked her back in the muck, pretending not to notice when she sold her body to keep my rotten soul alive!

I was pretty much bruised after the affair at the yard. And that wasn't all. I began to see things. Ugly things. Distorted. Frightening. Not only in my dreams, but as I lay there with Rose sitting beside the bed. Odd shapes billowing in the air, and I'd shout and scream, and thresh about in terror.

Yes, Rose was there. Soothing, quiet voiced. Her hand on my head, restraining me. I'd grasp at her wrist, entreating her not to leave me, and her face would disappear and I'd see my mother, my father and a hundred nameless things. Leering, jeering horrible things.

The doctor came often, sticking needles into me. Talking in quiet, solemn tones to Rose. Sometimes, Mrs Alcott would be there, sitting in the armchair, knitting. The sound of her needles clicking ominously as the ghouls of the past, and the nightmare shapes crowded round me.

I had a couple of weeks of that, then gradually, the visions receded. I felt calmer, cooler, and very weak.

One morning I opened my eyes to see Rose huddled in a chair beside me, her cheeks pale and pinched.

"Rose," I murmured, "I'd like a cup of tea."

She was up in an instant. Leaning over me.

"All right, dear," she said quietly. "Are you feeling a little better?"

"I suppose so," I muttered. "Given you a bit of a scare haven't I?"

"You didn't do yourself a lot of good. Oh, Steve! What am I going to do with you?"

She sat on the bed, looking at me earnestly. I stroked her arm. Tried to find words. Words to tell her of the shame I was feeling. The guilt. But when the words came, they were in the old mould. Evading blame.

"If it's not one thing it's another," I muttered. "When am I going to get a break?"

"That's up to you," she said, her voice suddenly tense. "It's no use talking about it until you're up and about again, but what good did it do? Drinking yourself stupid! Doing all that damage! Losing a good job!"

"It was Arthur. Hearing about him like that!" I told her. "There was something between him and me you'd never understand. I'd been thinking about him. About making things right between us. I was going to write. Let him know that things were working out okay for you and me..."

"Are they?" she broke in bitterly. "My God, Steve! What will it take to open your eyes? Something's got to be done - and soon! I can't go on like this!"

I gripped her arm tightly.

"Don't talk like that, Rose," I said urgently. "You're my wife. You're all I've got. The only one left in the whole bloody world!"

Impatiently she pulled herself away from me and stood up.

"Got a theory about that, Steve?" she asked harshly. "Only the good die young."

"That's not funny," I muttered, and fell into a morose silence.

"It wasn't meant to be." Her voice was flat and deliberate. "It's always you. You! You! No one else is allowed to have feelings! Well, I'm not going to take much more," and leaving me, she ran downstairs.

I suppose that was the beginning of the end of Rose and me. Perhaps that's when she stopped trying to be what I wanted her to be. Stopped kidding herself that I was anything other than a washout. The time we both realised that the only common ground we'd ever shared, was sex.

Sex! The answer to everything! Arguments, depression, bitterness, all ended there. Just to touch her, feeling her immediate response, and nothing else mattered but the excitement, the frenzy, the oblivion of that single purpose.

Only once it was over, the heat of desire spent, there was nothing. Only the restlessness and frustration all over again. Simmering - boiling - flowing over in abuse and anger, to be suffocated again by the surge of desire that started the pattern all over again.

"Steve," she said one morning, "I've been meaning to tell you. I know a chap who'll give you a good price for the piano."

Anger stirred. I tried to keep calm.

"It's not for sale," I said quietly.

"I know how you feel about it," she persisted. "It being your Dad's and all that. But you've got to be practical about it. You don't really need anything to remind you of him, do you? You don't use it, and it's a shame to let it stand there doing no good to anyone when some kid could put it to good use. Besides, we need the money."

"It's not for sale," I repeated doggedly.

"Suit yourself," she said, her lips tightening. "I should have thought it'd do us more good helping to pay a few bills, than just standing there picking up dust. I mean, what use is it? You can't play it."

"Perhaps I never could," I muttered. "You don't understand. Some have music in their fingers, but for some, it's just in the mind. Dad told me that. How it was all bottled up inside me, but never got to my fingers. Said I'd make a good teacher..."

"Taking you long enough to work round to that one," she sneered.

I thrust out my arms.

"How d'you think a kid would react to these?" I demanded.

"Better than you do," she retorted. "Kids accept that sort of thing. Maybe because they don't understand what it's all about. It's you who's making hard going of it. If you want to teach the piano and you think you can do it, why don't you do something about it? At least you can try! There's a woman I know. Hattie Gordon. She runs a small shop. Nearly new clothes. Does all right, what with rationing and all that. Perhaps some of her customers have kids who'd come to you, though it's not the best time I suppose, with so many kids being evacuated. Anyway, I'll ask her. Can't do any harm."

"It's an idea," I said thoughtfully. "I'll need to polish up. Haven't given much thought to teaching music in the last few years."

"Well there's no time like the present," she told me. "Start thinking about something constructive. It might as well be music. You're always harping on about it. I'm going to get some bread. I'll have a word with Hattie while I'm down at the shop."

When she'd gone, I sat down at the piano looking at the keyboard. Looked at my hands. It was true what Rose said. What use was a piano to a man who'd lost his fingers?

With a sigh, I closed the lid. Opened up the stool and took out the music Dad had left there. He'd been more prophetic than he knew when he said it would never reach my fingers. It was certain enough now.

I began to brood again. Opened a copy of Chopin's Ballads. Reading it like a book. The melodies sad and haunting in my brain. Hurting! My God! How they hurt! I put the book down. Tortured by melody. By chords that tore at my heart!

Took up a manuscript Dad had been working on. Simple accompaniments for beginners. I could finish them. As Rose said, someone could play them for me.

I tried to get interested, but the loneliness of the house irritated me, and after a little while, I left it, and went down to the Club and sat there playing cards.

At the end of April I did start looking for another job, but half-heartedly. Making excuses. Exaggerating the snags, amplifying the pain in my head. Staying in bed on the least pretext.

And after a while, Rose stopped nagging me. She'd lost a lot of weight, and her eyes, enormous in her thin cheeks, eternally reproached me.

I whispered promises. Went to the Labour Exchange. Actually began a series of jobs. In offices. Factories. Only in the offices, the walls seemed to close in on me. Suffocating. Unbearable. And there was the way the others looked at me, with that sickly mixture of revulsion and pity that made my short hairs rise. At those times, the pain in my head was really bad and I had a job to keep my anger under restraint.

In the factories there was the incessant noise and the same airlessness, choking me. With men and women, walls and machines bearing down on me until I had to get out.

I tried to explain it to Rose and to the chaps I met at the club and at the local. Explain or justify? Maybe that was it.

Why not admit that I enjoyed the days between jobs. Days when I stayed in bed until noon. Ambled down the road for a drink. Made up to Rose after our mid-day meal. Stretched out on the settee for the afternoon. Reading. Listening to the radio. Leisurely. Lazy!

An evening visit to the club. Yarning. A couple of drinks then home to Rose. Lying close to her in the darkness. Silencing her rebukes with kisses. Stifling the harsh shouting with caresses, until nothing else mattered to either of us.

On the ninth of May, the day after VE day, as the vast crowds gathered to celebrate in Whitehall, the end of the war in Europe, Rose brought Hattie Gordon to the house.

Until then, she had been only a name to me. Hattie was a bit of a hag. Fat and bloated looking. Over made up. A synthetic blonde with a perpetual cigarette hanging on her lips. But she was in the money all right. Her podgy fingers heavy with diamonds, and each time she opened her bulky handbag, she made a great show of churning up the roll of bank notes inside.

Yes, she was doing nicely. A secondhand clothes dealer, with a bit of dressmaking on the side - amongst other things. Only then, I didn't know about the room at the back of the shop.

"Nice little place you've got here," Hattie said expansively, as Rose introduced us. "Rose looks after you all right, eh, Steve?"

"I've no complaints," I told her.

She cocked her head knowingly.

"Had a bit of a rough time haven't you?" she went on sympathetically. "Lousy rotten wars! It's always the folk like you and me who get the dirty end of the stick. The High Ups who lead us into them, always seem to come out smelling of roses. Don't hear of many of them being maimed and killed, and their houses being blown to Kingdom Come, now do you?"

"That's true enough," I agreed.

"Well, at least the war in Europe is over," she declared brightly. "And I can't see the Japs going on much longer."

"Oh I don't know," put in Rose seriously, as she brought in cups of tea. "I mean - there are so many of them aren't there? And they don't seem to mind about getting killed. It's a special kind of glory for them to die in battle, isn't it?"

"It'll end soon," I put in vaguely. "It's a question of economics. So much money. So much blood, only for a few of us it can never really end, can it?"

"Then we just have to count our blessings, don't we?" Hattie replied. "Be grateful we're alive. There's always some poor devil a lot worse off. Look at you now. Nice little home. Attractive wife..."

"And how long d'you think it's going to stay that way on a bloody cripple's pension?" I demanded in a sudden burst of anger.

"Oh, something will turn up for you," Hattie said soothingly. "It all takes time. Stands to reason, doesn't it? You've got to have time to come to terms with yourself."

"And what do we live on in the meantime?"

"Hattie's offered me a job," Rose put in eagerly. "Helping in the shop. You wouldn't mind that, would you, Steve?"

"If that's what you want," I told her. "Doing plenty of business down there, are you, Hattie?"

"I'm not grumbling," she said. "I've got a good connection, and you can always sell top quality stuff, even without clothes rationing."

"Secondhand clothes have always been good for a living though, haven't they?" Rose added. "A lot of people would rather buy them than some shoddy new article, and now, with coupons and all..."

She shot a quick look at Hattie, left the words in the air, and I said thoughtfully.

"Should have thought it would be quite a job getting hold of the stock these days."

"Oh, I've got a lot of useful contacts," Hattie assured me, winking solemnly, "and one or two little sidelines to help things along. You know. Nylons. Odd bits of parachute material we make up into undies. Got hold of a nice lot of Service blankets. They make up into quite glamorous housecoats when they're dyed, and you can always sell a bit of coupon free glamour!"

"Good for you," I applauded. "You'll be all right among that lot, Rose - so long as you don't blow all your wages on Lady Whatsit's mink or something!"

"No fear of that," Rose said dryly. "We need the money."

A moment of uneasy silence, then Hattie put in lightly,

"Who doesn't? Don't you worry yourself, Steve. I'll look after Rose. It'll help things along a bit until you're feeling fit to cope."

"Yes," I muttered. "It sounds okay."

"Well, that's settled then," she said. "Come on now, Steve! Don't look so glum about it. Rose has told me all about you. You've had a rough time. There's no discredit in letting her take care of things for the time being, now is there She was telling me about your music..."?

She broke off suddenly, and getting up, went over to the piano and sat down on the stool.

"Rosewood," she said admiringly. "Lovely." She lifted the lid, ran her fingers over the keyboard. "Nice tone too. Been kept well tuned."

And then she started to play, and the rising resentment I felt, disappeared as her chubby fingers caressed the keys and the haunting strains of a Chopin ballad filled the room. Then she stopped abruptly and turned to look at me.

"I'm not much good without the music," she said. "Mind if I have a look at some of the things you're working on?"

"You're sitting on them," I told her, getting up. "They're mostly just melodies. No accompaniments. The idea was to compose pieces for children's tutors. Beginners, intermediaries, and advanced. They're all sketched out, but they need a lot of work to complete them."

I got out the manuscripts. Warmed to Hattie's interest. Took in her comments - her suggestions.

"You play really well, Hattie," I told her, as running through some of the melodies my father and I had arranged, she picked up the book of Chopin's music and, at my request, played one of his nocturns.

"Thank you," she smiled. "I must confess, I like to play. It relaxes me. Can't say I'm very taken with this modern stuff though."

"Nor me," I said eagerly. "You must come round here and play sometimes."

She beamed.

"Look forward to it," she told me. "And you, get to work on finishing those tutors. One of my customers has a contact in the publishing world. Don't know if it's music, but I can find out for you."

I was grateful to her. For restoring my interest in music - for giving Rose a job, and at first, everything seemed all right. Rose would go off about nine o'clock in the morning, return for a couple of hours at lunchtime, then go back to the shop until early evening.

Almost from the beginning, I was aware of a change in her attitude towards me. No longer did she nag and harangue me to go out and look for a job. Instead, she encouraged me to take things easy. To relax, cosseted with cigarettes and drinks, and paperbacks to read. Coaxed me to help out with the household chores.

I had money in my pocket. Time to spare, and it suited me.

In August, the war in Japan came to its macabre end when Hiroshima disappeared under a blanket of atomic dust, and with the Allies and the Russians growling over the bones of Berlin, an uneasy peace began.

Sometimes I toyed with Dad's music. Making it a facade of promise to bolster up my ego when the truth threatened to strip me of all pretence.

Hattie came more often to the house. Sometimes she came alone. Sometimes with a few friends.

I welcomed her.

"Hello, Steve," she'd say. "We've been having a bit of a party. Thought we'd come along and keep you company. Have a bit of a sing-song. Do you good. Can't leave a good man stagnating, can we?"

I enjoyed the breezy companionship. Laughing, drinking, singing. Not even resenting Hattie's fat little fingers beating hell out of the piano when we'd all had too much to drink, and the singing grew bawdier.

I don't know when I first began to wonder if Rose was back on the game. All the signs were there from the beginning I suppose. She looked different. Harder. Brazen even, and there was something in the way she carried herself. Sensuous. Inviting. Cheap.

And there were other things. Things she used in the toilet. Long sessions in the bathroom. The smells of disinfectant and cheap perfume.

I'd lie in bed waiting for her. Sweating like a pig. Bitter and seething. Working up to a showdown.

Then she'd come to me. Glowing. Her hair loose. Provocative. Lovely. Clean, and all the anger melted away as she climbed in beside me. Her eyes dark and hungry with wanting me.

I told myself I was wrong about her. The lie made me feel better. I didn't want to know. Life was good, and too easy.

Once a week I went down to Doctor Simpson's surgery for a check-up.

"You know," he said one day as he finished examining me. "I wish I could persuade you to see Doctor Eddison."

"What for?" I asked. "I'm not ready for the nut house yet."

He shook his head.

"Frankly," he said quietly. "I'm not happy about these headaches of yours."

"Nor me," I assured him, "but plenty of people suffer from migraine, don't they? Someone told me there's no known cure."

"All headaches aren't classified as migraine," he reminded me. "I'd like to know more about yours. Apart from that, how do you feel generally?"

I frowned. Shrugged vaguely.

"Not too bad I suppose," I told him. "Don't seem to have much energy. Feel tired all the time. Sort of flaked out. And another thing. I seem to run on a very short fuse."

He seemed puzzled.

"Lose my temper very easily," I explained. "You know. Go off at the deep end."

"You're not working?"

"No," I said shortly. "Don't feel up to it. Fortunately, my wife's got a good job. There's something I'm working on at home. I can rest..."

"Mr Stevens," he broke in emphatically. "Rest isn't the answer. We want to know the reason for this abnormal fatigue - this irrational temper. Believe me. It's important."

"I'm due at Greenleas in a couple of weeks," I reminded him. "Let it ride until then."

He was right. I knew it. The feeling of perpetual tiredness worried me. And the way I got het up with the slightest provocation. I tried to persuade myself that it was the natural reaction from having too much time on my hands. That too much ease was too relaxing, but the insidious lassitude was disturbing, the fatigue unnatural because when I went to bed, my sleep was shallow. Fretful. I would doze only fleetingly, and wake sweating and afraid of nameless things.

At those times I'd grope out for Rose. Clutching her to me. Entreating her never to leave me, and her arms would tighten round me. Reassuring. Safe. And there was the other side of the coin. When an ill chosen word from her would send me into a frenzy of anger. I'd lash out at her. Hate myself afterwards and descend into a snivelling wretch as I begged her forgiveness and swore it would never happen again. But of course it did!

And then on the morning I started off for Greenleas, I dropped in at the post office to pick up the local paper and my pension, and met one of the club stewards on my way out.

We stood on the pavement yarning for awhile and then, just as I was about to leave him, Hattie came hurrying towards us, greeting me cheerfully as she turned into the shop.

My companion winked knowingly as she disappeared from

sight.

"Bit of a dark horse then are you!" he declared grinning. "I didn't figure you for one of Ma Gordon's patrons!"

"What's that supposed to mean?" I asked him. "This is my demob suit..."

He laughed.

"Come off it, Steve!" he scoffed. "I wasn't talking about her clothes shop. What about the handy little knocking shop she runs at the back then? See 'em lining up like flies some afternoons! Cars, taxis, pushbikes - the lot! And all to see a tatty little blonde and a busty redhead who've never heard of meat rationing!"

He grinned knowingly, spat on the pavement, patted me on the shoulder, pushing me on my way.

I shivered. Felt clammy, and my head was a big balloon inside which my thoughts were vacuumed - frozen.

I went back to the car, and all the way to Greenleas, I hummed to myself, ditties from Gilbert and Sullivan. Concentrating on the words. Shutting out everything else.

The routine examination seemed to take longer than usual, and when it was over, Doctor Reynolds asked a lot of questions. About my head. The jobs I'd had, and why I'd left them. And what I thought about when I was alone.

"Nothing really," I told him. "Nothing in particular. What difference does it make anyway?"

"Mr Stevens," he said solemnly. "Physically you're in pretty good shape. So far as I can see there is no reason why you shouldn't have settled down to a near normal way of life. Got yourself a job..."

He broke off. Stared at me intently. Waiting for me to speak, but I had nothing to say to him. I avoided his eyes, and he walked away from me.

"Is something troubling you?" he asked abruptly.

"What do you think?" I answered irritably, holding out my arms.

He shook his head.

"We both know that's not the answer," he said quietly. "I've got a letter from Doctor Simpson. He wants me to persuade you to go to the Neurological Clinic."

"I know," I told him shortly. "Psychiatric wing."

"Well, what's wrong with that?" he asked rationally. "Your headaches are getting worse. Showing signs of increasing lassitude and inertia. Making hard work of rehabilitation. You tell me you can't stand confined places. That you're subject to unreasonable bouts of bad temper. It's outside my province to be able to help you. I can only advise you to go..."

"Don't tell me that every patient who complains of a headache is going round the bend," I cut in churlishly.

"You've got the wrong idea," he told me patiently. "Recommending psychiatric treatment doesn't necessarily consign you to a padded cell. Mental and physical health are interwoven. One is dependent on the other. Your headaches and the rest of your symptoms could well be caused by psychological stresses of which you yourself are unaware. Psychiatry can go a long way towards alleviating those stresses."

"It can't change anything that's happened," I muttered.

"It doesn't seek to," he replied. "It's purpose is primarily the relief of emotional tensions. Releasing repressed memories..."

"You're barking up the wrong tree," I grated, getting to my feet. "There's nothing repressed about my memories. They never sleep. Never leave me. My mother was a whore and they hanged my father for her murder. I have to live with that. Every day of my life I have to live with it!"

He looked shocked.

"That's quite a load to carry around," he said gravely. "But..."

"Oh, that's only half of it," I interrupted bitterly. "I tried to make a new life for myself. New interests. New friends. A wife, and one by one they paid for it. Dead! Every one of them! You see, you don't tie decent people up with the son of a murderer. You teach him a lesson. Make him learn the hard way. He's a pariah. Marked for eternity! And just so that he won't forget, you destroy everyone he touches. Butcher them. Keep the memory raw. Bleeding for evermore. Pile on the guilt."

"Good heavens!" he exclaimed. "I had no idea! You say your wife is dead?"

"How could you know," I demanded savagely. "You know

nothing of Cora."

"Cora?"

He looked puzzled, and I said solemnly,

"Cora was my first wife. She was killed in an air raid - with our son."

"I'm sorry," he answered, almost lost for words. "Deeply sorry. But your present wife?"

"Rose!" I told him bitterly as the hammers began to pound in my brain. "She'll be all right. Destruction is reserved for decent people. Rose is quite safe. She's a whore you see. Like my mother!"

Something trickled down my neck. Briefly I put up a hand to wipe it away, and only then, realised I was weeping.

He busied himself at a cabinet, then handed me a glass of water and a couple of tablets.

"Here take these," he said. "Then we'll let you rest for a while. You'll be all right."

A nurse suddenly appeared.

I didn't argue. I was very tired. I let them put me on a couch and went to sleep.

Rose was already home when I returned to Bursledon.

"Hello, love," she greeted me. "I've just put the kettle on. Haven't been home long myself."

I brushed her welcoming kiss away. Felt dispirited. Weak. Went into the kitchen and washed my face under the cold tap, letting the water soak into my burning head. Then I sat down.

"Is everything all right?" Rose asked, looking at me anxiously. "You look worn out."

"Reynolds is badgering me to go to that clinic," I told her.

"Well it won't do any harm will it?" she said reasonably. "After all, they must know what they're doing."

"Suppose so," I laughed suddenly. "He asked me a hell of a lot of questions today, and d'you know what? I gave him all the answers! Answers he didn't expect! I bet the 'phone wires between Greenleas and the Neuro place have been red hot with the old Freudian theories since I left!"

She frowned.

"I don't understand. What do you mean?"

"I told him the truth," I lied. "The whole bloody truth!"

"You mean about your Sandworth?"

"Right!"

"I'm glad," she told me calmly. "It's only right the doctors should know just what's eating you. Maybe they can help you get one thing straight in your head. It wasn't your fault!"

"Now what kind of anti-Christian dogma is that?" I demanded derisively. "What about the 'sins of the fathers' and all that?"

She shifted uncomfortably.

"You're tired," she said quietly. "I'll get you some tea then you can lie down for an hour or so. Get some rest."

"That's it!" I mocked her. "Rest! Can afford to do that now, can't I. Like I told the quack. I'm lucky. My wife's got a good job. Doing what she likes. Doing what she does best!"

I saw her stiffen.

"You know then," she said uncertainly.

"But of course, my love," I returned lightly. "You're doing fine at the shop. Ma Gordon's shop!"

She walked away from me. Lit a cigarette.

"All right," she declared. "So you know. It's a job. Just a job like when I first met you. It didn't make any difference then. You still wanted me. Still came back. Now you're ill. I'm trying to make things easy for us until you..."

"Don't know what you're going on about," I broke in calmly. "You wanted to work in Hattie's shop. Okay. Leave it at that. For Christ's sake, Rose. Leave it at that!"

So I knew about her, and she knew I knew. For most of the time I was content to leave it at that.

Why not? I'd never had it so good. For weeks she turned over backwards to make things easy for me. Anything I wanted. I had only to mention it, and there it was. Delicacies to tempt the palate. Brandy. Cigarettes. Money in my pocket. And she looked after me. Cooking. Cleaning. Comforting. Always tender. Desperately eager to please.

At the beginning of November an item in the Daily Echo caught my eye. A new panel had been added to the Sandworth

War Memorial, listing the names of local men and women of the Services who had given their lives in the Second World War.

The panel was to be consecrated in the forthcoming Armistice Day Service.

The War Memorial where it all began for me! Now to be a link for me between my father and Arthur. One for shame, the other for glory! One day soon, I promised myself, I would go there again.

I let the tears come. Wallowing in misery.

My days were spent moping about the house. Working myself into a black mood of self-recrimination, and at those times I came near to loathing Rose. But I loathed her, not for what she was, but because she made me despise myself.

The rows never ceased. Developed into ugly slanging matches that brought echoes of my childhood back in dreadful cadence. Ominous parallels that made me afraid.

One morning I went downstairs to find the letter to Doctor Eddison on the kitchen table. I fingered it for a long time as I sat over breakfast. Perhaps Rose was right. Anyway I thought, I had nothing better to do. Why not put the ball in Doctor Eddison's corner!

So I went to his clinic.

"I've been hoping you'd come along, Mr Stevens," he greeted me unexpectedly,

He was a pale, earnest man. He asked me a lot of questions. Painstakingly explained some of the medical jargon, then took me along to a small, pleasant room, to join a group of a dozen men and women who were sitting round in a circle, talking together.

The talking ceased as Doctor Eddison introduced me, and I took a seat amongst them.

Group Psychotherapy they called it. Everyone letting off steam. Talking about their grievances and problems with a psychiatrist trying to analyse the significance of the various revelations.

Sort of psycho-analysis. Bit of a laugh really. Everyone trying to sound unconcerned and unembarrassed as they laid bare their skeletons in the cupboard.

Soon it was my turn. I watched the various expressions as I became the cynosure of a dozen pairs of eyes. Shocked.

Incredulous. Excited! It was all there - only I wanted to laugh.

"Discuss it," Eddison urged. "Get it all out in the open. Talk it out of your system!"

Christ! Didn't he know?

Words! Words! Words! How could an avalanche of words wash out one single deed - or the consequences?

Rose was pleased I'd made the effort. Bought a few days peace at home. I even went back a couple of times. Enjoying the attention. Curious about the others. About their problems. Amused by their simple fervour.

"Waste of time," I announced when Rose asked me about it. "My problem's simple enough. No hidden meanings. No symbolism in what happened to me. Hell! I know why and what and when. Nobody and nothing can alter that!"

"Of course they can't," she said patiently. "They won't even try. They just want to help you live with your particular devils. Help you keep them in the past - where they belong."

"The past," I repeated heavily. "Sounds remote doesn't it? Yet even as we say 'Now', the moment is already behind us. The past had swallowed it up. The past is an instant away, no more..."

I broke off. Rose was watching me curiously. A frown creasing her forehead. Concern in her eyes.

"I don't understand you when you go off like that," she said uncertainly. "I just think you should give Doctor Eddison a chance. Let yourself unwind..."

But I didn't go back. Not then. I gave myself up to the easy life Rose provided for me. Lounging around. Mentally reviling her. Psychically drenching myself in her.

Some days I'd stay in bed. Lie there, thoughts festering around Rose. Remembering that stinking room at the bottom of the stairs. Picturing another at the back of Hattie Gordon's shop.

At those times I hated her. God, how I hated her. Yet in my brooding restlessness I longed for the sound of her key in the door. Her warm presence. Reassuring. Soothing my loneliness. Dispelling the spectre of my increasing impotence.

She took it all. The insults. The recriminations.

The shouting. The blows. The maudlin tears. She took it all, and still loved me. I never doubted that.

CHAPTER THIRTEEN

The weeks slipped by. The days a kaleidoscope of light and shade that merged one into the other. Endless. Frighteningly the same. I wrote a letter to Mrs Ryan. Tried to tell her what I felt about Arthur. I made hard going of it. Aware that I'd shamefully neglected her. The weeks went by, but she didn't reply. Maybe she was too hurt about the way I had treated her. Maybe her heart was broken by the news of Arthur's death... Maybe she was dead! Why not? She was a good woman!

Rose tried hard with me. But she couldn't reach me. Not anymore. I'd begun to take stock. Admitted to myself that she was my meal ticket. Nothing more.

I lazed around the house brooding. Had my fill in the pub to ease the turmoil in my head. The nightmares had started again. Rose and my mother. Forces of evil against me.

Rose grumbled that I disturbed her sleep. Taunted me about my conscience. How could she know! What damning indictment had my nocturnal ravings revealed!

I took to sleeping in the spare bedroom.

"You look awful," she greeted me one morning. "It's not doing you any good being on your own all day. You need something to occupy your mind. A little job..."

"I know what I need," I interrupted churlishly, "and as soon as I feel fit enough..."

I saw her look of contempt and lapsed into silence. Yes. In my own time I *would* look for something. For myself. To escape the twilight world that had enmeshed me. Freedom. Space to breathe.

As the days passed I watched Rose coarsen. Noticed the changed timbre of her voice when she spoke to me. How she soon became irritated, impatient, contemptuous. We exchanged insults. Nothing more, and suddenly, we were back to the long silences. They got on my nerves. Resentfully, I turned on her.

"What brought this on?" I demanded. "It's bad enough sitting on my own all day without having to spend the evenings with a bloody dummy!"

"You've got a remedy for both," she flashed back at me. "Get yourself off your backside in the morning, and find yourself a job!"

"So that's it!" I fumed. "Want me out of the house do you! Bad for business eh? You're singing a different tune these days aren't you? For weeks you been drumming it into me. Rest! Take it easy..."

"That's right," she interrupted me. "For weeks! Too many weeks! Weeks of waiting and hoping you'd turn out to be a man!"

I spluttered for words.

"Dammit, Rose! That's a rotten thing to say. What the hell can I do? They haven't discharged me from the clinic yet!"

"God Almighty!" she cried incredulously. "If you haven't got some nerve! You haven't been near the bloody clinic for weeks!"

"I haven't felt like it," I mumbled. "What's the use anyway? All that talk, talk, talk, and listening to other people's troubles. If you ask me, it's nothing but a waste of time."

"Oh stop it," she said wearily. "Sometimes you make me sick..."

The rows became more frequent. More bitter. More lasting. No longer did we share the warm sweet flame of reconciliation. No more could we discuss the future rationally. No pretense of love. The times of closeness were over. We no longer believed in each other.

She didn't understand that I really wasn't up to taking on a job. She didn't know how I felt. How my head played me up. At times almost driving me crazy. I needed time. I had to have time.

But time didn't help. The changes it brought grew uglier.

Rose began to talk openly of her life at the shop. Coarse, crude talk. Mocking me. Baiting me until the urge to silence that shrill, soul-destroying voice was almost unbearable.

And she'd stand there, defiant, daring me to lay hands on her. Taunting me with my father. I'd shudder and shake, somehow subduing my anger. Fear constraining me as, oh God, I groaned silently, let me find the strength to get out before my life goes full circle.

It must have been a month ago, that last day Hattie Gordon came home with Rose.

Rose was wearing a synthetic leopard skin coat draped casually across her shoulders and beneath it, a dress I hadn't seen before.

The skirt too short. The bodice sheath tight, forcing her breasts high. Voluptuous mounds above the neckline.

Looking what she was. It was there in every sexy flaunting inch of her.

"Come on in, Hattie," she invited, kicking off her stiletto heeled shoes. "Christ! This corn's killing me!"

I stared at her distastefully.

"Have you walked down the road in that outfit?" I demanded.

She looked surprised.

"I should hope so," she said with a laugh. "Cause a bit of a stir if I'd come home without it! I'd probably have been arrested!"

"What's wrong with it?" Hattie piped in. "Let a woman look like a woman I say! You see enough of the other sort these days. All these uniforms and that! You ought to think yourself lucky, Steve..."

"You keep out of this," I rasped at her. "Dammit, Rose! You don't have to hawk your wares right on our own doorstep - In front of the whole bloody neighbourhood!"

Her eyes widened.

"You hypocrite!" she blazed. "You don't mind me being a tart so long as it keeps you on easy street, and you don't see me at it!"

"Why don't you leave her alone," Hattie put in. "Just be thankful you've got a girl like Rose to work for you and..."

"Shut up you old cow!" I roared.

"Why you rotten pimp," she shouted. "You don't know when you're well off. If you take my tip, Rose, you'll get shot of him. Get him certified! He's not right..."

"Oh get lost, Hattie," Rose put in hastily as I took a threatening step forward. "It's none of your business, and you've no right to talk to Steve like that."

"Well, I like that!" Hattie declared indignantly. "If it wasn't for me..."

"Beat it," Rose said witheringly. "I don't owe you anything. You've done all right out of me!"

"I'm not the only one," the other answered viciously, looking at me. "Only I'm honest about it. I tell you, Rose, you'd be better off without this snivelling humbug. To tell you the truth I can't make up my mind whether he's barmy or just plain cunning! Either way, he's not worth a light, and one of these days he'll do you a mischief if he doesn't hold that temper of his in check."

"I told you to shut up," Rose said sharply. "You've said enough. You'd better go. This is between me and Steve."

With a last baleful glance at me, Hattie moved towards the door.

"I'll see you tomorrow then," she said uncertainly.

Rose eyed me.

"No," she answered. "I won't be working at the shop anymore. The time has come to make changes to my life."

With a shake of the head, Hattie let herself out.

"Well, that's that," Rose announced quietly. "Maybe she's right. I'd be better off without you. I'm going upstairs to change, then you and I are going to have a talk."

I watched her run up the stairs, leopard coat trailing. The sweat was rising. I trembled, suddenly afraid.

It was some time before she came down again. Perched herself on the settee and lit a cigarette.

Her face was a mask that told me nothing.

"One thing's certain," she said abruptly. "We can't go on like this. It's no use to either of us."

"I won't argue with that," I muttered. "I don't know what I'd have done without you."

"All water under the bridge," she said sharply. "I'll tell you straight, Steve, I've taken about all I can from you. You've got one option now. Tomorrow morning you go to see Doctor Eddison at the clinic, and you'll keep on going there until he's sorted you out. If you won't do that for me, we're through, and I don't care where you go. Maybe you should go back to Mrs Ryan. Anyway, I mean it. Get yourself sorted or we're finished."

"And you said you'd never leave me!" I murmured archly, attempting to be flippant.

"We've both said a lot of things," she said with a sigh. "You've got one more chance to make them stick. It's up to you."

She got up abruptly, and went into the kitchen to prepare a meal.

I stared after her moodily. This was no time for apologies and empty promises. I recognised the strength of her ultimatum. There was no other way of getting round her this time. But I had to play along. There would be a time to break free.

So I started at the clinic again. Went there regularly. Suffered the group therapy. Venting my bouts of anger, frustration and despair on the staff and on the other patients, until a couple of weeks ago, Doctor Eddison said he wanted me to go in for a while as a voluntary patient.

Said he wasn't satisfied with the progress I was making. Wanted me in for an x-ray and other tests.

I didn't like the idea. The thought of going in among mentally disturbed patients worried me. Suppose I couldn't get out again!

That the experience really sent me round the bend? Maybe it was some kind of trick to get me committed! An easy way for Rose to get rid of me!

When I discussed it with her, she was all for it and it didn't make me feel any easier when she told me she had talked to Doctor Simpson about it.

Simpson had told her about an operation, a leucotomy, which was sometimes performed to relieve severe mental tension. Something to do with surgical manipulation of certain nerve fibres in the brain. Altered the personality. Rose was pretty vague about it, so I went to see Simpson to find out for myself. Basically, what Rose had told me was right, but apparently it was an operation only performed as a last resort, and in extreme cases. And yes, in some cases things could go wrong.

"I don't know what you've been cooking up," I said wrathfully, returning home to Rose. "If you think you're going to turn me into a bloody zombie."

"Oh don't be so silly!" she interrupted me. "It's not going to come to that. It was in a book I read and I was interested. I asked Doctor Simpson about it that's all. It's something that's only done in extreme cases. The cure for your trouble is mostly in your own hands."

"Then why does Eddison want me in?"

"It's better to keep you under constant observation while they carry out the necessary tests," she said. "And it's only for a week or so."

"Sure of that are you?"

"No. I'm not, Steve, but I am sure of one thing. Anything that helps us make a life together, is worth trying. Oh Steve! I do want this to work for both our sakes. Doctor Simpson did tell me they're working on some revolutionary techniques that have been very successful in the States."

She came to me and, for the first time in weeks, cuddled me. Holding me close, and I murmured into her hair,

"All right. I'll give it a go. You'd better pack my gear, and I'll telephone Eddison, and tell him he's got himself a guinea pig."

Last night was a restless one. I lay in the darkness, prey to morbid thoughts, listening to Rose humming to herself as she came out of the bedroom and prepared for bed.

She'd certainly had the rotten end of the stick so far as our marriage was concerned. What had I contributed? Damn all! Unstintingly, she'd given me all she had to give. Borne the brunt of my moods, frustrations, insults and physical abuse - because she loved me! There was no doubting that. But had her feelings changed? Mine had. I'd never attempted to analyse what I felt for her. Been satisfied that she was there for whatever purpose I needed her. Now, I wanted rid of her.

Low life! That was me! No real contrition...

This morning, uneasy and tense, I listened to her singing as she finished packing my bag.

"Makes you happy does it?" I asked abruptly. "My going away."

"Yes it does," she said brightly. "Because you're doing something sensible at last."

"I want to go to Sandworth on my way," I told her. "I've been meaning to go for some time. Just like to pay my respects to Arthur..."

"The War Memorial," she frowned. "Are you sure that's a good idea? I mean... your father... D'you want to bring all those memories back again?"

"Can't bring back what's already there," I said. "Besides, if Eddison's going to work miracles, it'll be the last time won't it?

Anyway, I owe it to Arthur. If I'd had any guts I'd have gone to the consecration ceremony."

"You know best," she answered. "Anyway, I hope everything goes well at the clinic. 'Phone me and let me know what's happening and I'll see you soon."

"You won't be able to visit," I reminded her. "They don't allow visitors during the course."

"I know," she said. "But it won't be long before you're home again."

She kissed me warmly and stood in the doorway to see me off. It was twelve o'clock when I left the house, spent half an hour at the club, got my hair cut, and started off for Sandworth.

I had only gone a mile or so when I remembered Dad's manuscript folio. I had made up my mind to take it with me. There'd be plenty of time to work on it. Study it. Put some of my ideas into practise. Maybe I'd be able to surprise Rose with something really worth while.

Something practical. Something to prove I was trying...

Resolutely, I turned the car round and went back. And then, as I parked in a space a few yards from our house, I saw a man come out. He paused a moment, adjusted his dark glasses, and with a swift glance to left and right, hurried to get into a car parked on the other side of the road, and drove away. I wondered about him. Recognising him as a character I'd seen around the town and in the local pubs.

Suddenly, the hammers were pounding my head again. A clammy coldness spread over me. Surely Rose... the thought choked me... My vision clouded. I stumbled out of the car. Reached the front door and let myself in.

Rose was in the kitchen, lifting a bowl of hot water from the sink as I went in.

"Steve!" she exclaimed in astonishment. "What are you doing here?"

The bowl jerked from her hand sending a shower of water in all directions. Hurriedly she clutched at the gaping cotton robe that was all she wore. Fingered her neck, trying to hid the tell-tail marks. Shook back her dishevelled hair.

"You dirty, rotten tramp!" I ground out. "Had it all lined up did you?"

Her eyes narrowed. She stared hard at me, trying to weigh up the extent of my anger.

"Oh come off it, Steve," she said lightly. "You can't pretend things don't happen because they're not under your nose. I've never pretended. I am what I am..."

"You could hardly wait for me to get out of the house..."

"Well, what do you expect?" she demanded defiantly. "I've got to live haven't I? How am I supposed to manage?"

"Bringing them here," I said hoarsely. "Letting them come into our home! That's what you meant when you told Hattie you wouldn't be working at the shop! God..."

"Don't let's get maudlin!" she broke in impatiently, "Have you forgotten how we got this house?"

I looked at the crumpled bank notes on the table and she snatched them up.

"Five quid!" she shouted triumphantly. "He wasn't here more than fifteen minutes. That's twenty quid an hour! Can your pride afford to give up that kind of money? You know bloody well it can't."

The words had a familiar ring. I'd heard them before. Crouched trembling as a child.

My head was ballooning. Heard her laughing. I closed my eyes. When I opened them again it wasn't Rose I saw but my mother. Laughing as she always laughed. Taunting. Maddening...

With a wild cry I struck out at that hated face again and again.

Shook her like a rag doll then thrust her savagely away from me. Near naked, she sprawled against the wall blood running from her mouth. Shaking, dripping sweat, I glared down at her, and as suddenly as it had come, the frenzy left me. For a moment panic gripped me and the room was spinning. I clung to the table to stop myself falling. A distorted kaleidoscope of bodies tumbled in my brain. Hallucinations. Disorientation. And then I could see that still figure at my feet was Rose. Not my mother. Rose! Her face bloodied. Livid weals at her throat. All the time I was hitting her she'd never uttered a word. Never reproached. Never accused, and now, oh God! She was dead.

In the uncanny silence, I held my breath. And then as I staggered to my feet someone pressed the front door bell. Another client... ? I breathed in deeply, striving to control my trembling limbs, then closing the kitchen door behind me, went out into the hall. Fumbled the front door open to find Ralph Allcott standing there with a bundle in his arms.

"Mum sent the curtains," he announced. "Shall I bring them inside?"

"Thanks," I mumbled, indicating a chair in the hall. "Put them on there will you."

"Thought you were going away today," he said conversationally,

"I am," I told him. "Just off as a matter of fact. I have to make a call at Sandworth. Thank your mother for the curtains. Rose'll be in to see her later."

"Out then, is she?"

"No. She's upstairs," I said shortly, walking back through the hall to the front door.

He took the hint.

"I'll be off then," he said looking at me searchingly. "You're looking pretty rough old man. Feeling okay?"

"Not one of my best days," I returned.

"Well let's hope they'll be able to fix you up at the clinic. Good luck, anyway."

I thanked him, closed the door after him and watched him through the window until he disappeared into his own house.

I hovered a while at the kitchen door, but I couldn't open it. Couldn't bring myself to look at that still, crumpled figure on the floor.

Was this the end of the line for me? Full circle? Strange that it should have ended with a scenario like that where the story of my shame began. Even the rain had come to complete the tableau. I didn't go back into the kitchen again.

Pulling on my coat I went out to the car. Set off for Sandworth. It was right that it should end where it all began. Only this time, there was no desire. No one else to take the blame. Oddly enough, it was as though a great weight had been lifted from my mind. The time had come to rid myself of the burden of shame and guilt I had carried since that morning in Lawson Street which led to the death of a good man.

And suddenly I was back in that street. In the house I had left earlier with the shouting and screaming of my parents echoing through my head. Reaching my place of work, I discovered I had left the office keys behind and my boss sent me back to get them.

The back door was open and I went in silently hoping to retrieve the keys from the kitchen dresser, and get out without seeing my parents.

The first thing that struck me was the silence. An unnatural silence. I went through to the hall. And then I saw her. My mother, sprawled half naked on the floor. Her face bruised and bloodied. Her neck swollen, but my eyes were riveted on the smooth beauty of her long bare legs and the soft mound above. The firm stretch of her stomach and the one teasing nipple escaping from the crumpled dressing gown she wore.

Was she dead? I didn't know. I didn't care. I was only aware of the longing in my loins. The overwhelming desire to ease the hard pent-up ache became intolerable. I knelt astride and took her. As relief came her head lolled over. The sightless eyes stared straight at me and her mouth was stretched in the hideous parody of a smile. The movement of her body caused air to escape from her throat and she seemed to moan as though in sympathetic climax with me. I should have tried to help her, instead I fled and sealed my father's fate. I wanted her dead.

Shame and guilt have been my constant companions locked in the dark recesses of my mind. Yes, I wanted her dead, but who was really responsible for her death. Could I have saved her? Now I'll never know.

Outside, everything seems still. Waiting. Waiting for me to start that last walk. The walk I watched my father take as he went to confess his crime.

I had to come here. There's no one to talk to but I feel strangely at peace. No-one to burden with my inheritance. No need. With me it ends. Thank God it ends.

No heir. Perhaps after all, it was a blessing my son had died. Innocent. Unsullied. Never knowing. And Cora, my lovely Cora. Accepting my lie and loving me. But would she have loved me if she'd known the truth? Would Arthur have stood by me?

I look once more at his name. Wonder whether we'll meet again. All sin washed away.

The rain has stopped. A pale watery sun brings brief life to the plaques on the walls. The glory men. Honoured. Remembered.

Outside everything is still. Waiting. Gripping my stick, I go out on to the steps. Suck in a deep breath of fresh clean air.

It's time. Time for that walk but this time the shame and the guilt will go with me.

No one left to carry the burden. No one. No one left...

THE END